Of
Sand
and
Bone

Georgia Day

RHAPSODY

PRESS BOOKS

www.rhapsodypressbooks.com

Published 2022 by Rhapsody Press Books
ISBN 978-1-7367387-5-7

Cover and interior design by Heidi Sutherlin, mycreativepursuits.com
Cover art "Fractured Sky" by @SpaceFrogDesigns
Author Photo - Krystal Dawn Studios

First Edition

"We are funny creatures. We don't see the stars as they
    are, so why do we love them?
    They are not small gold objects, but endless fire."

Henderson the Rain King
Saul Bellow

Here is no water but only rock
Rock and no water and the sandy road
The road winding above among the mountains
Which are mountains of rock without water
If there were water we should stop and drink
Amongst the rock one cannot stop or think
Sweat is dry and feet are in the sand
If there were only water amongst the rock
Dead mountain mouth of carious teeth that cannot spit
Here one can neither stand nor lie nor sit
There is not even silence in the mountains
But dry sterile thunder without rain
There is not even solitude in the mountains
But red sullen faces sneer and snarl
From doors of mudcracked houses
                                              If there were water

  And no rock
  If there were rock
  And also water
  And water
  A spring
  A pool among the rock
  If there were the sound of water only
  Not the cicada
  And dry grass singing
  But sound of water over a rock
  Where the hermit-thrush sings in the pine trees
  Drip drop drip drop drop drop drop
  But there is no water

                          "What the Thunder Said," The Waste Land
                                          T.S. Eliot

Chapter 1

O nce, God and the Devil were traveling through eternity, arguing about creation. God pointed to the stars as they passed, proud of their beauty, and bragged of their perfection. The Devil nodded and smiled politely, but he was unimpressed.

So God showed the Devil the planets and sun he had created. He commanded them to move and orbit the sun, and the stars to shoot across the universe. The stars sparked and the planets whizzed by, but the Devil only nodded and smiled politely.

And God said, "The universe obeys my whim. I have made all that you see."

"But it is not true creation," replied the Devil, serenely.

So God plucked the third planet from its orbit and placed it between himself and the Devil. He created a blue paradise of oceans and mountains and deep wet jungles. He made creatures of every size and kind and gave them dominion over the planet. He commanded the rain to fall and the rivers to rush and the tides to ebb and flow.

The Devil saw the paradise and marveled at its perfection.

"It is truly a thing of beauty," he said. "Supreme in every way. A veritable Eden."

God smiled down at his little world, pleased.

"But—" the Devil continued, "it is not true creation."

"I have created something where there was nothing," God said. "I have made the heavens. I have made life and therefore all future life. I created creation. There is no truer act."

The Devil shook his wooly head and sighed. "I have been your constant companion since time began. I have seen you make wondrous things—things that would make the very universe weep with joy and cry out in abject terror. Long have I watched. Long have I felt you were capable of more, but I did not know what it could be. I fear your infinite talents have at last found their termination. You create supposed perfection with ease, but it is merely an illusion. The stars, *the universe, these beings—your every thought is their compulsion. It is not true creation because it cannot fail."*

God gazed down at the tiny planet with something akin to sadness, and he saw.

The Devil, watching the planet's surface, noticed strange new creatures among the animals. "You have made them soft, vulnerable," he said.

"But intelligent."

The Devil smiled. "They will do nicely."

"Perhaps."

"What do you call them?"

God thought for a moment. "Man."

And so, God and the Devil came down to Earth to walk among his creations. They were indeed intelligent. They made tools, and with these tools they made many wonderful things. They were ceaseless in their efforts. They built intricate machines and dazzling cities and sublime temples to God, and the Devil watched with jealousy as they created more and more and more.

And God said to the Devil, "Are you not satisfied?"

The Devil shrugged. "It is easy to be great in a paradise."

"A paradise is nothing. They do not need it."

The Devil looked at God. "Then take it away."

And so he did.

So great was his belief in his children that God made the world a wasteland. He dried up the seas and stopped the rains and commanded the sun to scorch the forests. He turned the animals against Man so that they learned to fear one another.

And Man suffered.

Many died, and those who did not die cried out to God for mercy.

And God said, "You have been blessed with eyes that see. Know that I am with you."

And so Man rebuilt the cities and invented machines to dig for water, and they found a new way to thrive.

But the Devil was not satisfied. "This is not creation. You are as a parent to a mewling infant. They would fall upon each other like beasts without your presence."

"They are good."

"Turn your back and they will fail."

"You cannot see," said God, "but you are the one who will fail."

God concealed himself in a stone in the farthest corner of the world where he could watch his creations, but Man was not fooled so easily. They made pilgrimages to the stone to worship. They did not tear at each other as the Devil thought they would, for they knew God was with them.

And so one day, the Devil made his own pilgrimage to the stone.

"You must leave them."

God emerged. "You are angry."

"Your stubbornness makes me so! You knew that wherever you went on this planet they would find you, and yet you refused to honor our agreement. You said you would turn your back."

"I said you would fail and nothing more."

The Devil would not be beaten. "Fear?"

"I do not fear losing to you, old friend. I do not fear being wrong. I do not fear failure. I simply cannot abide their suffering. My presence lessens their pain."

"Pain spurs them forward."

God said nothing.

The Devil sensed a change. "Then you concede?" he asked.

God shook his mighty head. "Will you never be content?"

"Perhaps I speak from experience."

"I see that you will not bend. You have much in common with these rocks— brittleness and all."

The Devil waited.

God looked at the sky, into the universe he created, and said, "I hope you realize the gamble you now make."

"It is my constant belief that to win against an opponent such as you, I have no choice but to gamble."

"Then I shall leave my children with one last gift...so that you can never again accuse me of cheating." God took a handful of sand from the ground and tossed it into the sky. "I do not need to gamble, for I already know who wins."

And he abandoned the world.

The Devil watched the sand drift through the sky, and as the wind carried it, each grain became a terrible creature of darkness and fear. The Devil commanded them to pursue Man, to torment and destroy any they could, and the demons dogged Man's every waking step. The Devil rained down terror and suffering, bleeding the life from the world, while his demons murdered and peeled flesh from bone.

And that is how the Devil inherited the earth.

Chapter 2

f only we could stop. Hot sand welled up behind my heels, rushing into my shoes with each step. In the distance, the sky turned the same white as the sand, obliterating the horizon so that we walked in a void. I couldn't stare or my eyes would spin, and so I concentrated on the back of Elyah's turbaned head and on my ever-present thirst. If only there were water.

It was our tenth day out since the Khamaseen winds had blown themselves out, and the heat was already immense. When I was younger, out in the open desert for the first time, I felt the heat wrap itself around me like a pad of cotton, and I could not breathe. I became convinced that by running and tearing at the air in front of my mouth, I could free myself, for cooler air must exist just beyond that suffocating veil. Afraid, my father struck me in the face and carried me home, where I lay in bed delirious with fever for three days. But I was older now. My permanent teeth had all come in, and I knew there was no escape.

There was no water, and to stop meant death. I learned to count on the constants in my life: there would always be the sun, there would always be the heat, and there would always be Elyah to walk before me. And at the end of my life, when I could walk no more, my body would be burned to prevent witches stealing my corpse.

Far ahead of the line, the priest repeatedly plunged his hand into the sack slung across his body as he walked, drew it out, and flung the black dust into the white sky, where it dispersed with a loud *crack*. He didn't bother watching the sky—that was the job of my brothers. They stood at the head and tail of the line, watching to see if anything fell to earth, but nothing had happened in weeks.

They looked bored, particularly Vargas, who had always been high-strung and restless. At the head of the line, he rested his machete on one shoulder and slowed his pace, occasionally pointing out snake tracks in the sand to no one in particular. I didn't have to look behind me to know that Cal was shaking his head at his brother's behavior, from the tail of the line.

Ahead, the priest's pace remained the same, and whether the rest of us lagged or kept up did not worry him. He walked on, flinging his dust in the air, tattered black robes streaming behind him—on and on until his bag was empty. Which was now. The priest stopped and sat in the burning sand, facing away from us, waiting for June the cartographer who mapped our daily routes. I looked over as June scratched his curly head and frowned at the map tacked to its box, the leather strap looped behind his neck. He cocked his head, mumbling to himself, then made a correction on the map. He looked up.

"Finished!"

The priest rose, and we turned to go back to the City. June rolled up the map with today's route and slid it into the cylindrical bag strapped to his back.

The priest had run out of his black powder just in time. There were only a few hours of daylight left. But then he had always had excellent timing.

The single spire of the capitol loomed high out of the sand as we approached the City, while the rest of the buildings sprawled in crouching squalor below. As we reached the edge of the City, the priest stopped while the rest of the witch hunters crossed into the slums. I looked back. The priest always walked with us to the capitol, but now he stood with his back to the City, light bearing down on his bald head. He seemed to be looking for someone.

"Rue!"

Cal was motioning for me to keep up. He looked angry and was pulling Vargas away from the vendors that had poured out of their shacks the moment we crossed the border. I shooed away a small, blister-skinned child bearing a fly-covered box of cooked meats and followed my brothers through the ghettos. More shanties sprang up every year, the slums spreading like cancer, its residents building wherever they chose. Dangerously narrow paths could dead end or dump its traveler out into the open sand without warning, but there was no way around them. Vendors in the outskirts made their living off the hunting parties that passed through the labyrinth every day. No one in the outskirts had ever seen a City resident. Only the hunters knew the way through.

Cal was scolding Vargas as we walked.

"...hot-headed and irresponsible, and you know it."

"There hasn't been a sign in weeks."

"Oh great, the short-sighted argument I've come to expect."

Vargas shook his head and tapped his machete on his shoulder. "No more. The day's over."

"If only you would be more vigilant tomorrow," Cal muttered.

"If it would shut you up."

We pressed our backs against a blue plastic shanty to let two snake hunters in high desert garb pass by.

The taller one nodded to us. "Bag yourself a witch today, Vargas?"

"Ten, but they're invisible."

The snake hunters laughed. "Maybe you should consider a change."

I watched Vargas eye the snake hunters' high, expensive boots and clean clothes as they walked away, the colored light from the plastic shacks turning his face blue.

"Bring you back a big one!" called the tall snake hunter.

Cal nudged his brother. "A boring day is a good one, remember?"

Vargas looked down at me instead. "Come on, Rue."

When we reached our small hamlet of sandstone huts, the tutors' circle was empty—no lessons tonight. I would be allowed to join my father and brothers by the community fires.

Vargas would not speak to any of us. Cal, sorry for his words, loaded Vargas' plate with food, leaving little for himself, and tried to draw him into conversation. Met with stubborn silence, Cal moved away and hunched over his plate.

My father merely shrugged. "Vargas is Vargas. You just have to wait."

I watched Vargas. Cal was right, a boring day was a good one. I hoped to never see a witch again. The last time—I shuddered, remembering the thing we had found in the sand. Injured but not dead, skin blistering in the sun, it had swiped at us. I remembered Cal's arm across my chest, letting the others take care of the creature. I remembered machete blades catching the light before the blood dulled their shine. Every time the priest's black dust cracked in the air, I prayed it wouldn't bring anything down, and my heart burned at Vargas' selfish need for excitement.

When the snake hunters returned, he went to their fire, and I watched him sit and laugh with them. The tall one pulled catch after catch from his leather bag, what he had not managed to sell in town, and children gathered while he cleaned the snakes for roasting.

Cal shoved his uneaten meal at me and stormed off. My father shrugged again, took Cal's food from me, and hefted his bulk up from his seat.

"We will save this. He gets peckish when he's angry. Do not stay up too late, little one."

"I won't."

"And no reading tonight. You use all the lantern fuel and then there is none for the next night."

Resigned, I nodded and pulled my knees into my chest, folding my arms over my legs.

"And do not sit so close to the fire."

With that, he left me alone. I stared into the flames, letting the white-hot glow fill my eyes, then looked up to the cold night sky, the phantom flames blotting out the stars. One by one, each pinprick of light poked back through as my eyes cleared, until the entire sky glittered with stars. I squinted, trying to find the three that made up Orion's belt. It was easier to see when I was younger; when my father sat me on his lap, pressing my cheek against his so that I could sight down his outstretched arm and see what he saw.

Right there, do you see?

I squinted again, stringing the three stars together, following up to Orion's shoulder, then hand, until a shout of laughter from the snake hunters startled me. Vargas was parading around their fire with a freshly butchered snakeskin draped across his shoulders while the other hunters pretended to clap delicately. When I looked back at the sky, I couldn't pick out the constellation again, as if the black had swallowed Orion whole. Or as though something had passed in front of it.

"I cannot find it either," said a voice next to me.

I gave a startled yelp and raised my hand to strike at the voice, until I saw it was the priest.

The priest cocked his head at me. "A strange noise for a child to make. It's Rueda, isn't it."

It wasn't a question. He knew who I was. The firelight flickered against his bald head, throwing a shadow across his eyes. I had never heard him speak before. I did not think he could speak, which was silly. He waited, completely still. I lowered my hand and swallowed.

"My brothers call me Rue."

He nodded slowly, then looked at the fire. "Rueda is a good name for you. I have been thinking about that."

I pulled my father's blanket around my shoulders and shifted a little away from the priest. If he noticed, he did not mention it. He watched the fire with great intensity, as if it had something to say.

"I cannot sleep," he said. He was smiling faintly. "I dreamed of a miracle."

He looked at me, still smiling.

"A miracle?" I asked.

"Two nights ago. I dreamed of an animal that did not fly in the sky nor crawl on the ground."

I shook my head, confused. "What did it look like?"

"Ah, that is the trick to dreams. I don't remember anything else except that its body shined as bright as the sun. It was leading me."

"Where?"

"Paradise."

There was something in the way he said the word that made my heart stop. His voice had lost the wonder it had previously held and become bittersweet.

"Why can't you sleep?" I asked.

The priest was no longer smiling. "Because I know this miracle will come true."

"But—"

"But not for me."

"You said the animal led you."

"I thought it was, but I feel that time is narrowing to a point. I feel a heaviness weighing on my brain, and a crushing hand around my soul. I sense darkness. I fear the night."

"I don't—"

He looked over at me.

"I do not understand," I whispered. All my life the priest had seemed to be a rock, a heartbeat, steady and ceaseless—no pain, no joy, simply present.

"There is no reason why you should, but I felt it must be said." He smiled sadly and rose to leave.

"What are you afraid of? Why are you afraid?"

"I don't know."

I stood up. "Wait."

He looked down at me, for he was still much taller than I.

"You're the priest. Aren't you supposed to know everything?"

"Who told you that?"

"Told me? No one. That is the way it is."

He studied my face. I knew he could see my bewilderment and the fear that came from it, but he seemed to look past it, past the Rue in this place, on to another Rue in another time in another place. His mouth drooped, and I suddenly noticed how time had creased his face. I remember him younger.

"I am nothing," he said finally. "And none of us really know anything."

Alone in my room that night, I watched the moon cross the sky, and I did not sleep.

Chapter 3

n the morning, I washed my face in the basin and looked at myself in the mirror. I could hear the streets coming alive outside my bedroom window. Today was market day. The merchants would be setting up their stalls, and soon the air would be filled with spices and shouts and laughter. I loved market day. Willa had promised me that pink beads would be in stock this week, but I knew the pink beads would have been sold hours before the hunting party returned this evening, probably to a City wife. I examined my face in the mirror, noting the darkness of my skin with disappointment. City wives' and daughters' skin was rarely touched by sunlight. I had heard my father say once that City wives were a waste, that they got their fair skin from sitting indoors growing fat off their husbands like house cats. He had said that real women were not house cats and real men would make strays of them.

I smiled, closed my lips over my teeth, and then smiled again and pushed my mouth closer to the mirror. My permanent teeth were much bigger than my baby teeth had been. I clicked my teeth together and crossed my eyes at my reflection just as Cal walked in. He shook his head at me and tossed my turban at the mirror.

"Let's go," he said.

We made for the capitol, same as always, but today Vargas and Cal did not joke together and walk far ahead of me. Cal walked next to me, tugging my arm to make me keep pace with him while Vargas strolled well behind. Ahead, the spire of the capitol building jutted into the sky like a great white needle. Capitol families, their living quarters at the larger base of the tower, were getting their children ready for school. Mothers kissed their children goodbye. Husbands made small talk with one another. A boy in a starched tunic gaped at me as we passed. His eyes were blue. I pulled at Cal's sleeve and pointed, but Cal slapped my hand down and told me not to be rude. Blue-eyed children almost always went blind, so they were kept indoors after the age of ten to preserve their sight. In a few years, that boy would never see the light of day again.

I think I would rather be blind.

We paused at the Founders Fountain in the square to savor the last few mouthfuls of water before going out into the desert. Older hunters carried enough water to survive for one day, but I was young and still learning. I did not carry my own provisions or weapons. Cal carried my water and machete because it was his job to look after me until I turned fifteen. I would be a real hunter then. I cupped water from the fountain into my hands and drank, the explorers Copernicus and Magellan on horseback carved in stone above me. They had charted this entire region, founding this and five other cities. The capitol building now stood where Copernicus' original home had been, hundreds of years ago. The base of the capitol building spread wide, narrowing to a point some thirty stories above. I thought it looked like a nail on the ground waiting to pierce the foot of an unsuspecting giant.

City families in starched and embroidered clothes milled about us, keeping their distance. Cal always said the City families tolerated us, but they did not like us. We kept them safe, but they did not want to think about it. I watched a lady in pale blue skirts swish by, her yellow umbrella cocked to the side to keep us out of her field of vision. She probably lived in one of the great houses that lined the square, maybe that black and white one with the red sandstone path and paper birds in the windows.

I often wondered what it would be like to live in one of those houses. I would wear red dresses and cream-colored trousers and leather shoes. I would have a girl that did my hair every day and a white umbrella to keep the sun off my fair skin. I would read books about faraway adventures and fantasize about running away to become a hunter because I would have no idea what it was really like.

Cal called to me to catch up, and we walked through the City, the houses gradually becoming smaller and less grand until we were very far from the lady in the blue skirts and yellow umbrella who did not want to look at us. She didn't know how to get through the maze of plastic shacks, but I did. There, she would die without my help.

Cal would say that they would all die without us.

Chapter 4

W here the desert met the ghettos, I fell into line behind Elyah just as the sun broke the horizon. The priest stood away from us, facing the desert, waiting. He did not turn his head or acknowledge me. Instead, he reached into his bag and tossed the black dust into the morning sky.

Crack

Vargas and Cal were not speaking to each other. At the head of the line, Vargas had the same cocky swagger from the day before, but this time I knew he was doing it to make Cal angry. I peeked back at Cal, who was grinding his teeth, his eyes boring a hole in the back of Vargas' head. I was sure Vargas was delighted—nothing pleased him more than to know he was annoying his brother.

Crack.

As the sun climbed higher, Elyah pulled at her turban, trying to let the wind cool her neck. It was hotter than it was yesterday, and I began to dread the midday heat. Behind me, June fidgeted, wiping his sweat off the map. Up and down the line, the black-robed figures sprouted limbs that plucked at their turbans and sleeves, trying to find a moment's relief. Only the priest seemed immune.

Crack.

The sun reached its zenith and squatted over the desert, its merciless heat pressing us into the ground, buckling our knees. Elyah stumbled but didn't fall. Vargas lost his swagger. His feet made drag marks in the sand, and his machete gradually grew heavy. I didn't look around anymore, worrying that my legs would give out from under me.

Crack.

I kept my eyes on the priest. I made my steps match his, forced each leg in front of the other. To stop meant death for all of us. I tormented myself with thoughts of water. My tongue was like sandpaper. I tried to swallow to moisten my throat, but only brought on a coughing fit that scratched it raw. I needed water, and the blood rushed to my head when I remembered there wasn't any. I rubbed my face with my hands and prayed for the sun to go down.

Crack.

Elyah screamed. Everyone looked to the sky, then in the direction of her outstretched arm.

"Sidewinder!" she screamed.

It was close—close enough that I could see the pebbled diamond stripes of its back and the pointed hoods over its eyes. It rippled towards our line so quickly that it seemed to float over the sand, but Vargas was faster. He struck, slicing the animal in two, and Elyah whimpered as the halves flipped and curled and then lay still. Vargas bent to pick them up but was stopped by a large hand on his shoulder.

The priest stood over the snake, his brows knitted together. Everyone backed away a little in surprise. He looked up, and for a split second our eyes met, before he turned his face to the sky, searching. He pushed through the rest of us, stumbling against June, driven past us out into the desert. Away from us, he paused. His feet didn't seem to want to move further. Even at this distance, I could hear his breath coming in ragged gasps. The rest of the hunters watched him, afraid of what they had never seen. His shoulders tensed. His right hand came up, forced itself down into the bag of black dust, but came out clean. Looking down at his empty hand, his breath slowed and his body relaxed. I watched a single bead of sweat trace its way down the back of his head and disappear into his collar as he looked out into the vast desert ahead.

And the priest sat in the sand.

Vargas and Cal had been trying to get us back into line but froze when a shadow fell over us all. There was nothing in the sky, not one cloud, and there was no way I could have known what would happen next, but I did. I saw the priest sitting out in the sand, watched the shadow slide over him—before it had been shapeless, but now the edges became jagged, pointed slices of black like wings. The priest did not look up, and I could not look away.

A bird, large as a building, black as a nightmare, appeared out of the air and plunged its claws into the priest's back, lifting him as if he were nothing— merely a twig—into the atmosphere. The hunters panicked around me. I could hear someone screaming, someone calling me, but I had no control. My feet stuck in the sand as if they had grown from there. He was dead. I knew he was dead. He hadn't made a sound. He must be dead. *Dear God, please be dead.* The bird lifted him higher and higher. Its ragged wings spread and spread, blotting out the sun, casting us into darkness. Its talons melted into the sky, and it ripped the priest in two, crushing what was left and letting it fall back to the now cold earth.

I felt a hand on my shoulder. Cal was pulling me to him, his machete ready, when we felt the sand tremble under our feet. In the semi-darkness, I saw a black wall of sand moving toward us, and I heard the snarling of dogs.

"Damn the Devil," whispered Cal. "It's an ambush!"

The earth rumbled, and I heard the terrible laughing of a hundred hyenas made of wind and black sand bearing down on us, hungry jaws snapping, eyes glowing. And in the face of open, wretched, abject horror, I realized I had never before known fear. This was fear—unholy, terrible, all-consuming terror.

Cal grabbed my arm and we ran, but I could not match his stride. Ahead of us, the hunters fled. I could see Vargas staring at us in open-mouthed panic, his arms making useless gestures, as if he could make us go faster.

"Run!" screamed Cal.

Vargas dropped his machete and ran. Cal pulled me harder. I felt the dogs closing in on me—the hot breath on the back of my neck and snarling laughter in my ear. Cal had lost his grip on my hand. I stumbled and fell, curling into a ball, covering my head with my hands, sobbing with terror. Suddenly, the earth shifted and gave way beneath me, burying me in a shallow depression. I heard screaming amid the deranged laughing of the hyenas. I heard the hunters cry out, and I screamed with them—I screamed for Elyah, for June, for my brothers. *Oh dear God, my brothers.*

Sand filled my mouth, and I spat and tried to draw breath before sand rushed in again. My lungs burned, but I held my breath and listened. Silence. The terrible noises had stopped. I could no longer hear the rushing wind digging at the pit. Unable to wait any longer, I clawed at the sand above me. The pit could not have been any more than a meter deep, and I dug myself out easily, gasping for a breath of the early evening air.

I was not prepared for the carnage that awaited me above. Waist-deep in sand, I scrabbled at the earth, trying to free myself and not look at the bodies that surrounded me. I didn't want to see their faces. I closed my eyes and wished I was blind, but my nostrils still registered the sickening metallic smell of blood. My hand touched something wet, and I yanked it back, unable to draw breath.

I had pulled myself onto all fours when I realized that the sun was going down, I was exhausted, and I had no idea where I was. I couldn't see the City on the horizon, and a cold lump of fear settled in my stomach. I was going to have to spend the night out here.

I tried to stand, but I couldn't. I had twisted my knee when I fell. I crouched, trying to stretch it when I heard a sound. Some dozen yards before me, its back to the setting sun, a bony, hairless figure squatted among the bodies, picking at the meat. My breath froze in my chest as I realized what I was looking at. The long, emaciated legs jutted out over its prey; a small, wet speck of a sound reached me with every pluck of long fingers traveling back and forth to a grotesquely bloated head.

Very slowly, I pressed myself against the ground and looked for somewhere to hide, but it was no use. We had been walking in completely open desert that day. Not so much as a boulder dotted the horizon—nothing except me and the dead, and I did not intend to join them. There was only one place to go. My left foot toed the edge of the pit, and I inched back, quietly scooping sand with my foot and pushing it out, my breath coming in choked gasps. Little by little, my eyes glued to the bony figure, I inched myself down into the shallow depression, covering myself again as much as I could.

At first, I heard nothing. Soon, however, an odd halting noise reached me—*shuf shuf,* and then a long pause. In my mind's eye, I could see it moving among the bodies, making its way closer. Could it smell me? I had left a small opening so that I could breathe, and I feared now it would be spotted. Each muffled *shuf shuf* was louder than the last. A spray of sand and swift tearing with skeletal fingers—my mind tormented me with images of being discovered. In the otherwise still evening, I tried to smother my breath for it sounded like a gale wind in my own ears. A few grains of sand trickled down the hole as the beast shuffled less than a meter from my pit, until an avalanche filled the hole entirely as a heavy weight settled on top of me. My fingers curled in panic. Trapped! If I moved, it would sense me, but I could not hold my breath much longer. Its weight pressed down on me. It was only a matter of time now. Lungs screaming for air I could not give, stomach twisting into itself, eyes clenched shut, I waited. I would not move. I would not give in.

The sand suddenly felt weightless as the witch moved off. I strained my ears, trying to gauge its distance, but either it was gone or I was simply too desperate for air to hear anything. Pushing my fingers upward through the sand, I gratefully took a breath. Listening again, I still heard nothing, so I dug my way out of the pit for what I hoped would be the last time.

The moon was just rising in the sky, already bright enough that I could travel by it. I hobbled away from the pit and the bodies, then sat in the sand to think.

There would be no search party.

Without June and his maps no one would know where to begin. The most that could be done would be to send word to other cities to be on the lookout for the missing hunters. I was on my own. Traveling would be difficult enough, but my knee would slow me down further. I had no water, which meant I needed to make for the nearest settled city. The only problem was, I had no idea what that route would be.

With some reluctance, I stood and looked over at the remains of the hunting party, but even from here, I could see it was hopeless. Not a single paper fluttered in the night wind. All of June's maps had either blown away or been destroyed. Scanning the empty horizon, I settled on a direction I thought might take me to a city. I left the bodies of the hunting party as they were and started to walk. I was exhausted. My knee hurt with every step, and in my heart, I felt a flicker of anger.

The Devil would not get me tonight.

I walked all night, jumping at every sound and every startled desert hare rushing into the dark. I thought I heard dogs.

At first, the cold night air kept me alert—each breath like frost on my raw throat—but eventually fatigue slipped over, calm, comfortable, and uncaring. The throbbing in my knee had numbed some hours ago, but the swelling made it stiff. Still, I kept going, marking an *X* in the sand to record my trail. I feared going in circles.

I do not remember the sun coming up. I remember little about the night except the constant need to continue. No thoughts, no tears, only one foot in front of the other over and over until I noticed the world around me had changed and the sun was already over the horizon.

For a moment, I stopped and stared. I had not slept in two nights, and I had not had any water in twenty-four hours. I would die in two days. If I had been walking in a straight line—and I could not be sure—I probably walked eight miles during the night without any sign of the City. I was walking in the wrong direction. My knee throbbed, my head ached, and I was alone. I didn't care what city I came to, and I felt confident I would see some sign in a few hours.

I watched the sun climb in the sky.

"My name is Rueda Cole," I told it, "And I am not going to die here."

And so I walked on.

Chapter 5

I once saw a battle between a white fox and a golden eagle.
My father and Cal had taken me far from the City and were teaching me
how to dig for water. As my father showed me how to look for signs of
where the water ran, I saw a white-hot streak barreling down the next dune,
orange dust in its wake. I raised my arm to point it out to Cal and my father when
an eagle, like an arrow loosed by the deadliest of archers, hurtled down out of
the clear blue sky onto the white streak, stopping it in its tracks.

Sand flew, concealing both, the brown and gold ailerons just visible above
the fray. Its wingspan seemed longer than my whole body. As we watched, a
little white fox emerged from the dust, snarling and rolling, twisting itself out
of the eagle's grasp. The eagle made another leap, hefting its body forward,
its talons ready to snatch up the soft fox. The fox was quicker, and instead of
running, it turned, leaped, and tore at the eagle's chest and eyes. The dust took
them again as the eagle spun and flapped to regain the advantage. The two
tumbled down the dune, the jaws of the little white fox firmly clamped to the
golden down of the eagle's throat as it clawed the fox's belly with its black
talons. In a moment, the eagle seemed to change its mind about this particular
prey and pushed against the dune with its wings. Twice was all it took before the
eagle gained enough momentum to lift off from the ground. The fox, in mutual
agreement, released its grasp and made for the base of the dune and the patches
of scrubby brush below.

My father shook his head in wonder and chuckled to himself. He said there
really was no such thing as a hopeless fight.

I marked another *X* in the sand and scanned the still empty horizon. I could
no longer bend my knee, and as the sun reached its zenith my need for water
was becoming overpowering. I covered my face with my hands, trying to

think, trying to remember all of the things Cal and my father had taught me. I remembered where to dig for water, how to find it, but there was nothing around me. Not even the smallest bit of brown vegetation poked out of the sand. Not one agave I could peel for moisture. Nothing. This was a dead place. I needed stars. I needed Orion. I had just seen it the night the priest—

I looked around again, straining my eyes past the heat rising into a deep blue sky that was burned white at the edges. I thought I could see a rocky rise somewhere at the end of the horizon. Maybe it was there, and maybe it was something I could climb to get a better idea of where I was. Maybe I could see the City from there.

It wasn't there. No matter how far I walked, the landscape never seemed to change. The rocks never got any closer, and the more I hobbled the more I felt a lump rising in my throat. I was not getting anywhere. Maybe I wasn't even walking.

I should have stopped—bedded down for the day, traveled at night, taken my time. Time was not something I had, and I was beginning to feel I was being watched. My brain was a muddled haze, and I drifted—one foot in front of the other—remembering stories my mother used to tell.

How did God make the world, little baby?

"He burned it. He laid waste to everything that was beautiful. We burned. We all burned. Why didn't he just take it all away?"

That is the question.

Once, in the high mountains to the East, there lived a great phoenix. A rare and solitary creature, it lived alone on the tallest peak, away from the world of Man. Every morning, as the first rays of sunlight touched the phoenix's nest, the bird would sing in its high, clear voice. The villagers in the valley below rose to this melancholy sound each morning, for it meant that it was time to start the day.

In those times, the villagers believed the phoenix called the sun to rise, and they sang songs of their own in praise to the great phoenix. But that was in the Beginning. Soon enough, they came to know the phoenix did not call the sun— the sun would rise with or without the bird, with or without anyone—and they began to wonder about the nature of the ever-present soul in the highest peak. None had ever seen it. Poets and bards had written for so long that the phoenix called the sun that legend and fact blurred together, and people began to say that the great phoenix's feathers were as golden as the sun itself. Others said they were also the deepest vermillion and richest purple. The bird must indeed be very beautiful, and the village treasured it all the more. Men dressed in red shirts and women bleached crow feathers to wear in their hair.

But why did the phoenix live so far away? Why did it keep itself from the village? It must be afraid of them, as most beasts are, they reasoned. The phoenix continued, as it always had, to sing its mournful song as the first rays touched its nest, and the villagers grew restless.

They must see the phoenix, they said. There was no reason for it to fear, and no need for it to keep its beauty from the village. Yes, yes, they knew best. They would make a great expedition—the first of its kind—to the highest peak to see their bird. Some said it would be best to capture the phoenix and bring it to the village so that they might protect it. The villagers argued amongst themselves, and it was decided that they would go see the phoenix, but it would only be captured if necessary—if it were in danger. So they mounted an expedition to the highest peak, selecting three of the best men in the village to make the journey: Curiosity, Bravery, and Wisdom. The travelers were loaded with food, supplies, and a large golden cage, just in case. The morning of the trek, they were awakened as they always had been by the song of the phoenix.

It took a week for them to reach the phoenix's nest. Each morning the mournful song was their cue to continue, and each night they exchanged old stories of the phoenix's beauty and theories of its existence. Curiosity said it must be immortal, for it had never ceased its song. The others laughed at him because such a thing could not exist. Wisdom believed that it must be a female singing for its mate. Bravery confided that he intended to pluck a golden tail feather as a present for his wife, but the others shook their heads and discouraged him. The phoenix must remain untouched. This was a peaceful mission to determine the safety of their phoenix. No harm must come to it.

On the morning of the seventh day, the men rose as they always had to the song of the phoenix, but today was different. Today, the sound was just above their heads. They must be close, they said. Excited, the travelers scrabbled over the rocks, pulling each other up over the ledges.

It was Curiosity who saw the nest first. But something was wrong. He stood dumbfounded before it, then his body shuddered with laughter. He laughed and laughed. The others approached, demanding to know what it was he found funny. Curiosity pointed to the nest. Inside, a smallish bird of moldy gray and black squatted in the twigs, blinking at them. Its twisted green beak issued a long croak. It was a horrible sound. Wisdom reasoned that it was the height of the mountain, the morning wind, the echo, that had made the song so beautiful. Bravery winced as Curiosity snatched a tattered gray feather from the nest and laughed in his face. Wouldn't Bravery's wife be pleased with this present? Curiosity grabbed another feather, this one plucked from the bird's back, and waved it in Bravery's face. The bird squawked in pain. Annoyed and angry, Bravery pushed Curiosity's hand away, took up a stone, and hurled it at the nest. The stone struck the phoenix, and it cried again in pain. Bravery hurled another stone, then another to silence the disgusting sounds the bird made. Curiosity joined in. Wisdom stood quietly, fearful of Bravery's wrath. He watched as they killed the phoenix.

That night, they went back down the mountain. They would never tell what happened, why the phoenix no longer sang. The villagers built temples and danced in their fake phoenix feathers to mourn the loss of their guardian's song. The sun still rose every day, but each one was empty for the people of the little village below the mountain. They had lost a part of themselves, and they did not know why.

"What does it mean, Mommy?"

It's about truth, little baby. Sometimes even the best of us are not good enough.

I knew I was dying. I wasn't hungry anymore. I had been before, but I wasn't now. I was not thirsty, either. I couldn't think. My head buzzed and buzzed so that I confused the horizon sometimes. There was something out there—something that watched me. Witches would come. Why had they not killed me yet? I wasn't enough. I was too small, and they were too hungry. They needed more. They always needed more. That's why we hunted in packs—to draw them out, to bring them down, and then we killed them. We should kill them. I wanted to be a witch hunter just like Cal. Where's Cal? I had to find Cal. He would take care of me, carry me home. *Carry me, Cal.* There's something out there.

I wanted to be just like you.

One foot in front of the other, little baby.
"I can't. I don't want to, Mommy."
Just one more step.
There was something in the sand in front of me, like a drawing.
You are going in circles, little one. My father walked next to me, smiling quietly to himself as he always did. *Do you not remember the rules?*
"A hunter never travels alone. A hunter always marks his route. A hunter always makes the kill."
You are a poor hunter, little one.
"Useless."
But you are being watched.
"I know."
Where is Cal? He would never leave you alone like this.
I stumbled.

"He won't come back, he won't, and neither will Vargas. No one is coming back."

My father shrugged. *Vargas is Vargas. You just have to wait.*

"I tried to run. I wanted them to run. I'm sorry I was not faster. I couldn't run faster. I was too slow. I'm sorry. I'm sorry."

You are going in circles, little one.

I stood staring at the *X* in the sand. Somewhere in the distance, a coyote barked once. I looked at the sand dunes and rocky formations around me. I looked but I didn't see. I breathed, but I couldn't feel my breath in my lungs. I couldn't feel the burns on my skin. I was leaving my body. I had failed.

And so I fell.

The horizon blurred like clouds in my eyes as my head hit the sand. Nothing hurt anymore. I was floating. I drifted as the world quietly went dark. Just before everything went away, a shape split the fading horizon, growing larger, and before I closed my eyes I saw an animal with neither wings nor legs flashing gold, bright as the sun.

How did God make the world, little baby?

"He burned it. He burned it all."

No, baby. Not all.

Chapter 6

I remember water. Water poured across my lips, cold in the cracks. I tasted blood, but more than that I tasted the water flowing down my throat and cooling me to my fingertips. I wanted to cry, but I had no tears. I drank more and more and cried again when it was taken away. I must have woken up because I remember a fire in front of me and the smell of cooking. I thought I was home around the community fires. I thought I would sit up and there would be my father, passing me my dinner, and Cal and Vargas arguing about the day. I thought I was safe.

I dreamed of terrible things—Cal and Vargas yelling in the dark, yelling for me, my father's eyes begging me for his sons, hyenas laughing in the night, and a dark cave. I had never seen that cave before, but I felt I had known it all my life. As I approached the mouth, it vomited black sand that engulfed me and pulled me down into it, down into the inky darkness where thousands of voices were waiting for me. I tore at the darkness around me. I screamed and screamed, but I couldn't breathe.

A rag was being shoved into my mouth. I sat bolt upright, swinging and pulling at the rag. A hand on my chest pushed me firmly back down, and another covered my mouth. I scratched at the hands with my fingernails, but they only pressed down harder. I remember a pair of hard, anxious eyes over me and then nothing. The world tilted and blackness took me, and I dreamed no more.

When I awoke again it was day. A wind was blowing my hair across my face, the strands tickling my sunburned nose. I brushed them away, tucking them behind my ear and wincing at the stiffness in my body. I squeezed my eyes shut and opened them again, trying to get my vision to focus. I felt slow, lazy, my brain stuffed with cotton wool. Objects around me didn't make sense. I felt a scratchy blanket of braided animal hair under my fingers and draped over my body. A water bag sat on a rag nearby, next to some strips of what looked like roasted cactus and dried meat. Charred logs and mounds of gray ash smoked a meter in front of my face, and on the other side of that dying fire sat a woman. The wind caught up the smoke and shielded her face, but I knew she was watching me.

I sat up and nausea rose up to lay me back down. I rolled on my side, cradled my head in my hands, and drew my knees up to my chest. Through my fingers, I could see she was still watching me. She sat silent as a stone and didn't offer to help me. Something about her seemed round. Not round as the shape, but round like time—past, present, future, repeat. Like the rock on which she sat, she seemed to have always been there. There was a weight to her presence, a solidity, as if stillness could be measured in grams and ounces.

The wind took a deep breath and puffed away the haze, and I could see she was indeed watching me. I had no doubt those hard brown eyes could see right through me. Short, bristled black lashes held their positions around those eyes. An ugly, jagged line split her left eyebrow and disappeared into the head of thick black hair that she had carefully brushed and braided into one heavy plait down her back. She was neither beautiful nor ugly, tall or short, fat or thin, just there. Solid and undeniable.

She shifted her gaze to the water bag and food beside my makeshift pallet. I sat up, gingerly this time, and reached for the water bag. She watched me. I unscrewed the cap and lifted it to my lips, my eyes meeting hers. I froze. She had been the one watching me in the desert. I sniffed the mouth of the water bag, poured a little out into my hand—cold, clear water—and sniffed again. I slurped a little out of my hand, rolling it around my mouth, testing for poison, and swallowed carefully. The woman's eyes narrowed ever so slightly. I sipped a little more water out of the bag, trying to wait to see if I became nauseous, but I could not hold back. I drank in great gulps, trying to fill the last few days with water. I could feel it cold in my belly and still I kept drinking, reaching for the food with my other hand. I sniffed the cactus strips, testing, but gobbled them down and tore the dried meat into bits, shoving it in my mouth and wanting to cry it tasted so good.

I drained the water bag and lay back on the animal hair blanket, suddenly tired. I felt myself drifting away again, and I turned my head to look at the woman.

I was alive.

Her hard eyes regarded me for a moment before looking away, out to the horizon and the sky. But I had seen something pass over her face—a shadow of sorts—just before she looked away, a flicker in her eyes that turned my heart cold.

It was disappointment.

I slept on and off for the rest of the day. When I awoke, there was a full water bag and a little food by my pallet. She sat on the rock—she was never anywhere else—and watched me eat and drink and fall asleep again. She did not say a word to me, and I never said a word to her. I ate and drank and slept, pulling the animal blanket over my head for shade. From time to time I looked around, scanning the horizon, trying to get my bearings, but it was useless. I did not know where I was when I started my journey, let alone where I was now. I was here. Simple as that. Whether she would take me back to the City or not, I could not say. I ate and drank and slept. I was not afraid of her. She would not kill me now that she had shared her rations with me. It wouldn't make sense to do that.

When I awoke again it was night. She had made a fire and was in her spot, watching me. I drank and ate. My joints were less stiff, and my head no longer buzzed. I felt a little like myself again. We watched each other across the fire, crickets singing in the dark. Somewhere a coyote howled.

I set the empty water bag down and crossed my ankles, drawing the animal blanket around my shoulders.

"What now?" I asked.

She looked off into the sky, the flames flickering against her throat, and I noticed for the first time that she was wearing the strangest collection of clothing. I searched, but that was the best word for it—a collection. It was as though she had pieced together some sort of mosaic from other people's lives—stand close and see only one piece, step back and see the whole. Her legs were encased in the high, black, flat-heeled boots of the snake hunters. They swallowed the light, but I knew what they were. True snake hunters sew tiny strips of snakeskin into their boots to signify their prowess, and I saw a glint of light from a scale somewhere at her ankles. Her black leggings were thick and wrapped with soft leather like an equestrian's, the kind that would protect them on long rides chasing the wild herds of mustang that were common to our region.

But what I could not stop staring at was her tunic. Despite the cold air, she did not wrap a blanket around her shoulders as I had, and I could see the fine embroidery that covered every bit of the garment, even down the long sleeves. The cloth was dyed the very deepest of blues, the thread dyed to match, so that it was a maze of texture. The blue was unlike anything I had ever seen—deeper than the bluest sky on the clearest day, but with a hint of gray, like the color had been laid over a storm. It was an expensive piece—too expensive for her—and it had clearly been made for a man. The fabric gaped at the shoulders and drowned her frame so that she had to cinch the waist with a wide leather belt, the kind favored by builders for its many loops and pouches. She shifted her weight to see a constellation just behind her, and the tunic's embroidery glowed in the light of the fire. It was too beautiful for her. It had been made for a City man, maybe someone in the capitol building, not a woman with an ugly scar. My eye caught sight of a metal disc on a chain at her waist. It was June's compass.

Anger rose in my throat.

"That is not yours," I growled.

She glanced down at me, then looked back up at the sky, unconcerned.

"That is not yours," I repeated loudly, startled by the strength in my voice.

"I needed a compass." Her voice was dark, quiet, but like a firm hand. She was not ashamed.

"Then buy one."

Her scarred eyebrow twitched. She was laughing at me.

"There is not anyone to sell me one."

"Then leave it." My fingers gripped the edges of the animal hair blanket wrapped around me.

She tilted her head. "The sand does not need to know where to go. What does the moon care about north or south? Sidewinders go with the dunes. It is foolish to leave useful things behind." Her hard brown eyes caught the light of the fire. "What kind of a hunter are you that you leave behind useful things?"

A dead one, I thought to myself and tried to swallow my anger.

"What else did you find?" I asked after a while.

"Nothing worth carrying," she answered flatly.

I wondered if that now included me.

She pulled another animal hair blanket up from where it had been warming by the fire and laid down on the rock, drawing the blanket over herself to cover even her head. I could only guess if she would take me back to the City in the morning. I had the feeling she would not answer me even if I asked her.

Chapter 7

I was awakened the next morning by the woman nudging me in the side with the toe of her snake hunter boot. The sun had just peeked out over the edge of the horizon, the light catching her face and tinging it pink. She had carefully brushed and braided her thick hair in a coil on top of her head. She hadn't bothered to wrap her turban but left draped it over her head so that the edges cupped the wind, funneling the air to her face and neck. She was scanning the horizon.

"Get up." Her voice was low, as though she thought someone might hear.

I stood, surprised at how shaky my legs were. I had not fully recovered, but it did not matter because I was going home. I stooped to wrap my makeshift pallet, but she pulled it away from me, compressing the skins even more and binding them together with strips of leather until they were a fraction of the size I had made them. She removed the bulkier travel robes from her pack and put them on, then she pushed my pallet and hers to the bottom of the pack, and tossed the whole onto her back, adjusting the straps over her shoulders. She had many items strapped to her belt, but my eye was drawn to the long blade of the machete at her side. She kept it well sharpened. June's compass swung in slow circles on its chain from her belt as she bent over. She tucked it into her robes and looked around. I tried to see what it was she was looking at, but I could not see anything.

She picked a direction—how, I don't know—and started walking. She took great long strides, planting her feet powerfully, pulling herself forward without hesitation, as if nothing would ever be in front of her that she could not dominate.

I trotted after her, each of her steps covering two of mine despite her being only slightly taller than me.

"Where are we going?" I asked, slightly breathless. I had not gotten up from the pallet at all yesterday, but it felt as though it had been a month.

She did not answer me. She only moved forward.

"Wait."

She did not answer. She did not stop. She only moved forward.

"Hello?"

She did not answer. She did not stop. She only moved forward.

I grabbed the back of her pack and yanked. She whipped around and caught me under the chin with the heel of her hand. It was only a pop, but it knocked me down easily. She was strong.

"What is *wrong* with you?" I yelped, sitting in the sand looking up at her stony face. Her expression did not change, and for some reason, it made me even angrier. I wanted to yell at her, but kept my voice low. "You cannot expect me to follow you. Where are we going? You can't just—You have to tell me *something*."

And then I realized—I had assumed she was taking me back to the City. I had assumed that I was supposed to go with her, but she had not told me any of that. She had not said anything. She had not told me to follow her. She had not expected me to follow her. She did not want me to follow her.

I started to cry—not for her or my brothers or my father, but for myself. I was afraid to be alone again in the open sand. I was afraid that I would fail again, and this time there would not be anyone there to save me.

She looked surprised—unsympathetic but surprised.

I wiped my face, angry at her for her coldness, angry at myself not only for despairing but for my complete inability to conceal it. She stood silently while I cried. I cried so long I almost forgot she was there, but she never said a word. I thought she would tell me to stop feeling sorry for myself, that I was embarrassing myself, that she would take me home, but she did not. But she didn't leave me, either.

So I cried myself out, wiping snot and tears on my sleeve until my sobs faded and I was left hiccupping quietly. My head hurt again. I was not embarrassed. I did not really care anymore. I stood, dusted off the back of my robes, and faced her. I could almost look her right in the eyes without tilting my head too far. I waited. If she left me there, I would probably die. If she took me with her, she might know how to get me home, she might not, but I could be sure that I would live. It was up to her. I would not beg.

She faced me, unmoved by my blotchy face and swollen eyes. And then she walked away. I felt as though the wind had been knocked out of me. I watched her go, her long powerful stride propelling her up a near dune. I looked around, wondering which way I should try, which one would take me home, when I heard a low whistle.

She stood facing me on the dune's crest, the sun behind her.

Not waiting to be asked twice, I sprinted to catch up, my feet sinking in the soft sand. My legs pushed into the side of the dune, sand welling up past my ankles and over the lip of my soft boots. I paused with her at the rise, taking a moment to dump the sand out of my shoes. The sun had not yet reached its midpoint and the sand already burned. When I glanced at her, her eyes were fixed on something in the distance. I shoved my foot back into my boot and looked. Some ways in the distance, a single white spire pierced the sky like a needle. My heart beat hard in my chest.

"That's it!" I jumped in the air and waved my arms as if anyone could see me. I giggled and covered my face. I had never been so happy to see the City.

She nodded once and started to walk along the ridge of the dune, away from the City.

"Wait!" I called to her. "Are you not coming?"

She kept walking. "I do not have any reason," she answered over her shoulder.

"But my father will want to thank you," I said lamely. I did not want her to go yet.

"Why does that matter?"

"What about supplies?"

"I have no money."

"We can give you provisions for your journey. Where is it you are going?"

"Go home."

I do not know why I chased her. I don't even remember telling my legs to run, but I was suddenly in front of her, trying to convince her to come to the City with me. She was hesitant, but eventually agreed, on the condition that she be allowed to trade for her supplies. Nothing would be given.

She walked ahead of me, her head swiveling from side to side, watching for movement. She was watching for anything she could use to trade when we got to the City. Every so often, she would take off after something in the sand that only she could see. By the time we reached where the desert met the ghettos, five rattlers and one sidewinder were slung dead over her shoulder.

Chapter 8

S omething was different. I felt wrong.

The moment my foot crossed into the maze of plastic shanties I felt like a bead of oil on water. The plastic shacks seemed to close in, crossing over the path to swallow me up. I quickened my step.

We were instantly swarmed by vendors offering boxes of roasted meats, braided cords, and tiny painted figurines made from clay. There seemed to be more of them than ever today, and maybe it was because there had always been that many. I had just never seen them because I followed Cal.

Vargas had bought meats and trinkets off them at random, some days more generous than others, but to me it seemed cruel. Vargas got their hopes up. I never knew whether he did it intentionally or not. Cal never looked at them. He thought *that* was cruel. He was always angry at my indecisiveness. I could never choose a way, so I followed him.

Today, I pushed by on my own, checking to see if the woman was following me.

She was looking at them. She met their eyes. She considered their goods without speaking before walking on. I had never seen anyone do that before. The vendors watched us go, their boxes gripped to their chest a little tighter, their eyes a little sadder. Why had she done that to them?

We made our way through the ghettos and out into the sunlight, the houses gradually getting bigger the closer we got to the capitol building. I had hoped she would be impressed, but if she was she did not say anything. She glanced at the fine people walking by, none of whom returned her gaze. We paused at the Founders Fountain while she refilled her water bags. She seemed to contemplate the figures in marble above her. Her eyes traveled from Copernicus to Magellan and up the spire of the capitol building. She read the names engraved in the fountain and studied the faces in marble, then sealed the bags without a word.

Out of the corner of my eye, I noticed a whiskered City man in a waistcoat standing near her at the fountain. He had a small silver cup attached to a chain above his pocket watch. As he bent slightly to dip his cup in the fountain, he paused, noticing something on the woman's left hand. He squinted at it, then at her face which was turned away from him. He seemed about to say something when she motioned for me to lead on. I turned to look at his face after we walked away. I could not describe it—he looked blankly surprised. His silver cup in his hand was forgotten, and he seemed to want to call us back but he did not. I looked at her before turning my eyes back to the road. For one fleeting moment, I wondered who she could be. I knew she was not a Bedouin. Her left hand swung by her side as she walked. Something glinted there, but when I looked she almost trampled me. She made a frustrated sound in her throat.

"Almost there," I said, turning back to the road.

I could feel her eyes boring into the back of my head, but I did not look around.

The great houses gave way to smaller ones as we crossed through the City, to the red sandstone mounds of the hunters spaced far apart from each other. We preferred the space. Closer to the capitol building, the houses were built right on top of each other.

"We need breathing room," my father always said.

We wanted room for community fires and space to see the stars. I had believed him when I was smaller, but now I thought the City residents did not want us any closer than we had to be. Or maybe that is just what Cal thought. Had thought.

Even here, the sandstone mounds felt cramped together. I was sure the space between them had shrunk somehow when I saw the one that was my own.

My stomach dropped as we approached. The hunting parties would not return until much later in the day, but my father would be home. He had not hunted since Cal and Vargas had lifted their first machetes. I saw him now, standing in the red doorway of our home, looking out at us. He gaped at me, gripping the doorway for support. He tottered out, unsteady on his legs, his tunic spattered and dirty. His eyes were wet, and I felt his callused hands on my face. He pulled me close to him and I buried my face in his chest.

He held me tight and whispered, "Vargas? Cal?"

I shook my head, my nose squashed against his chest. I felt him take a trembling breath that caught in his throat. He nodded, his bristly beard brushing the top of my head. He loosened his grip and I saw he was looking at the woman.

She had stayed well behind me, her hard eyes watching us.

"She saved me. Out in the open." I told my father.

He pulled me close to him.

"Thank you," he said to her. He paused, waiting for her to give her name. She didn't.

"I told her we could help get provisions."

He nodded. "Where is it you are going?"

In response, she swung the snakes down from her back and held them up for my father to see. "I have these for trade," she said in her dark, quiet voice.

My father smiled and spread his arms wide, shaking his head. "Please, you saved my Rue's life. I couldn't—"

"Trade only," she interrupted. "I will not take anything for free."

My father was puzzled but motioned her inside anyway, holding me close by his side. "Well, let's see what we can find."

They haggled in the den—the woman, my father, and a dried meat vendor named David who had happened to be passing by. David's loud voice carried, my father's booming intermittently, and patches of the woman's voice rolling over them both. I listened to them from my room, picking apathetically at my things.

I went into Cal and Vargas' room. My father had not packed any of it away, but I was sure he would now that he knew they were never coming home. They had collected a number of weapons and a good amount of survival gear in their five years as hunters. A thought seized me. I started taking things: a machete with a blade as long as my torso, a water bag, a leather belt with a loop for the machete and a pouch for rations, a pack, and bandages. I dragged a box from under Cal's bed and pulled out the cloth bag where he kept his savings. I spread the money on the bed and took half of it, leaving the other half for my father. I hesitated and then put the money back, leaving the bag on the bed where my father would easily find it.

I took the rest of the supplies to my room and folded my spare robes as I had seen the woman fold the blankets, making them as small as possible and shoving them down to the bottom of the pack. I put everything in the pack and set it in the corner of my bed when I was finished. Then I unpacked it and tried again, making the folds in my robes tighter, compressing the bundle even more. I wanted to save as much room as possible. I slid my arms through the straps, testing the weight of it, trying to estimate how long I could carry it. I put the pack back on the corner of my bed.

For the first time since I crossed into the City that day, I did not feel apart, out of place. The pack felt right. The machete felt at home in the belt around my waist, the flat of the blade against my thigh. I left the pack in my room and walked toward the den. I could hear my father's voice and paused to listen.

"…different. What happened out there?"

Silence. I peeked around the corner. David and the snakes were gone. My father and the woman were alone. She was packing dried meat into strips of cloth and leather. His back was to me.

His voice came again. "You do not know then."

The woman shook her head but did not stop packing away the dried meat.

My father went on. "How could she have survived? You found her, of course, but before. She is so small, only still learning. And yet she is alive. She lives. It is a miracle."

The woman's hands slowed, her eyes looking at something barely a meter in front of her face—something that was not there—and then they slid in my direction. She looked at me very intently, like a layer had been added to my skin that she had not noticed before.

My father looked around and then noticed the machete at my side. He looked very sad.

My father avoided me around the community fires that night, choosing another fire away from me. The other hunters avoided me, too, maybe fearing I would bring them bad luck. The tutors' circle was full of children, but I felt no desire to join them. I sat alone, looking up at the stars, my plate untouched on the ground in front of me. Orion was there again. I felt like I had not seen him in ages. Sand crunched near my hand, and when I looked over the woman was seated on the rock beside mine, looking up at the stars. She sat quietly for a long time. If I had not looked at her, I would not have known she was there. She was a master of silence—I couldn't even hear her breathing.

"My name is Connor Fadi," she said softly, her face still turned to the stars.

"Connor is a boy's name."

"It's my name." She looked over at me and shrugged. "My parents wanted a boy. They got me."

"Why are you telling me?"

"Who says I was telling *you*?" She looked back up at the sky, up at Orion. "Perhaps I just wanted to say it out loud to someone."

I studied her for a while. Her scar, her hodgepodge collection of clothing, her chapped lips, the way she seemed *apart*. "How long have you been in the desert?" I asked, not really expecting her to answer. It seemed as though she spoke only when she felt like it, not to oblige someone else's curiosity.

"A year. I think. Maybe longer."

"Alone?"

"Now."

"How? How could you possibly have survived that long alone?"

Her left eyebrow twitched, and she did not answer me for some time. Across the community fires, my father watched us with a heavy expression.

"Do you watch the stars often?" she asked.

I nodded. "I like their stories."

She glanced at me. Again, that look. Her stare bore through me, as though I was being figured out.

"A book my father used to read to me," I said. "My brothers…" I faltered, and my voice sealed itself inside me.

She shifted a little before she spoke again. "They are not really demons, the witches. They kill us. They kill anything they think they can eat, but—" she shrugged her shoulders slightly, "They are predators, like wolves. Only we do not understand them in the same way."

"You're wrong."

"I'm not." Her face was hard again, but the volume of her voice never changed. "I know you saw something out there. It may not have been real."

"What?"

"Fear alters the mind, hides the truth. What is real and what you saw may be different."

I looked away from her, back up at the sky. Anger curled over my heart. But I was still curious. "Why will you not tell anyone where you are going?" I asked.

"Because they would not understand."

I shook my head. What nonsense.

It was a while before she spoke again. "I am not going to a *where*. I am going to a *what*."

"What are you looking for?"

Connor hesitated. "A miracle."

A glint near the fire caught my eye. On the fourth finger of her left hand was a thick gold ring, the kind a man would wear. The ring was molded into a shape—that of an animal with no legs or wings, an animal that neither crawled on the ground nor flew in the sky and shined bright as the sun.

"I am going with you," I said, my eyes fixed on the ring. It was not a question.

Her brown eyes searched my face, studying me right down to my core.

She nodded.

Chapter 9

To talk of destiny would cheapen it—my choice to go with Connor. *Destiny* was a word people used to make themselves feel important. It carried no weight with me. I wanted to go because I wanted something else besides a life of death and fear.

This was rebirth.

I stood in my room later that night, sorting the supplies I would take with me. My fingers ran excitedly over each item, but I hardly saw any of them. My eyes looked ahead to the open sand, the wide sky, the new day.

"You are going with her," said a voice behind me.

I turned. My father stood in the doorway. He leaned heavily against the frame, his mouth drooped behind his curled beard. His dark eyes held mine and I felt the creep of guilt at the edges of my heart.

I was the last of his children.

I wanted to tell him that I was leaving but that I would be safe. I wanted to say that I was old enough. Service children and apprenticed children left at a much younger age. I wanted to say that I would be all right.

But I was his last child, walking away with a stranger, and when I left he would be alone.

Selfish. Willful. Ungrateful.

I swallowed. His eyes left mine and he shifted a little against the frame. "I had hoped," he said quietly, "that you would stay. The City will always need witch hunters. I had hoped that you would continue your training."

I shook my head. I did not understand how he could think so. Not after my brothers.

He hefted his body away from the frame and away to his own room. He did not have anything else to say to me.

In the morning, Connor stood outside the door of the hut as my father and I said goodbye, not wanting to intrude, or perhaps simply anxious to get started.

My father took my hand in his. He had spoken little to me that morning, and when he had his voice had sounded thin and small. I do not think he had slept at all the night before.

"Rue," he whispered, "how will you care for yourself?"

"I was old enough to walk with witch hunters."

"With your brothers to protect you."

I shook my head, not wanting to say anything more that would hurt him. My brothers had not been able to protect me. My brothers had died. I had seen their bodies picked over like meat.

"I want to go," I said gently as I could.

"Where is she taking you?" His eyes wrinkled and his mouth creased with emotion. "What if she is killed? Who will take care of you?"

"If she dies," I whispered, "I promise I will find a way home."

"Alone?"

"Alone is never a choice," came Connor's voice from outside the door. "We are always alone."

My father gripped my hand tightly in his. "She is *wrong*, Rue."

I hugged him. "I know."

And I did know. My father had been with me in the desert, as had my mother, as had Connor. I had not been alone when I fell, and I would not be alone now.

Connor and I set out toward the edge of the City. As we came to the Founder's Fountain, I looked up at Magellan's face and thought, *I will never be here again.*

Connor paused to let us drink from the fountain, but we did not speak to each other. I was lost in thought, but Connor was simply still. Given months or even years, I felt I would never know all there was to Connor Fadi. Most of her would always be hidden somewhere far out of my reach.

And I was following her into the Devil's playground.

⸻

We climbed our first dune just as the sun was reaching its zenith. The first day had flown by. I was lost in the drama and romance of a new adventure—the vast unknown filling me with excitement. Connor mastered the dune with her long, powerful stride and left me to scuttle in the sand like a beetle, trying to catch up. Burning sand swelled over my ankles and into my short boots with every step up the dunes. Connor stood at the apex with her back to me, fiddling with June's compass. I took the opportunity to empty my shoes.

"We will have to keep an eye out for something more suitable," said Connor, her eyes on the horizon.

"Witch hunters keep to the lowlands," I answered from where I sat, sand spilling out of my boots and piling in a little cone in front of me.

"You will slow us down."

She scanned the horizon, looking from it to the compass.

"You need a map," I quipped.

"I lost it," she replied darkly.

I went back to my shoes, not wanting to annoy her by asking more questions.

"How do you know where to go?" I asked.

She didn't answer, which irked me. I shoved my feet back in my shoes and watched the sky out of habit. I caught myself wondering who stood behind Elyah in line now before I remembered that no one stood with Elyah anymore. I had forgotten Elyah, and I hadn't even remembered that I had forgotten her. My stomach sank a little.

After a few moments, Connor spoke again. "There are canyons to the west of us, flats to the north. The flats are difficult to cross, too difficult with what little we have on us. We will have to head west first through the canyons. There are small towns there where we can get what we need to cross the flats. We need to move. The nearest safe place to camp is almost thirty kilometers from here."

"What is on the other side of the flats?" I asked.

She glanced at me.

I tried again, attempting to stay as still as she did, hoping she would see I was like her. "Why do we want to cross them?"

She looked away, her breath slightly shallow, and it crossed my mind that she might not like this. She probably had not had to speak to anyone in a long time. She was not used to explaining herself.

I might have had the smallest hope that she would respond to me, at least in some helpful way, but she did not. Instead, she made her way down the dune heading west toward the canyons. Her confident stride became more of a slide and step down the dunes, less of a hacking and stabbing and more of a negotiation. She melded with the desert much better than she did with people; there was grace to her movements that was better than words. She conveyed more about her relationship with the desert in one walk down a dune than she could ever tell me.

Not that she would tell me, I thought, perhaps a little bitterly, as I followed her down, doing my best not to fill my shoes again.

You never get used to the desert heat, not really. I wished I could say that after the few years I have spent in its vastness, I no longer noticed the heat, but there is no preparing yourself for the crushing hand that is midday. Desert garb is designed to protect the skin from burns and the sting of sandstorms, but the heat—there is nothing. Nothing can protect or lessen. It just is, and I think that might be why Connor thrived out here. They were the same, she and the desert.

Or maybe I was thinking nonsense because I was thirsty.

Conserving the water was the hardest part. Cal had carried my supplies because I was not old enough, but now I had to learn how to not just carry but to save. I had to learn because there was nothing out here to keep us alive but ourselves. It was a frightening and exciting thought.

I picked at my turban, inviting the meager breeze to cool my neck. I realized that I had automatically started to walk directly behind her, as part of a line, and by the way she looked over her shoulder I guessed that it was unnerving. It felt unnatural to walk next to her, and I could barely keep up as it was, so I fell behind. She stopped for a moment, waiting for me.

"I will leave you here," she hissed as soon as I reached her. Her voice was angry. "Keep. Up."

She broke into a trot and I jogged after her, my pack bouncing on my back, making annoying *shunk shunk* noises with each of my steps. I struggled to tighten the straps and jog, but I could not do both. Connor slipped behind me and easily yanked my straps into place in one smooth motion. The pack jammed against my back and the straps pinched my armpits, but I did not say anything. She was already ahead of me again anyway.

I trotted after her, determined not to fall behind. No one ever said it would be easy, certainly not Connor, who had told me precious little about the journey as it was—what we were actually looking for, what we would do if we found it, or indeed how long that might take. I watched her jogging along the sand at an easy pace, her shoulders still, her arms bent at her sides. For the first time, I wondered just what I thought I was doing.

Chapter 10

The first day passed quickly, as most first days do. My father would say it was the excitement of something new, and I was excited—wary but excited. We were bound for the unknown, and the unknown was always both thrilling and frightening.

We bedded down at the edge of the Red Canyons, discovered by Cortez some three hundred years ago and mapped by another explorer a hundred years later. I had never been, but Vargas and Cal used to camp there when they were boys. It was part of their survival training. They would catch and roast lizards and insects, learn the names of the cacti, how to tap a Saguaro for water, and travel up and down the canyons using the constellations. They did not worry about witches, who never hunted in the canyons. It was easier to patrol outside more populated areas for food. Even so, I remember wandering into the den when I was five years old, my brothers gone for two days, and finding my father sitting in the open entry of our home. His back was to me and the night was very cold, but he would not come in or close the door. I remember how bright the stars shone over his then black hair. He had told me to go back to bed, but he would not look at me. His voice was tight. It is my earliest memory.

When we got to the Red Canyons, Connor left me to build a fire while she climbed the canyon wall to get her bearings. I did not tell her I had never built a fire before.

She set her pack on the ground, stripped off her outer robe and head scarf, and walked along the base, picking her spot. She chose a craggy, wrinkled slab with easy handholds and footholds. She pulled herself up, keeping her body close to the rock and testing her holds before transferring her weight. Below, I gathered brush and twigs and watched her progress. The striped faces of the canyons jutted some six or seven meters out of the ground and snaked west for days. I did not know where the next city was, but it would not be less than three days away. If she fell, there would be no saving her.

When she disappeared over the top of the canyon wall, I returned to my task. I made a cone with the twigs, going on no other previous experience than something Vargas had told me once. I then tucked the brush inside for fuel and dug through Connor's pack for flint and steel. I pulled out her animal hair blankets and set them neatly to the side, shaking the pack to see within. I felt around with my hand, pulling out rations wrapped in leather and cloth, small knives in leather sheaths, sharpening stones, a pot of aloe for burns, and a hairbrush. In the very bottom were flint and steel. I repacked her bag, leaving the blankets out, and squatted in front of the kindling to shield the sparks from the wind. I heard her soft, snake hunter boots hitting the ground behind me just as the brush caught fire. She toed her pack, glancing at me. I passed the flint and steel back to her, and she inspected the fire I had built. I was quite proud, even if she didn't care. Why would she? She did not know it was my first fire. She reached into her pack and tossed me a packet of rations, removing another for herself.

"We should not eat these," I said. "We should hunt instead and leave the rations for when there is nothing to hunt." I was exhausted from the quick pace she had set to cover the 30 kilometers to get here. I did not want to move and was perfectly happy to eat rations tonight, but I wanted to show her I knew proper survival procedures. I did not want her to think I was useless.

She bit into a piece of dried meat. "Tomorrow," was all she said.

We ate quietly, listening to the land come alive. A pack of coyotes howled, and night birds whistled. The brush shuddered whenever a hare or mouse passed through. The fire popped every so often as the kindling crisped and the last of the air escaped the twigs. I loved the smell.

Connor finished and folded the empty packet under her blanket, taking a sip from her water bag. I made sure to do the same. We both spread our blankets and bedded down, Connor on her back and me on my side facing the fire.

"Connor," I said, not bothering to whisper. "What did you see up there?"

"Rock," she answered.

I glanced at her across the fire. Her mouth twitched in the barest of smirks, or maybe it was only the shadows playing across her face.

"What else?" I tried again.

"There is a small town I know less than a day from here. It isn't much, but we will be able to find all we need to cross the flats. The town is due west, but the canyon divides a few kilometers from here. One way goes to the town, the other becomes a maze—divides another four times or more."

"We might get lost?"

"No."

"You know where to go?"

"Yes."

"What town is it?"

"Would you know it?"

"No," I conceded.

"It is just a town."

"Connor, I have nothing to trade."

She was quiet a moment. "I would not worry about it," she said finally.

I wanted to ask more, but I felt heavy. My eyes had been slowly opening and closing as we talked, and now they were too tired to do that anymore. I felt myself slipping down, very gratefully, into a deep sleep. My last thought before losing consciousness completely was if one of us should be keeping watch.

Someone was shaking me. I rolled over. In the darkness, I could see Cal's face over me. His eyes were wide and anxious, and he shook me hard. His mouth kept opening and closing but I could not hear him. He was saying my name, but I could not hear him. It frightened me that I couldn't hear him. I tried to sit up, but I could not move. I tried to tell him, but he pulled at my arm to get me to stand, his mouth opening and closing like a toy. I looked at his mouth. It was *Rue, Rue*, but then it wasn't. His mouth opened and closed in one syllable, one word over and over, but I still could not hear him.

"What are you saying? What are you telling me?" I cried.

He stopped and pulled my face close to his. His eyes were dark from fear. He opened his mouth and the word filled my brain, loud like a clap of thunder.

RUN.

I bolted upright just as sparks showered over my bedding. I spun out of the blanket and to my feet, chaos erupting around me, dogs snarling, flashes, screams. I reached for my machete as darkness knocked me back, pinning me down, and a hundred fangs bore down on my face. I plunged my hands into coarse fur, pushing, and twisting my body away. Suddenly, it was gone, replaced by Connor hauling me to my feet.

"Run!" she yelled in my face.

I turned and ran for the canyons, Connor right behind me, or so I hoped. I turned to look for her and saw coyotes tearing through our camp, one dead and one howling. The rest snarled and bounded after us. Connor had grabbed our packs and was sprinting after me.

"Don't look back!" she cried. There were two coyotes between us. I lifted my knees and sprinted harder as sharp teeth nipped at my ankles. Coyotes are faster than people. It was only a matter of time. I heard heavy sounds and yelping, and suddenly Connor was next to me. I looked back. The coyotes were gone.

I fell against the nearest canyon wall, gasping for breath.

"What happened?" I asked.

Connor wiped her machete. "They got brave," she gasped, out of breath. She leaned against the opposite wall for a moment. "We cannot stop here. We have to keep going. It isn't safe."

I stayed where I was. My heart was beating too fast. All I could see was a wall of sand coming at me, and I heard the hysterical laughter of hyenas chasing me through the desert. Connor chunked my pack at my chest, bringing me back to the cold canyons. I slipped the leather straps over my shoulders and shivered. The night air was a sharp cold in my nostrils that left me wide awake.

She wanted to travel to where the canyons divided before we rested, but her voice seemed far away still. I closed my eyes for a moment and opened them again. Behind us, the dying fire threw shadows up the red canyon walls, where the coyotes danced and snarled and howled at the moon before melting into the ground and disappearing completely.

The fire should have kept them away. They should have been frightened of us. I shivered in the night air before turning to follow Connor further into the canyon.

Chapter 11

We walked at an easy pace, but it still seemed like hours before we got to the great divide in the rock. The jagged edge sliced the red rock in two; each path snaked away quiet and still in the dark. You could not see past the openings, but Connor strode confidently forward, not waiting for me to follow. I plunged into the left fork after her, not bothering to ask for a break.

I could not see her or anything else. The moon was still bright, bathing the top of the canyon in bluish grey light, but none filtered down to us on the ground. I watched for the glint of Connor's machete to tell me that she was still there, and I dragged my fingertips along one side of the canyon wall to keep from walking into the other. Things skittered along the rock above my head, sometimes sending down pebbles and dust. I swallowed and tried not to think about it. My only real concern was the soft noises along the base of the wall that indicated a startled snake. I dreaded getting a snakebite, especially now when I had no idea how much further it was to the town or indeed if anyone there would be able to help me. Small towns sprang up every few years over shallow wells or mineral deposits, but they were often for only a handful of inhabitants, and they never lasted long.

I did not want to sleep in the canyons. The walls were so close, and I was greatly relieved that Connor never stopped. I could hear her footsteps ahead of me, and a second dragging sound that never stopped. She was following the wall with her fingers as I was. I looked up at the night sky. A trail of white light told me the moon was just behind the edge of the opposite wall—black in the dark. I could see the edges of constellations but could never be sure of what I was looking at. Where was Orion? Was that bright one Rigel or Betelgeuse? Or neither? Where was I?

A feeling of unease came over me as the dark seeped out of the canyon walls and up into the sky. The stars faded away and the walls opened into a circle a half kilometer wide. A large stone sat just outside the circle with letters carved into it that were worn almost smooth. We had reached the town. I ran my hand over the faded marks.

Welcome Home.

Chapter 12

T here was nothing there but fragments of buildings, nothing but ghosts of what had been, and not a soul left. Jagged husks seemed to grow from the ground, small flags of paper fluttered against the earth, and bits of belongings dotted the ground—reading glasses here, a broken comb there. Something flashed in the sand. I reached down and pulled out a hand mirror painted with horses in fantastic colors—a child's mirror. If their well had dried up they would have taken the time to pack their things, but they had not. They had left everything behind as though they were planning to come back one day.

"Witches were here," I said softly.

Connor brushed past me. "Stop calling them that."

I watched her stride up to the nearest building, the mirror still in my hand. She did not hesitate at the door but walked right in as if she had been there a hundred times. I stayed outside, picking over the pieces of other people's lives in the sand, while Connor banged around inside. I did not want to go in. It felt wrong to disturb the town like this, like walking over someone's grave. I pulled at some half-buried papers. The edges were bleached and brittle after so much time in the sun, but the papers were bound and came out altogether, pouring sand and sending a small cream-colored snake the size of my finger wiggling to the safety of the brush at the canyon wall. I thumbed the pages, listening to the soft *thhhh* of paper on paper. It was a book. The cracked burgundy leather was flaked with gold—the pattern almost like stars, the title worn to pieces—and the pages were written in a language I did not know.

A bit of color among the black and white caught my eye, and I turned the pages to a picture of a beast. I sat cross-legged in the sand, unable to look away. It was blue—the whole page was blue. The picture had been done in shades, from indigo to cobalt to turquoise to the palest morning sky. It was not a color seen every day, but here it was, buried in the sand and forgotten. Outlined in thin strokes—a suggestion of shape—was an animal of sorts, with the head and talons of an eagle and the body and brushy tail of a coyote. The animal slinked along the ridge of a sand dune under a starry night, the lines of its body echoing the lines of the dune. A dimpled blue moon hung low in the sky, filling half the page.

A hand appeared in the middle of the cobalt night, and I looked up. Connor was staring down at the page, her chapped lips slightly parted. She stroked the page delicately, far more gently than I would have expected her to be capable of, her brown eyes soft.

"I found it," I said, for lack of something better to say.

She was not listening. My heart sank as she pulled the book out of my hands and flipped through the pages, looking for more pictures. She stopped on one page, running her finger over it, tracing something, but I could not see what she was looking at. Just as I opened my mouth to ask for it back, she stepped behind me. My pack shifted against my back, and when she stood in front of me again her hands were empty. She glanced at me for a moment, then turned on her heel and headed for another ruined building. I adjusted the straps on my pack and followed.

The building she went into was all that remained of their supply store. It was the most intact building in the town, the four walls erect and undamaged save for where they ended quite abruptly just above our heads, as if a giant had ripped the top off the building to look inside. I watched her go through what was left. She swung her pack off her shoulder and filled it with any bit of harsh weather gear she could lay her hands on: a small tent, dried food, small pots of aloe vera for burns, packets of liquid mixed with potassium compounds to keep water in our bodies, and so on. She crossed to me and pulled my pack off, dividing the supplies between us, and adding an extra bit of flint and steel for me.

For a while she stared at the wall of supplies before us, pressing her body away from it with the palms of her hands against the edge of the counter. She wanted more; I knew it. She wanted to be able to take more with us in the flats, but we could not carry more. I watched her think, a bead of sweat forming at her hairline. She glanced at the packs, running through the list of supplies in her head. I could practically see the numbers—the number of days for the distance over the flats, food and water divided by two people over that number of days. I wondered how much further we had to go.

I had heard eerie tales of the salt flats—adventure seekers lost on day trips with no hope of rescue, pioneers wandering in circles until dying of thirst, whole armies swallowed up as though they were nothing. In school, I had learned that Magellan, on his failed journey to circumnavigate the globe, had lost twenty of his two-hundred-man party in the salt flats alone. Students had asked how it was possible to lose anyone when the salt flats go on unbroken by so much as a boulder for over a hundred kilometers, but the light does strange things in the flats. A man could be standing meters away and you would have no idea.

When I looked up again, Connor had her eyes on me. I wondered if she was also thinking of Magellan. She reached below the counter, then straightened and slapped a bundle of thin cord on the countertop, which I wordlessly bundled in with my gear. She meant to tie us together in the flats. She could not have everything she wanted on her back, and she did not want to lose what was on mine either.

We left the town that same day. As we crossed back into the canyons, Connor glanced back at the ruins, her brows knitted together.

"What?" I asked.

She looked at me for a moment, then shook her head and kept walking.

"What?" I asked again.

She stopped, her head down, thinking. "Did you see any bodies?"

"No."

"Not even blood," she said, looking at me.

"Not even blood."

Connor looked troubled, but would not say anything more. I followed her, glancing back at what was left of the town just before we crossed over into the canyons. There had not been any bodies; no pieces, no bits. Witches may have been here, but it had been years since the attack. Why that troubled Connor, though, I could not understand.

We reached the edge of the flats at sunset. The journey that day had been an easy one as the high red walls of the canyons protected us from the sun. Just before it dipped below the horizon, the rock walls ended, and the hot breath of the open desert enveloped us once more.

Connor stopped at the edge of the flats, looking out over—

I dropped my pack and stared. The orange sun dipping below the horizon did not end at the horizon. There was no horizon. The sun bled into the desert in front of us, becoming two halves of the same star stacked on top of each other. It was so close. Thirty steps and I could touch it. Where was the sand? I took a step and the ground shifted, tilting under me. I stumbled and fell onto my hands and knees.

"You are confusing your mind," came Connor's voice somewhere behind me. "Don't look at the horizon."

"There is no horizon," I gasped, trying to look up.

"The salt flats are a weapon the desert wields. The light will trick you, so we travel by night."

Turning my head away from the flats, I saw Connor was tying my pack to hers. "We can't start now," I told her. "We have been traveling all day."

"Wait now and we wait through the day as well. We are too exposed here. It is better to go now and rest in the morning."

"Nothing lives here—nothing could survive."

She straightened, her jawline set. "You'd be surprised."

She was right, things did live here. Night things. Crawling things. Things I could hear but could not see. Skitterings in the salt beside my foot every time I took a step. Shrieks in the distance. The soft slide of scales over the crumbled ground.

We traveled at night, the line of cord connecting us, and made crude tents out of blankets we pulled from our bags during the day, tilting the openings to try to catch the wind. I preferred this to sharing the tent from the town's supply store. It gave me time to be alone. When I could not sleep, I would cock the edge of my blanket tent and look out at the shimmering flats. The mirages made my stomach drop but I kept looking. I'm not sure why. Maybe I thought I could get used to it, like taking tiny doses of poison to build up an immunity. Maybe I thought I could conquer the flats.

Connor tied the edges of our blankets together and then tied the blankets to our packs. We kept every bit of supplies close to us. For the first couple of days, I watched the shaded sun cross my blanket tent and did not sleep. I wondered if Connor could sleep. I listened outside for signs of life. I missed the shade of the canyons.

We saw bones in the dark. Night after night, staves of ribs bleached white by the sun jutted out of the salt and tripped us up as we walked. Some skeletons were animals I could recognize—lions, jackals and other dog-like creatures, birds and snakes whose thin bones were easily crushed under my feet—and then we came upon something that could not be real.

Our way was blocked by bones. Tusks longer than my body stabbed upward into the night sky, the other ends of which were fitted into blocky skulls with huge eye sockets and short, flat teeth. Four long limb bones reaching out from a cavernous rib cage ended in strange half-toes. The tails were indicated by only a tiny line of vertebrae, stopping well before the feet. When it had been alive, this animal was taller than the two of us standing on each other's shoulders. Then I realized there were more. Limbs disappeared into the dark, and farther away shards of bone stood out against the black sky. Death lay before us, and we could not see how long it went on. I shuddered.

Connor took a step forward, but I grabbed the line between us and yanked. I heard her stop but that was all.

"No," I whispered. If the Devil lived anywhere, it was here.

"This is the way we have to go," I heard Connor reply softly. The bones hushed us, made us small. The living should not speak here.

Before I could speak again, she tugged the cord out of my hands, pulling me forward. I stumbled and put my hand out to steady myself. My palm landed on the nearest creature's skull. It felt smooth under my hand. I looked and found myself staring into its left eye socket. The hole, like the darkest cave, sent a shiver down my spine. I quickly pulled my hand away and followed Connor.

We picked our way along, winding between the skeletons, which sometimes overlapped each other so that the creatures appeared to have two heads, bisecting rib cages, and double spines. The normal sounds of the desert at night had stopped, as if the bones had formed a barrier that no life could cross—no life but us. Bones rose high above our heads, closing in and crowding out the stars. I pulled my lips into my mouth and bit down hard whenever I brushed against a tusk or skull. I thought I saw things in the dark—demons lurking in the shadows, witches waiting for fresh meat. They would smash our heads against the bones as easily as splitting a melon on a rock. I imagined them scooping out our brains with their long fingers, adding our corpses to this collection. We would never be found.

Connor walked faster than I could, the cord yanking me forward. Angry and afraid, I would yank back and hear her stumble. Finally, she reached back and grabbed the front of my robes, pulling me up to walk next to her. Now we would have to go together, walk through this place at the same time. For just a moment, I thought of my brothers and the witch hunters, all dead on another patch of sand; how long it would be before they were nothing but bones bleaching in the sun. I wondered how much of the world was a graveyard. My eyes stung and I wiped them with my sleeve, the salt from my clothes burning my face.

It seemed as though we walked for hours, passing creature after creature. I had not thought to count how many there were, but eventually there were no more in front of us. We had passed through and come to the other side. I thought of the creatures with their huge bodies and blunt teeth. Connor and I had been walking for days in the salt flats. How long had they been walking? I looked behind me at the last skeleton. It lay on its side with its front limbs reaching out. It was smaller than the others. *Family*, I thought. *They didn't know. They died together.*

We walked on.

On the fifth night, I started to wonder how we got anywhere, how we made our way in the dark, how we moved. To me, we were blind. Were we not tied together, we would slowly drift away from each other and not even notice. Then one night the moon rose high in the sky, spreading her silver face wide and smiling down on us like the shiniest of coins. By her light I finally saw Connor, her strong back firmly in front of me, her head tilted up, slowly turning from left to right. The sky glittered with a million tiny points of light—stars spread thick as jam in the deep black sky. The belt of the galaxy stretched itself directly over our heads, descending the night sky in a vertical line, and disappearing into the horizon directly in front of us. Connor's face tilted toward the line like a worshipper. She pursued the end of the galaxy, leading me to the place where the stars met the horizon.

I followed Connor, and Connor followed the stars.

Soon, I was too tired to stay awake. In the early mornings, as the sky became rosy, Connor would stop and leave me to build the blanket tents while she distributed the rations. Some mornings, I pulled our tents into place, crawled into mine, and would be asleep before Connor had finished. She would put my rations back on those days. At night, we followed the stars.

On the tenth day, we heard something new. Something sighing over the flat ground. Something human. I cocked the edge of my blanket tent and looked out over the flats—what little I could see.

"Do you hear that?"

She shifted in the tent next to mine. We both listened. In the distance, we heard the sound of many feet traveling slowly toward us, but we saw nothing. Again, I thought of Magellan's twenty lost men who strayed too far from the group and could not find their way back. And then there came another sound. The sound of low singing. I shook my head and listened again. Connor had thrown back her blanket and come to stand next to the entrance of my tent. I looked up at her. She was squinting out into the shimmering horizon, straining to see what was coming, the thin scar on her face pink under the glare of the sun.

Suddenly, five figures appeared, stepping out as if from behind a veil. They were covered head to toe in heavy white robes that trailed the ground behind them, the hoods of their robes pulled up over their heads. Rope belts encircled their waists. The tail of each belt was tied to the one behind it, forming a human chain as more and more figures stepped out of the shimmering horizon. They were singing very softly in a language I did not understand, and they did not appear to notice us.

I crawled out from my tent and stood beside Connor. "What are they doing?" I asked.

Connor shook her head. This was madness. No one entered the salt flats without water, supplies—something, anything—but these people had nothing. They carried no packs, no water pouches, nothing but themselves.

We watched the line of figures, ten in all, walk out just past our tents. Just as the first in line was about to disappear into the horizon again, it turned and circled back in toward the group, leading the others in a circle, before going back the way they came.

"They are leaving," said Connor. She turned and started quickly disassembling her blanket tent. "Come on."

I started pulling down my tent and packing it away.

Connor shoved her blankets back into her pack, keeping an eye on the figures disappearing into the mirage of the horizon. "Didn't you see?" She asked. "No supplies. No water. They are not traveling; that means the edge is close."

She swung her pack onto her back, checking the rope that led to mine, before following the line of robed figures. I swung my pack onto my shoulders and followed her.

As we pursued the train of figures, we started to notice long scratches in the salt. They could not have been made by an animal. The scratches were few at first, and then more and more appeared, scarring the whole ground.

Further on, I noticed movement along the salt and stopped. A shiny rod, its end somewhere far ahead of us, was advancing in our direction a few centimeters above the salt ground. It stopped near my feet. Its end was the size and shape of a cupped hand. Connor and I watched the cup dig its edge into the ground, fill itself with salt, and then the rod was pulled away from us. We watched it retreat in the same direction as the white-clad figures.

Connor sighed. "Salt dippers."

Chapter 13

We emerged with the train of white-clad figures, who still had not noticed us, into a bustle of activity and color that grated against my senses after so much silence and solitude. Skinny, sun-browned salt dippers squatted at the edge of the flats, maneuvering their long silver poles into and out of the flats, emptying the gathered contents into large clay pots next to them. They were nearly naked, wearing only wrappings of white linen. Some had draped cloth over their heads and backs to keep off the sun. Behind the dippers, men and women in absurdly vibrant traveling garb shouted at each other and at the dippers, arguing over space at the edge. These were the merchants.

One dipper looked up as we approached and squinted at us. Behind him, a man elbowed his neighbor and pointed in our direction. As the line of white-clad figures pressed past the crowd, one turned and seemed to look at us before continuing onward.

A man riding a chestnut horse swung down and pushed his way past the other traders. His shirt and trousers were plain, and he wore a beige hat with a funny tassel. A red-and-white striped shawl was thrown over one shoulder. He wore soft boots and the leather leg wraps of an equestrian. As he passed the dippers, he raised his hand in our direction in a tentative greeting.

I glanced at Connor. Her lips were set in a line, her face unreadable. I turned back to the man with the striped shawl. Everything about him looked soft. His round face was framed with curly black and gray hair that almost brushed his broad, rounded shoulders, and he had the beginnings of a paunch. Deep lines creased his mouth and eyes. He was now waving at us, his mouth open in surprise. I waved back.

This seemed to encourage him. "Are you hurt?" He called.

I looked at Connor. Why didn't she answer him?

"No," I called back.

The man hurried out to us. Behind him, the salt dippers had paused in their work and were watching us. The other traders stopped shouting and pitched their voices low, whispering to each other and watching.

"My god," said the man as he approached us. "What are you doing out here? Are you lost? Where is your party? Are you thirsty?"

His brown eyes searched our faces, glancing at our clothes, and scanning the horizon for signs of other people like us. Sweat beaded his forehead and soaked the baby curls at his sideburns. His mouth, under a black and gray mustache, was still open in amazement.

Finally, Connor spoke. "We are thirsty."

The man did not hesitate. "Of course!" He made to put his arm around Connor but thought better of it. "Please. We have water." He motioned for the traders to clear a path and we followed him. Connor walked with her chin up, her back straight, looking each trader in the face as we approached. She did not smile. A few of the male traders looked at her with interest, but most ignored us and yelled to the dippers to finish their work.

A small boy held the reigns of the man's chestnut horse. The man took them and swatted him away. The boy backed up but kept his eyes on Connor and me. He could not have been more than ten or eleven. The man pulled open one of the side flaps of his pack just behind the saddle and pulled out a small water pouch.

"Here," he said, giving it to me first.

I tipped my head back to drink and noticed the heel of an embroidered boot in a stirrup very close to my head. A woman with dark, wild hair was looking down at me from astride a brown horse with white speckles across its flanks. Everything about her face was too big, from her wide eyes to her thick eyebrows that met over her large nose. She was studying me. I swallowed and passed the pouch to Connor, who handed it back to the man without drinking anything. She jutted her chin toward the line of people in white robes, their receding backs still disappearing into the wall of traders and horses.

"Who are they?"

The man looked and then turned back to her. "Who are they? Who are you? They are worshippers come to test their faith against the mirages of the salt flats. Who are you that you've never seen them? They come every day. They spend ten minutes in the flats and then leave. They're a nuisance, and they can't see a thing in those stupid robes. I'll bet they didn't even see you. You two appeared like ghosts—mirages come to life. Who are you?"

"What faith?" Connor asked, watching the last one disappear.

"That's what I say," the man replied, chuckling at his own joke. "Who knows? Who cares? They come, they sing, they leave. Who are you? What is wrong with you that you cannot answer a question?"

I sighed. I knew how he felt.

"Maybe they're spies," said a languorous voice above our heads. The woman with the wild hair smiled down from her perch on the white speckled mare.

"Spies?" The man put his hands on his hips. "Spies for what? We don't have anything except salt. Fine, steal that. Who cares? Get on the horse. We're leaving."

Connor did not move.

"We are just travelers," I said, stepping forward. I could feel Connor tensing beside me. She hated that I had spoken up, but I did not care. Frustration welled in my throat, and I refused to look at her. There were rules about hospitality to strangers in the wilderness. This chubby-faced man was not going to hurt us. Why could she not see that?

"Why? To where?" The man asked. I did not know how to answer him. "Fine," he said. "Don't tell me. But the nearest city is Morra—that's my city. The one after that is another five days walk. You want to walk there? Fine, but I bet you don't. Get on the horse."

"I'll take the little one," said the wild-haired woman, reaching down to help me scramble up and sit behind her.

"Good. Take her." The man waved his hand dismissively. "It's hot. Let's go."

I was angry at Connor, but I did not want to be separated from her. What if she could not find me when we got to Morra? What if she left me there? I gripped the woman's waist and turned my head to keep her hair out of my nose. Connor reluctantly mounted the chestnut stallion and did not look at me as we rode away.

Morra was not beautiful. Its spires were not as tall as my city, and there were too many people. Bodies clogged every available space on the street, pushing and shouting—vendors to be heard over other vendors, passersby when the horses came too close—everything seemed to be fighting for space. Even the mangy street dogs barked and snapped at each other. After so many days in the wide sands, the press of bodies against the flanks of the speckled horse made me feel like I could not breathe.

Ahead of us, the man roared at people to get out of the way, the funny tassel on his hat bouncing up and down, but they barely looked at him. He nudged his chestnut stallion through the crowds, waving vendors away and sometimes slapping their wares to the ground if they got too close.

"What are you doing?" He shouted. "What would I want with your junk? Get away!"

I hid my face in the woman's back and squeezed my eyes shut until the voices subsided.

"These people," the man grumbled to himself. I looked up and saw we had traveled deeper into the city, to a street where the high buildings towered over us and hid the sun's harsh light. The air was cooler and the people kept to the side paths. "Immigrants," the man continued. "Will we never be rid of them?"

"*We're* immigrants, my love," the woman replied.

The man snorted. "*Us?* We're *taxpayers*. Don't start with me."

The woman chuckled to herself and then said in a low voice, "Merchants always think they're better than everyone else." She turned her head and winked at me. "He's just mad he's not the only one who thought of coming here. He thinks he's an original."

"An original what?" I asked.

"You know," she said. "An original. Different. Better."

"But he is not?"

"Of course not," she said with a smirk. "No one is."

Her voice was dark as honey, muddled with a very slight accent that matched the man's. When she turned her head, her large nose looked hawkish, bent at the bridge at an angle that would have looked wicked on anyone else. But under her large eyes and thick eyebrows, a smaller nose would have been laughable. I peered around her cloud of black curls at Connor, whose straight back told me nothing.

The man gave a theatrical sigh of relief and stopped his horse in front of a large white house. "Here we are," he said loudly, swinging one leg over his horse's neck and dismounting. The movement seemed too awkward to be correct. He turned to help Connor down only to find her right beside him, brushing the horsehair from her black snake hunter boots. I did not want to be rude, so I did not resist when the woman helped me down. She seemed a far more competent rider than her companion, but I felt slightly ashamed for allowing a rude thought about someone who had shared water with us.

The two-level white house was trimmed with blue and had a knee-high white fence around a tiny gravel yard, like something out of a story. Two terra cotta pots stood on either side of the door. They held one sunflower each. I had never seen a sunflower outside of a picture in a book. No one had them. Plants required water—more than most had to spare—and were a luxury. I stared open-mouthed at the broad, nodding heads wreathed in gold. And green leaves. How beautiful such a color could be, and how rare. I looked over at Connor. She stood with her toes to the edge of the white fence. Her eyes, which could be flat and harsh as polished wood, were soft. Her lips parted and she slowly exhaled as though she had been holding her breath for a long time.

"Beautiful, aren't they?" The man was suddenly at her elbow, grinning. The woman walked past us and up the path to the house. She looked back at us, extended her thumb and middle finger, and flicked the head of one of the sunflowers. Hard. Connor and I both jerked, and my heart sank as I realized—

"They're fake," the woman said, and swept into the house.

Connor's eyes went hard again and her mouth set in a line.

The man shrugged. "Cloth. Who can afford the real thing? But these are good fakes. You couldn't tell." He nudged Connor with his elbow as though to include her in his joke. She did not look at him, so he shrugged again and motioned for us to go into the house.

Chapter 14

I have heard my father speak of the obligation to strangers my whole life. Water, shelter, food—share what you have with those who are lost. Those words were law. How Things Are. And yet neither he nor anyone else ever spoke of the threat that stood just behind those words—just out of sight, but I could feel the shadow underneath. Give, or be taken from. Share, or risk the wrath of the desperate.

The man and the woman looked at me with open friendship, but Connor was different. Despite their willingness to be hospitable, they could not come to grips with her, and her presence unnerved them. Their smiles slid from their faces when they met her gaze. She was not harsh with them, just impassive, unreadable, so I smiled for both of us to put them at ease. Still, our machetes were taken away by the boy who had held the man's horse at the edge of the flats. He was not their child. They had no children. I assumed he was a servant—there were other servants in the house. How many, I could not tell for they were silent and did not meet my eyes.

Connor and I were given separate rooms—small, but comfortable—and baths. I could not remember the last time I had bathed. Even then, it was never in anything as luxurious as a room just for bathing. I stood in a stone room while one of the servants covered my body from head to toe in perfumed powder that gripped my skin, bonding to the dirt and sweat and grime. My skin prickled in response and I sighed, enjoying the wonderful anticipation of being clean. The powder expanded into a caked mud that she scraped off me with a wooden blade. I wiggled my toes on the cool, smooth rock beneath my feet. A light breeze from the window just above my head touched my clean skin. I felt new as a baby. The servant combed my hair and applied oils before braiding it around my head. I thanked her, but she did not acknowledge me. She handed me a pair of linen trousers and a tunic and quietly left the room. I dressed myself, smelling the perfume from the bath powder on my wrists and hands. I covered my face with my hands and inhaled. When I spread my fingers, Connor was standing in front of me. How was it she made no noise?

She was dressed in plain trousers and a tunic similar to my own—guest clothes, I supposed—and her hair was plaited and wound around her head in the same style. Her skin had the freshly scrubbed glow that mine did, but her face was blank. She looked at me for a moment and then announced there was food laid out downstairs. Another servant in the doorway behind her motioned the way.

The man was called Cyril, and the woman was Zazi. They had come from a region further north, eighteen years ago, and settled in Morra, but they still preferred the northern style of eating—reclining on pillows around a low table. Aside from the ornately embroidered pillows, the room was simple. The dark wood of the table was unfinished, and the legs were carved into little pig-faced demons holding up the tabletop. I struggled to get comfortable, and in the end decided it was better to sit up with my knees bent and legs crossed underneath me. We ate snake meat in a spicy sauce with flatbread and persimmons, and there were honeyed dates for dessert.

As we ate, Cyril chattered like a wild parakeet, and Zazi showed me the necklace Cyril had given her the day he asked her to share her life with him. The chain of green malachite beads encircled her neck, and the pendant was a chunk of unfinished malachite. A copper wire monkey was woven into the natural creases of the stone. She called the monkey *elwala*. Cyril held up his left hand so that I could see the ring she had given him in return—the same copper *elwala* monkey grasped his finger. I wondered how long they had been together.

They seemed bound to one another, connected, and I marveled at them. Cyril smiled and snuck glances at Zazi as he told wild stories of his time in the salt flats, and she laughed and told us he was the biggest liar. There could be one hundred people in the room, and Cyril would only see Zazi. I thought of my father and mother. I could not remember how he had looked at her, but I hoped he had loved her as madly as Cyril loved Zazi.

A change came over me. Cyril spoke continuously and never seemed to take a breath, and yet a knot in my stomach that I hadn't known was there was starting to uncoil. Was it them? Was it the noise and warmth of the house? Zazi's laughter filled the room as Cyril finished yet another impossible tale, and he reached over to touch her outstretched hand. She looked at him and shook her head.

"You liar," she said, still smiling. She turned to me and rested a hand on mine. "Are you enjoying the food?"

The touch made me feel favored, singled out. I felt a swell of pride. "Yes, everything is delicious."

"The snake can be too spicy for some," she whispered conspiratorially, leaning in and rolling her eyes, "but you eat like a northerner. You can handle a little spice."

I smiled and repeated that the meal was excellent and then fumbled for something else to say. I wanted so much for her to keep talking to me. "Your house is beautiful," I said lamely.

She looked around as if seeing the room for the first time. "It is, isn't it? I'm glad you approve. So tell me about yourself, Rue. Where do you come from? Where are you going? Tell me everything."

She held my hand in hers and leaned her face closer to me. She smiled, revealing a row of large, white, perfect teeth. I was completely enchanted. I felt as though I were talking to a sister or a beloved aunt. I never had either, but I had always wanted one so desperately. As a small child, I had an image in my mind of growing up with another warm female presence—someone to braid my hair and tell me secrets. Elyah had five sisters, which made me jealous. I only had brothers. The thought evaporated—Elyah's parents were mourning their sixth child, and I did not have brothers anymore.

"Are you all right?"

Zazi's large eyes were searching my face, her brows knit together in concern.

I forced a smile and hoped it looked genuine. How long had I been quiet? "Oh," I managed to answer, "there is not much to tell. It would be boring."

Zazi tilted her chin, as though trying to see the truth through my lie. I forced a smile again, hoping it would hide the lump rising in my throat.

"Do you like jewelry?" she asked.

When I was small, I woke one morning too sick to get out of bed. My skin was burning with fever; my bed wet with sweat. I cried out of sheer discomfort, and my mother went to the market to buy a jug of cool water mixed with aloe jelly, into which she dipped clean linens. She stripped off my nightshirt and wrapped me up in the wet fabric to keep my skin cold. Still, I could not sleep, and so she read me the story of Mani Singh and the magic cave.

Mani Singh was an explorer who loved to climb the rocky cliffs outside of his village. He was scaling an unfamiliar outcrop when he slipped, nearly tumbling into the ravine below. He managed to grab onto a rock and was dangling by one hand when a jinni appeared beside him.

"What are you doing?" asked the jinni.

"I was climbing the cliff when I fell," cried Mani Singh. "Please help me!"

The jinni considered his request for a moment. "This cliff conceals my home. I will save your life," he said, "but in exchange, you must leave and never return. If you come back or reveal my secret to anyone else, you will be punished."

Desperate, Mani Singh agreed.

The jinni waved his hand, and Mani Singh found himself standing on solid ground just outside the gates of his own village. He was so grateful that he resolved to build an altar to the jinni to show how thankful he was. He considered building it there next to the village gate, but he knew there was a much better place for it.

That night, under the cover of darkness, Mani Singh returned to the spot where he fell and built an altar, for surely the jinni would not object to that. He piled the altar with dates and sweet bread in offering to the jinni and was just about to leave when he noticed a cave concealed in the rocks.

"That must be the jinni's house," Mani Singh said to himself.

He knew the jinni would be sure to see his altar in the morning. Mani Singh felt very proud of himself but also curious to see what the jinni kept inside his cave.

"Surely the jinni would want to see his altar now," he thought to himself. "And maybe it will make him happy and grateful, and he will invite me into his home."

Mani Singh crept to the entrance of the cave. "Hello?" he called out. There was no answer, and he felt a little thrill of excitement right down to his toes. The jinni was not home, and so in the manner of explorers everywhere, Mani Singh walked right in.

It was the deepest, darkest cave he had ever explored. It was too dark to see, and so he lit a torch. In the glow of the flame, Mani Singh realized the ceiling of the cave was so tall that it soared out of reach of the light. Stalactites hung low like chandeliers, dripping fresh, clean water onto spires of white crystals jutting out of the ground. The walls glittered like stars, and when Mani Singh managed to pry one out of the rock, he saw he held a diamond as big as his thumb. Everywhere he looked there was treasure—rubies, emeralds, and opals—arranged in piles throughout the cave. He had discovered the wealth of an entire kingdom—no, two kingdoms—in one chamber of this cave. How many other chambers were there? How much more treasure was waiting to be found?

Mani Singh's throat went dry as he struggled to calculate just how rich he had become. Giddy with excitement, he started filling his pockets with as many gems as he could carry, when the jinni emerged from behind a tower of crystals. Mani Singh did not even notice. His eyes were bulging from his skull as he shoved more and more treasure into his pockets.

"What are you doing?" the jinni asked.

Mani Singh whirled around, his clothes heavy with gems.

"You have returned," growled the jinni, "and you are stealing from me."

Mani Singh sputtered, but the words would not come out. It was hardly

Standing in Zazi's bedroom, watching her unlock a massive silver cabinet, seeing the glimmers from the darkness within, I understood how Mani Singh must have felt when he first saw the jinni's treasure.

The cabinet was lined with shelf upon shelf of gem-laden pendants, collars, cuffs, headpieces, anklets, rings, and earrings. She slid each shelf from its place and emptied the contents onto the massive bed she and Cyril shared, before reclining onto it and draping several heavy necklaces over her slim body. She motioned for me to do the same before lying back and pulling a string of jade over her eyes.

I sat on the edge of the bed and fingered a silver choker carved into the shape of a serpent. Its body was made up of interlocking segments, allowing it to bend and curl like a real snake. I took either end and made it slither across the bed.

I glanced up. Zazi had lifted the jade necklace slightly and was regarding me from the corner of her eye, smiling so that I could see her large teeth. She lifted one leg and used her toes to push a bracelet toward me.

"Don't be shy," she said, drawing a heavy gold chain over her throat.

The bracelet was silver set with a gold lion surrounded by a cloud of diamonds. I felt the weight of it in my hand and circled it over my wrist. It slid off immediately. The gold lion had emeralds for eyes. I picked it up again and draped it over the middle of my head, just over the part in my hair, letting the diamond-crusted clasp dangle between my eyes. The metal felt gloriously cool against my scalp and forehead. I coiled the snake choker around my neck, feeling the heavy head against my breastbone. Sliding my feet across the floor so that the bracelet would stay on my head, I made my way to the mirror next to the silver cabinet. Turning from left to right, I watched the diamond clasp dance on my forehead and catch the light like a star. Then, as always, I bared my teeth and examined my reflection. These were so much bigger than my baby teeth.

Zazi chuckled behind me and lifted herself from the bed, sending necklace after necklace back down to the others. She stood next to me and bared her teeth as well, crossing her enormous eyes at me.

"Come," she said, and she opened another cabinet.

This one was full of dresses, robes, printed scarves, and pot after pot of colored pigments. She pulled out a scarf red as blood and covered her hair with a flourish. She layered a gold chain headpiece over the scarf, then put her hands on her hips, looking up and away and jutting her chin out like a statue.

"What do you think?"

She was glorious.

She took my hand and told me it was my turn to pick. Fabric of every color greeted me from within the cabinet, but there was one that called to me louder than the rest. I pulled it gently from its place and let it fall over my face like a veil. Zazi made a sound of approval and folded the deep blue gauze back from my face.

"I have just the thing," she said, crossing to the silver cabinet and, winking at me, touched a hidden latch. The latch released another drawer—one that, when closed, had been completely invisible to the eye. She reached in and withdrew the most beautiful object I had ever seen. "I wore this the day I married Cyril," she said softly, holding it in both hands with a kind of reverence.

She motioned for me to stand in front of the mirror. She stood behind me and lowered the circlet of gold onto my head. It was carved into curls to resemble a bank of clouds; from each cloud dangled a tear-shaped diamond. When I moved my head, the gems shivered and danced, their light echoing a light in my eyes. I looked like a queen.

Zazi gently stroked one cloud. "Two hundred years ago, a merchant commissioned this for his bride to wear on their wedding day. She was his relief, his comfort, and his life. No jewel was good enough for her. He rejected every piece he saw. He loved her so much that he wanted her to wear the holiest thing he could think of, and so he asked the jeweler for a gentle rain. After her death, this was passed to her daughter, who passed it to her daughter, and so on until it came to me." Her voice sounded far away, as though she were remembering something, but after a moment she smiled and squeezed my shoulders. "You look beautiful."

I smiled back at her in the mirror, and she gently removed the crown and returned it to its secret compartment. The drawer slid shut, melting into the rest of the wood. She returned to the other cabinet and pulled out some pots of red and black pigment.

Dipping her finger into the black powder, she smudged it over my eyelids and then hers, batting her eyelashes at me in the mirror. "Did you ever do this with your mother?" she asked suddenly.

I took a deep breath. My mother had not owned any jewelry. She had not painted her face. Her clothes were plain cream robes, the same as mine. I had once tried on her boots to see if they fit, but by that time my feet were bigger than hers had been. I did not want to tell Zazi any of that, so I just shook my head.

Zazi looked surprised. "First time, then? I got into so much trouble as a little girl, digging through my mother's clothes and trying on her jewelry. Once, I tried to climb onto her vanity to see myself in the mirror better, and I knocked a bottle of her perfume onto the floor. It broke and soaked into her favorite rug, and then it stank so badly she had to throw it out. I do not think she had ever been so angry with me." She told me all of this while expertly smudging red pigment over her lips. "There," she declared, putting her arm around me and admiring us in the mirror. "The lovely ladies of Morra."

She walked me to my room that night, and we talked and laughed all the way. I had returned the scarf to her cabinet, but my eyes were still streaked with kohl. It was not until she was wishing me a good night at the door that we both noticed Connor. She stood in the hall, a few steps from her room, peering at us in the dim light.

Zazi started. She seemed put off by Connor's presence but managed a small smile. "And goodnight to you as well," she said, nodding at Connor.

Connor nodded back but did not leave. I thought maybe she wanted to talk to Zazi alone, so I said goodnight and closed my door.

I listened for a moment, but they did not speak to each other. Connor's door closed, and I heard Zazi's footsteps on the hall floor, retreating away from the guest area of the house.

I climbed into bed without washing my face and dreamed of storm clouds gathered over the dunes. When they released their burden, they rained gems onto the sand below.

Chapter 15

I passed the next day in quiet solitude, wandering the halls of the house and looking into empty rooms. I did not see Connor at all, and Cyril and Zazi remained at the salt flats until the early evening. I heard when their horses approached the house and greeted them at the door. I thought for a moment they looked troubled, but Zazi's face lit up when she saw me. She took my hand briefly before heading to her room to change.

At dinner, Connor reappeared, and though she had spent the day avoiding me, her face was as inscrutable as ever.

Cyril entertained us with stories from the day, all of which Zazi disputed. He made her laugh. He made me laugh, too. I marveled at his storytelling, his bright eyes that pulled you into each and every tall tale, and his laugh that boomed out of his body like a cannon.

Leaning back from the table, Zazi gave the deep, satisfied sigh of one whose belly is full and whose heart is happy. She took Cyril's hand.

He smiled back and then looked at Connor. "So where will you head now?"

Connor was lost in thought, looking down at the last few dates on her plate. I do not think she realized Cyril was speaking to her. She looked up and saw we all were looking at her.

Cyril tried again. "Where are you heading?"

Connor blinked. "West," she answered.

"West," Cyril repeated flatly.

She would not tell them. Why wouldn't she tell them?

"There is nothing west of Morra," said Zazi, looking at Connor doubtfully and then at me. I could not meet her eyes. I did not want to lie to her.

There was a heavy silence. The air had changed in an instant, so quickly I had not even noticed the shift. It was different now. I squirmed, longing to fill the quiet but not able to think of anything to say.

"Rue," said Cyril, "how old are you?"

"*Cyril,*" whispered Zazi.

"What is this?" asked Connor.

"It's a simple question," said Cyril. "Not that you would know how to answer one of those. Rue, how old are you?"

Something was wrong. I did not know what to say, so I told the truth.

"Twelve."

"Connor is not your mother." He was not asking.

"No," I said quietly, not knowing why this would be wrong.

"Cyril, stop," Zazi whispered again. "Northern children leave much earlier; you know that."

"For work," Cyril said sternly. "I do not know what this is."

Connor scoffed and Zazi turned on her. "Well then, what is it?" she snapped.

"Ask *her*," Conner replied darkly. "If you doubt me, then do not ask me."

Their voices made my skin crawl. We had just been laughing. Why were they angry?

"You took a child through the salt flats—why?" Cyril was facing Connor with his fist on the table. "What are you doing out here with her?"

"If you do not want us here, we can leave," said Connor darkly.

"Stop!" I cried. They all looked at me, and I realized I was standing. Why were they angry? What had happened? "We're not doing anything wrong! We're—we are just looking for something. My father knows I'm here." Which wasn't entirely true. He just knew I was with Connor. But all children left. I could not be the one to stay. "Can't we eat? Can't we talk? Everything is fine." I did not know what I was saying now. I wanted their faces to stop being angry. I wanted to hear more of Cyril's stories and Zazi's laughter. I wanted everything to stop.

I looked down. Zazi was gripping my arm and looking up at me. She pulled me down to where she sat and held me for a moment. I breathed in the smell of cinnamon and honey. Her malachite pendant pressed painfully into my chest, but I did not pull away.

"What are you looking for?" she whispered.

I turned my face to Connor, who shook her head ever so slightly.

"My father's family lives further west," I said. The lie came to me suddenly and poured out of my mouth like a fountain. "I want to go live with them. Bedouins. Their camp is four days from here. My father was not well enough to take me, so Connor is my guide. We took the salt flat route as a shortcut. We did not know how dangerous it was. Thank you for saving us."

Zazi gave me a sidelong look and Cyril searched Connor's face for a lie. True to form, Connor stared him down with eyes hard as stone.

"Some guide," Cyril grunted. "You should be more careful." He shrugged and looked away. "I thought…"

"Of course," Connor said quickly "I would have thought the same."

He nodded and glanced at Zazi, who had released me. After a moment, Cyril leaned toward me conspiratorially and said, "You know, I was once imprisoned by pirates and had to wrestle a full-grown warthog for my freedom."

"Oh, you lie!" cried Zazi.

Cyril looked abashed and raised his arms over his head. "It's true! Oh, it was many years before we met, but—"

As his story went on, building and spiraling higher and higher into the stratosphere of impossibility, I looked across the table and met Connor's gaze. From now on, the truth would be a secret; the lie would be shared, but I would go no further until I knew why.

Chapter 16

I came to Connor's room that night after Cyril and Zazi had gone to bed. I could feel my determination waning. She had made me lie to them, and now my whole body was warm with shame. I was sweating through my shirt.

She did everything in the dark. The candle on her bedside table had never been lit, and there was no light coming from the toilet room where she was. Instead, she had folded back the painted screen in front of the window to let the room be bathed in moonlight. As my eyes adjusted, I could see the outline of every stone in the floor, all the way to the bed that had been piled with embroidered blankets by one of the silent servants. I stood by the foot of the bed so that she would see me when she came out. The moon was so bright tonight. I held my hand up to see how it looked in the blue-white light. Light does strange things to the dark. The wood of the bed seemed to glow, and then I noticed the legs had been carved into human shapes with faces that looked up at the sky. Eyes that bulged. Mouths pulled open into screams. Cal grabbing my hand. Vargas yelling at us, begging us to hurry. The wall of sand. Laughter like hyenas snapping at our heels. Cal and Vargas on the ground. *Run. Run.*

"What are you doing in here?"

I whipped around. Connor was centimeters from my face. She looked angry. Her scar was painfully visible in the moonlight.

I swallowed, but I could not get the words out. My head felt like it had been stuffed with cotton, and her voice was too loud. I shook my head and stared up at her. She loomed over me, dark as a storm cloud. I could not remember my shame, my words. It was as though my mind and my body were reaching out, trying to find each other.

Where's Cal?

"Get out."

The command tore the cotton from my head. My mind and body joined again. I found my anger.

"No!" I snapped. The force of my voice shocked me, but I made myself keep talking—the second I stopped I would not be able to start again. "I am *here.*

We have been walking for weeks now, and—and you tell me nothing. Every day is silence. Every *thing* is silence, and I just lied for you to people who are nice. They are *nice* and they do not like you and I think I don't like you either but I'm here and you never tell me *anything*. And I have been quiet. And I have not asked questions. And now I'm asking you a question and you are going to answer me because if you don't I'm staying *here*."

She looked surprised but didn't say anything.

"Well?" I demanded.

"Well, what?"

I looked around and threw my arms out in frustration. "Where are we going? What are we doing?"

She looked at me, but not at me. Through me, to another time and another place. "It does seem mad, doesn't it," she murmured. "Searching and searching and never finding. How can I explain it? There is something else—something more—something no one has ever seen."

I shivered and thought of the priest staring into the fire.

"I dreamed of a miracle…an animal that did not fly in the sky nor crawl on the ground. It was leading me."

"Where?"

"Paradise."

I looked and could see the ring on her finger—the ring that never left her finger—glowing in the moonlight.

"Who gave that to you?" I asked.

She held my gaze for a moment. "Someone important."

"Who?" I demanded.

Her face, normally so hard, wavered. "I can't." Her voice was quiet, heavy, sad.

I had to accept it. I had tested her walls and gone as far as she would let me. I would never know who gave her the ring, who started her journey, but I knew I would finish it with her. She had chosen me. That was the truth. There was something out there—something no one had ever seen—and she and I would find it.

Where we went, we would go together.

I padded to the door and looked out into the black, unlit passage back to my room. I felt eyes in the darkness, and I remembered something else the priest had said that night. *"I feel that time is narrowing to a point. I feel a heaviness weighing on my brain, and a crushing hand around my soul. I sense darkness. I fear the night."*

I turned back to Connor. "Can I stay here tonight?"

She hesitated and I looked back out into the passage. Someone was out there. Not waiting for permission, I shut the door and climbed into Connor's bed, pulling the embroidered blankets up to my chin. After a short pause, Connor too got into the bed. She was turned away from me, her thick hair spread between us, and warmth radiating off her body like an oven. I inched down further under the covers and lay on my back to see outside. The moon, bright as a coin, hung just below the arch of the window. I felt warm. I felt safe. Just before I drifted off to sleep, I remembered something.

"Why were Cyril and Zazi mad at you? Why did they ask what you were doing with me?"

She did not answer for a long while. I thought she was already asleep until her voice floated up into the darkness. "They thought I was a trader."

"Like Cyril?"

"No. Not like Cyril. A trader of flesh. Of human lives."

There was something in the way she said it that made my heart grow cold. *A trader of flesh.* I tried to imagine the cruelty of someone who sold people for money.

"Have you seen one before?"

"Why would you ask me that?"

I did not know why I had asked. Because she had traveled far and seen many things. She knew things I did not. Before I could answer, her voice floated up again, low and edged with abhorrence.

"Yes. I've seen them."

Them. They. More than one. More than one.

"Some travel alone; some in packs. The packs will destroy a town if it's small enough. They take everyone. The town before the flats... We won't see them," she added quickly. "Not west."

"Zazi said there's nothing west of Morra."

Connor paused and then spoke again. "There is never nothing. There is always something. There can't be nothing."

I only had one more question. "Why can we not tell anyone what we're looking for? Try to explain?"

"It's safer. Do you think you can sleep now?"

I nodded, but the moon outside had taken on a sinister light. There was evil in the world—evil that was human, not witches. There was danger, and I did not know what it looked like. How would I know who was evil?

Chapter 17

The next morning when I awoke, everything felt different. The light streaming over my face coaxed my eyes open, and I lay watching the dust fairies floating in the narrow beam. I was alone. Connor must have gotten up before sunrise. But there was something else. The knot in my stomach was back, coiled tightly as ever. It was then that I noticed the open door and the face of Zazi, her skin caught by the light of the new day, eyes like twin caves, hawk nose casting a shadow along one cheek, and her beautiful mouth twisted in disgust. She fled almost immediately, the fabric of her black dress lifting and retreating like crow's wings into the dark hallway.

My stomach dropped. Cyril and Zazi thought Connor was a flesh trader. A vile worm of suspicion had made Zazi come to Connor's room this morning, and she had fled after seeing me in the bed. She must believe her home to be tainted. I threw the blankets back and took off after her.

I did not need to guess where she was going. I heard the crashes, the raised voices, and I followed. My bare feet slapped the stone as I rounded the corner to the dining room, which was now in chaos. Zazi's hair stood up at all angles like a storm cloud, her mouth gaping in a scream of rage as she hurled every bit of pottery and cutlery within reach at Connor, who was backed against the wall on the other side of the massive table.

Cyril was trying to hold Zazi's arms, but she twisted away and lunged across the table at Connor. Cyril saw me and, quick as a snake, wrenched me away from the doorway and behind him. I yelped and Zazi finally noticed me. She pulled me to her side and screamed at Connor, "Get out! Now!"

With a grip like iron, she dragged me from the dining room. The last thing I saw was Cyril advancing on Connor with his large hands balled into fists.

I tried. Zazi dragged me by the arms, hands, my tunic, switching her grip whenever I managed to pull free. One of her servants joined and grabbed my legs.

"It is all right now," said Zazi. "We're going to take care of you."

"Stop!" I screamed. "Please!"

"You never have to see her again," I heard Zazi say as she and her servant shoved me into a room. "I promise. No, no, no, everything is all right now," as the door slammed and metal clicked. I was locked in.

I hammered the door with my hands and called out for help.

"Rue, it's all right. You're safe now." Zazi's muffled voice came from the other side of the door.

"No! You don't understand!"

"I do. I understand more than you could possibly know. That woman is sick. She was hurting you."

"No, she wasn't. What are you doing with her? You cannot leave me in here!"

Zazi was silent for a minute. "Rue, I know you are too young to understand, but this is for your own good."

"Let me out! She will leave me here! I won't know where to go!"

"Rue, I'm sorry. I need you to stay in there just for a little while. You can come out when it is safe." Zazi's footsteps retreated down the hallway.

"Let me out!" I screamed and slapped the door. I looked wildly around the room. *I have to get out. I have to get out. What if she leaves? I won't know where to go. What if they hurt her? What if they kill her?*

Zazi and her servant had thrown me back into my room. My pack was still in the corner, and the window was open. I grabbed my pack and looked out. The drop was not far. Without thinking, I threw my pack out the window and followed, hitting the ground and banging the same knee I had recently twisted. I felt like the wind had been knocked out of me, but I hoisted my pack on my back and looked up into the face of Cyril's boy servant. He made a grab for me, but I spun past him, pushing him to the ground with all my might and running toward the street. I heard him shouting, but I kept running. *Left or right?* I turned left and sprinted to the next alleyway, which was lined with bags of refuse and loose paper. I dove behind the nearest pile and pulled a bag of trash in front to cover myself.

I listened for the sound of pursuing feet but heard none. Zazi's voice floated up from further down the street. I heard her calling my name. Cyril's voice echoing hers. They were coming closer. I froze, listening for them.

"Rue!" Zazi was crying. My name sounded ragged as she called between sobs. Cyril's voice followed, quieter, gentler. He was trying to comfort her. "Why did she run?" Zazi sobbed.

"It is not your fault, my love."

"We tried to save her," Zazi said.

"You did your best. We did our best."

"You should have killed that monster."

Their voices were getting further away. They had come closer and were now going back to the house, but all I could hear were the last words Zazi said. *You should have killed that monster.*

Where was Connor?

<h1 style="text-align:right">Chapter 18</h1>

I waited in the alleyway for a little while, making sure they did not come back. When I felt sure they were no longer looking for me, I edged my way out into the street, checking corners before coming out. I had to find Connor. The streets were crowded with people on their way to work. They chatted with one another or looked straight ahead. Few glanced at me.

She will leave me here. I will never find her.

I saw a woman with a soft face. Her dark eyes slid in my direction, and so I asked her if she had seen Connor. I described her. I told her I needed to find her. The woman shook her head, barely slowing down, not looking back as she walked away.

I asked a few other people as they walked by. I asked a street vendor who was selling persimmons, but he brushed me away. I was distracting his customers.

No one had seen her. Were they even looking? Would they even notice her?

I found myself at a small fountain built into the side of a gray building. A metal demon's mouth vomited a continuous trickle of water into the basin below, and I suddenly realized I was very thirsty. As I bent to drink, I noticed a man in rags crouched on the other side of the basin. His brown eyes were huge, popping from his wrinkled head. Dust covered every part of him that I could see. He smiled at me over the top of the basin, his wrinkles gathering in an arch at his forehead. I did my best to smile back, to be polite. He smiled wider, his chapped lips peeling back so that every brown and rotten tooth he had left was visible. His few teeth parted, a dark and spotted tongue peering out of its stinking cave like a snake, sliding out from between his lips and down to the surface of the water in the basin. His eyes bulged out of their sockets as he grinned at me, his tongue flicking the surface of the water.

I backed away. His eyes, big as eggs in twin cups, swiveling as far as they could, never leaving my face. I moved around him, keeping my distance, and ran as soon as I turned the next corner. I turned down side streets and kept going until I was sure the man with the bulging eyes was not following me.

And that was when I saw her.

The buildings met in an arch over the street some ten or fifteen meters ahead of me. There, in the semidarkness of that alcove, stood my mother. She was wearing dusky pink robes—a color I had never seen her in—with her hair hidden under a scarf of the same color. I could not make out her face, but it was her. As surely as I stood there in the street, it was her.

"Mama?" I called softly. My feet were already taking me to her. My heart hurt. "Mama?"

She hesitated, her face slowly resolving into something unfamiliar. It was not my mother.

My feet stopped immediately. The lump in my throat was too hard to even let me apologize. I simply stood, letting the salt sting my eyes. My hands clenched and unclenched at my sides, still fighting to grasp my mother's hand.

The woman peered at me. "Are you lost?" She asked. Her voice was so like my mother's—so very much. Like warm honey and dark thunderclouds. Like water from the sky. Like a miracle.

I tried to swallow. The lump in my throat would not let me.

"It is all right," said the woman. "You're all right." She bent toward me and stretched out her hand. "What is your name?"

I sniffed. "Rueda. Rue."

She smiled. "I am Asha." Her teeth were different from my mother's. My mother had very large, white teeth. "Would you like some tea, Rue?"

Her eyes were the same. I nodded and took her hand and let her lead me through the darkness of the arch and into a side door painted dark blue.

Chapter 19

The dim room was a cavern. The ceiling spiraled up so far above us that it seemed lost in the dark, but as my eyes adjusted to the low light I saw the ornately carved arches above me—lizards, birds, humans with demon faces—rising like the heavens. The earth below was lined with shelf after shelf of books. The walls were also lined with shelves that reached for the vaulted ceiling. They were so tall that ladders and metal walkways had been constructed, some of which were occupied. I thought of the blue book in my pack. This was its home.

I reached out to the nearest shelf. Its dark wood held leather spines of every color. I lightly ran my fingers over them and tilted my head to read their names. My fingers stopped on one called *Beasts of the Southern Lowlands* and pulled it from its nest. The spine cracked a little when I opened it, landing on a pen sketch of a male and female lion at rest on a rocky outcrop. I pushed my face close to the pages and breathed deeply before closing the book and returning it to its brothers and sisters.

Asha was smiling at me. "Come," she said, leading the way through a maze of shelves to a door off to one side, behind a section called *Anthropology*.

Asha lived in a small, one-room apartment hidden behind the library walls. The kitchen—nothing more than a basin and small stove—was sectioned off from the rest of the apartment by a half-wall. The floor of the main room was piled with pillows and poufs of every color, interrupted by the occasional column of books, and the faded walls were covered with heavy tapestries depicting myths and fables. I noticed the story of the journey to the phoenix's mountain on the half-wall of the kitchen. A gray, long-haired cat sleeping on a deep blue cushion stirred long enough to slide its gold eyes in my direction before closing them again.

Asha motioned for me to sit down, then unwound her head scarf and made her way into the kitchen. I attempted to sit gingerly on a pouf ottoman but was sucked down like quicksand until I was nearly horizontal. The gray cat, like a spider sensing a helpless fly in her web, deftly picked her way over to me and curled up on my legs to continue her nap. I ran my hand over her soft head, and she purred gently in response. I had always wanted a pet. I had asked my father for a dog when I was younger, but he had said no. Cal used to say—

The sound of water and the clatter of crockery in the kitchen brought my thoughts back to the apartment, and I took in my surroundings. On the opposite wall hung a tapestry showing the story of the lion and the bear. The lion was stitched in gold thread as standing on his hind legs, grasping the bear in a violent embrace. The bear and lion's mouths were open, revealing white fangs and red maws. Behind a boulder in the background, the Devil held the hand of a little girl, both watching the battle with interest. On the wall to my right was the story of Magellan and the salt spirit. Magellan's men were scattered throughout the tapestry, blinded by the salt spirit's minions, while the explorer himself plotted to dissolve the spirit in a water jug.

"Here we are," said Asha, setting a tray on a large brown ottoman. She handed me a steaming cup and took one for herself. The tea was black and smelled of strong spices. I put my face over the steam and breathed. "Nice, isn't it?" she asked. "It is my own blend. Good for the skin." She passed a dish of semolina cakes, and I took one. "I see Mow found you." She gestured to the cat. "That one is a real whore. She doesn't care who sits down as long as they keep her warm."

I blushed hard. "Why is her name Mow?"

Asha shrugged. "It is the sounds she makes. It sounds like *mow, mow, mow*." She imitated the cat's mewling. Mow opened her eyes long enough to be sure the sound was only Asha. I laughed.

"So," said Asha, looking at me expectantly over her teacup. I felt nervous. Asha hesitated, "You do not have to say anything now, but I think you should tell me where you are supposed to be."

I looked down at Mow and brushed a pink toe pad of her front paw, which contracted at my touch. "I don't know where I should be."

"Did you run away?"

"No," I said quickly. "My father knows I went away."

Asha shifted. "Did you leave an apprenticeship? You look about the right age."

"No," I said again. I searched for the right words. "I was traveling with someone. We got separated."

Asha pulled her long hair over one shoulder. It had been dyed with henna and shone slightly red in the dim light. "Who were you traveling with?"

"Her name is Connor Fadi. Do you know her?"

Asha shook her head. "Where were you going? Perhaps I can show you where you can meet her."

I hesitated. "I do not know where. We had stopped here, but we were going west, I think."

Asha frowned and thought for a moment. "I do not think so," she said finally. "No. No, that cannot be right."

I thought about telling Asha everything. I did. I wanted to. I opened my mouth to tell her the entire story: the witches, the storm, my brothers, Connor and our journey, Zazi and Cyril, everything. I wanted her to look at me with my mother's eyes and tell me with my mother's voice that everything would be all right. But the lump in my throat reminded me that my mother was not here. My mother was dead. I swallowed and said nothing and looked away from my mother's eyes.

Asha sighed. "I understand," she said softly. "I was lost once, too."

I looked down at Mow, and Asha took my hand.

"It is all right," she said gently. "Would you like to stay here tonight? We can look for your friend tomorrow."

I nodded.

"Now, there is just one more thing, and this is most important." Asha looked at me very seriously. "What would you like for dinner?"

That night I slept soundly among the pile of pillows and pouf ottomans. Asha read to me from one of the books from a stack near the kitchen, a story of a magician who conjured sandstorms and animals to do his bidding but gave up his powers for the love of a Bedouin. I fell asleep looking at the gold-threaded lion in its tapestry, struggling with the bear while the Devil and the little girl watched.

In the morning, we searched for Connor. We asked Asha's neighbors and the library attendants. We waited by the communal fountain and asked everyone who passed if they had seen someone who looked like Connor. I kept an eye on the faces passing us, fearful one of them would be Zazi or Cyril. If they took me away, I did not know what would happen.

At midday, the food vendors opened their carts, and Asha bought me a pastry from a woman with a face like a raisin. As Asha opened her purse, the woman looked at me and smiled. "You have a beautiful daughter."

Asha looked up in surprise and then at me. "Oh," she said. She passed a few coins to the woman. "She's... Thank you." She seemed to be waiting for me to say something, to correct the old woman, but I did not see why I should.

We ate pastries by the fountain and after that Asha took me back to her apartment in the library. I spent the afternoon pulling books out of their piles and reading stories about explorers, sorcerers, and spirits. My favorites were the stories of magic, of people who could pull water from stones and cure all sickness. Asha made tea and sat with me as I read to her. I liked reading to her. I would make my voice deep for the kings, raspy for the spirits, and silly and high for the princesses. She would laugh at my voices and pull Mow closer when the heroes were in danger.

We spent days combing the Morra streets. Asha had grown up there and showed me the small neighborhood of her youth. The houses were narrow and little more than shacks, but she took great pride in showing me. I told her about my home, the white spire of my City, and my father. I did not tell her about my brothers, and we never went down Cyril and Zazi's street, though I still looked for them. I never saw Connor and began to understand that she had abandoned me. Asha had stopped asking me about her, and our daily searches became daily walks. At midday, Asha would stop and buy pastries or street meats for us to eat, and we would sit at the communal fountain to watch the people go by. At night, she read me stories of magic and adventure. When the night chill crept in, she pulled heavy blankets over me and tucked them under my chin.

One night, she fell asleep before I did, book open on her chest, henna-dyed hair laid across a pink and gold pillow, and Mow curled against her side. I felt warm. Not on my skin, but inside. I did not feel out of place in the tiny apartment and its stacks of books and floor swollen with poufs and pillows. I did not have to be a witch hunter like my brothers and father, and I did not have to be afraid to die in the sand. But I missed the open desert. I missed the wide sky. I missed the wind. I wanted to keep the desert with me—wrap it around me like this blanket and keep it with me here. I wanted this apartment with Asha and Mow, and I wanted to walk in the expanse of sand and sky.

On the wall above Asha, the gold thread of the lion glinted in the dim light, softening and fading as sleep came for me.

Chapter 20

Something is wriggling in the dark.

Something small is burrowing its way in. Just outside of my vision. Just gone when I turn my head. But it's there. It wants. It tastes and it needs. I cannot see it. But it's there.

Caleb.

Cal. Help me.

My eyes opened but could not see. It was dark. Where was I? There were pillows piled on either side of my body. Asha snored gently a little further off, Mow curled into a tight ball on her belly, rising and falling with Asha's breath.

Sweat stung my forehead and upper lip. My chest still heaved. As with all nightmares, this one clung to my brain, and I held myself still as a corpse, listening for the slightest sound, for the danger I was sure was still there. When nothing happened, I let my body relax and tried to remember dreams. Normal dreams. Nice dreams.

A heavy weight shifted on the other side of the wall, and my breath caught in my chest. I turned my ear against the wall and listened. Something moved on the other side. Something was in the library. As if pulled by strings, I crept to the door and opened it just a crack, just a sliver, and pressed one eye to the gap. In the darkness, the shelves rose like black cliffs—a light from somewhere on the street too far away to do much more than make the dust in the air glow a faint blue—and a darker shape moved less than two meters away. I held my breath. Had it seen me? The dark shape expanded, and a part broke away from the whole. It was a hand reaching out to the books lined along the nearest shelf. The skin glowed in the light from the street, but something else caught the light and threw off a glint. Gold. A gold ring on the fourth finger of the left hand.

I threw the door open. "Connor!"

The shape darted back but stopped, breathing heavily. "Yes."

A light from behind me—Asha had woken up—threw a warm glow onto Connor's face. A bruise painted one cheekbone, a second bruise over her mouth, and a scab where her lower lip had split. Normally straight-backed and solid, she carried herself delicately, slightly hunched over to one side. Her hair and clothes were dirty, and I could have sworn she looked relieved to see me. Or maybe it was I who was relieved to see her. Asha appeared at my side. She looked wide-eyed into the library, afraid of the woman there, and she reached for my hand. Her touch sent a pang to my heart, and I felt another when, despite herself, Asha invited Connor into the apartment.

Connor did not tell us what happened to her after we were separated. The marks on her face told a shadow of the story for her, and we did not ask. She only said that she had heard an old woman and young girl were looking for her. She ran her hands over the embroidery of the pillows around her and stroked Mow's head gently. It had taken her some time to find us.

"And now here you are," said Asha quietly.

Connor contemplated the tapestries around her and nodded.

"Rue," Asha said turning to me, "why don't you help me make some tea for your friend?"

In the tiny kitchen, Asha grasped my hands in hers. She bent low and looked at me with my mother's eyes.

"You do not have to go with her," she whispered.

But I thought of the open desert and the wide sky. I thought of Connor and the promise I had made myself. I thought of the priest and my father and my brothers. My heart twisted in its cage. I had to leave.

Asha was sad. The next day, she held herself away from me and told Connor where to find supplies. Connor made a list for herself and checked my pack, noting what was still needed, but Asha wrenched my pack away and refused to let her get anything for me. She gathered my supplies herself, carefully folding every item or wrapping it with strips of cloth that could be useful later. She bought high boots to keep the sand out, new robes, a machete, and a small packet of tea leaves mixed with strong spices. She watched me store this all in my pack, making sure I did not forget anything.

That night, knowing she was not wanted, Connor slept in the library. Asha made one last pot of tea for the two of us and pulled a book of magical stories from the pile. She gathered Mow close to one side, and I curled up on the other, letting my head rest on her shoulder. She pulled her henna-red hair away so that it would not tickle my nose. She read to me with my mother's voice, but the hands that turned the pages were Asha's—dark, and with skin delicate as the thinnest linen. She smelled of tea and the musty comfort of old paper.

Asha, my caretaker. Asha, the home that I could not keep.

And for one last night, I fell asleep listening to stories of sorcerers, kings, and queens.

Chapter 21

n the morning I said goodbye, scratching Mow's head one more time and taking a last walk through the library, inhaling its slightly sharp musk once more. I closed my eyes and willed that scent to stay with me. I wanted to embed the smell of crumbling paper, soft vellum, tapestries, and tea into my memory. Only when I was sure it was there did I pick up my pack.

Outside, Asha held me tightly.

"Thank you," I said, my face pressed into her neck, salt stinging my eyes.

Connor stood away from us, pretending to adjust her pack.

Asha pulled away and looked me over. She tugged my desert robes and folded the edges of my head covering against my cheeks to keep the sand out of my ears. Her eyes were wet.

"You look like a true Bedouin," she said, smiling slightly. "Be careful, my little Rue."

I nodded. The lump in my throat caught my words so that I could not answer her.

The first steps were the hardest. I kept looking back. Asha raised one hand to wave to me before clasping her arms tightly over her chest. She held herself and watched me go, tears staining her skin. She did not wipe them away or hide her face. When I could no longer see her, I cried, letting the tears soak into the cloth at my cheeks. Connor did not hurry me or look back. She seemed to know when she had gotten too far ahead and would simply wait with her back to me until I caught up. My first thought was that she felt ashamed of me for crying, but perhaps it was really her way of giving me some privacy. People stared but did not bother us. I kept my eyes on the ground until we reached the edge of Morra. Avenues widened, buildings shrank, homes became huts, huts became tents, and then there was nothing but the sand. Rocks jutted out at the edge of the horizon, like crooked fingers reaching toward the sky.

Connor stopped. I stood next to her, and she looked down at me. "You do not have to do this," she said. Her eyes, hard and dark as polished wood, searched my face.

I looked out at the sand and stepped into the desert. Connor was wrong. I had to go with her. My brothers, my nightmares, the priest—they all had to mean something. Something was leading me away from the City, away from Morra, pointing me toward the horizon.

Chapter 22

I scanned the sky for witches out of habit, I did not want to die a witch hunter. There was something out there, something different—a *more* that felt just out of reach. And despite Connor's harsh exterior, I sensed a thrum just below the surface where the strength of her conviction blazed, hollowing her out and leaving only the search for *more*.

The sand outside Morra was soft, and when my foot sank to the ankle with each step, I was grateful for the new boots Asha had given to me. Even so, the way was slow and tiring. The cloth at my forehead kept the sweat out of my eyes, but nothing stopped it from beading on my upper lip. I wiped it with my sleeve, but it soon returned. My legs burned with fatigue. Ahead of me, Connor trudged through the sand. She sank deeper than I did, but she moved steadily. She seemed to be made of metal and gears rather than flesh and bone—she never faltered, never slowed, never tired. She and the land were one.

As for me, the first break for water could not come soon enough. When it finally did, I sat in the sand and pulled my pack to my stomach, feeling the muscles in my legs relax gratefully underneath me. I sipped the water from my bag slowly like my brothers had shown me years ago. *Water is life. Hold back. Hold back.*

Tying the water bag back to my pack, I noticed a lump near the top, a rectangular shape with sharp corners that pushed the cloth from within. I had not done this. Easing the pack open, I felt for the object, grasped it, and withdrew my hand. Gold lettering on brown leather proclaimed *The Land of Magic.* It was the book Asha had been reading last night—the last story she had ever read to me. I opened the cover. Inside, in Asha's handwriting, *My little wanderer, do not forget your Asha. All my love.* I held the book to my chest and looked back toward Morra, still visible at the horizon.

Within a day, the city had become a faded haze behind us, by the second it had sunk into the sand entirely, as if it had never existed. But I knew Asha was there. Connor never looked back, and I could not blame her. The city meant very different things to us.

The sky stretched above us and ahead in the brightest blue streaked with faint white clouds. At the horizon, the fingers of stone we had seen from the edge of the city had broadened into high towers of craggy rock with eight narrow canyons. The first rounded a corner and turned into a dead end within an hour. The second did not run smooth and would require climbing the walls to edge our way around boulders that blocked the way. The third was blocked completely after the first two kilometers. We would lose the light before we could reach the other canyons, and we would need the shelter of the rocks after sunset. Connor did not like sleeping on open sand, and she regarded me with her dark eyes. I knew which path she wanted to take.

"I can climb," I said.

She adjusted the straps on her pack to bring its weight as close to her body as possible, and she showed me how to do the same. Approaching the wall next to the bolder, she pointed out the path we would have to climb, and where we could rest when we needed to. She gripped the canyon wall and pulled herself up, moving steadily up and away. Loose shale slid under my feet as I tried to grip the same crannies in the rocks that she had, but it was useless. She was bigger than I and could reach further. I could not follow the same way.

Something small skittered along the wall and I looked up. A tiny brown lizard was looking down at me, just out of reach. He sat on a thrust of rock I had not noticed before. Planting one foot, I reached. My fingers found the edge, scaring the lizard away. I looked and found other handholds along the wall. My own little way.

Ahead, Connor had wedged herself between the boulder and the canyon wall to wait for me. When I reached her, she gripped my pack and pulled me up next to her. Her face was streaked with grit, one of her hands was bleeding, and she looked almost happy. We edged our way around the boulder and found solid ground on the other side. There had been a rock slide some time ago that had cleared the walls of the canyon. The rocks slid under our feet, and we had to climb twice more to get around the larger boulders, but after another kilometer or so, the ground was smooth and straight under our feet. We descended the last climb with a sigh from exertion and tried to rub the life back into our limbs. Every muscle in my body ached and my stomach rumbled with hunger as we prepared the fire for the night. Connor sent me to find brush we could burn, but when I returned, she was studying the canyon wall to the south. I followed her gaze but saw nothing.

"What is it?"

"Black rock," she said quietly.

I looked. There was a large black rock topped with a tuft of dried grass on a ledge on the southern wall of the canyon.

"What?" I asked.

Connor shook her head, turned, and went back to building a fire.

As the sun disappeared behind the canyon walls, I saw her looking toward the southern canyon wall again. The black rock was still there, but the grass was gone.

Chapter 23

The next day, I was awakened just before sunrise by Connor's foot digging into my side. "We need to move," she whispered. In the gray light of early dawn, I saw her eyes were trained on the southern canyon wall.

Shaken, I did not ask questions. We packed and hastily continued our way through the canyon. Connor raced ahead of me, practically running along the path. By the time the sun peeked over the rim we were far from our campsite, streaming with sweat, breathing heavily. Connor let me stop to catch my breath while she scanned the walls for something only she knew to look for. We both faced the southern wall as she crouched down low next to me. I started to ask what had frightened her, but her rough hand immediately closed around my mouth. Three pebbles tumbled down the southern wall, clacking against ledges, and skittering into the undergrowth below. My heart hammered against my rib cage; the hair raised at the back of my neck. We were being watched.

Connor pulled me up, pushed me ahead of her, and we rushed on. Black beasts rose in my mind, darkness coming down from the wall to take us. I looked back, expecting to see it right behind us. Connor grabbed the back of my skull and turned my head forward again. She kept one hand on my right shoulder to push me ahead, to not let me slow down. The canyon split into two routes, one leading southwest, and the other branching northwest. We took the northwest path. Whatever was following us, if it was still following us, would have to come down to the ground to get to the northwest passage.

There was a mound in the earth ahead of me and an open crag in the rocks to one side. Connor shoved me hard into the crag, stripped the pack off her back, and wedged it into the fissure so that it covered as much of my body as possible. Sharp rocks dug into my shoulders, but I could see out just over the top of her pack. She strode slowly to the middle of the path. The machete at her hip gleamed. Her face was wet with sweat, jaw set like iron. She turned her back to me and drew her machete, waiting.

But nothing happened.

I watched her shoulders rise and fall with her breath, a slight breeze touched the edges of her head covering. A rock spiraled down from the southern wall, now too far away for me to see, but it rolled, bounced, and settled at Connor's feet. She slid her machete back into its hilt, picked up the rock, aimed, and threw it back at the southern wall. Nothing. No sound, no movement.

She wrenched her pack out of the crag and let me out.

I looked to the southern wall but could not see anything. "Is it gone?" I asked.

"No," she answered, keeping her voice low, "but it will have to show itself if it wants to keep following us."

"What do you think it is?"

She pushed me ahead of her. As we walked past the mound in the earth, Connor gently toed its edge with her boot and looked behind her. "Do not touch that," she said to me.

"What is it?"

"Something that will get us into trouble."

I looked. It was an ankle-high mound as wide as a dinner plate. The earth looked damp. It even smelled damp. Connor pushed me ahead.

Hours passed in the northwest passage of the canyon, but nothing followed. No rocks fell from the walls. All was quiet, except for the lizards. Dark brown with frilled heads, they stretched themselves over the path—next to each other, piled on one another—warming their bodies in the sun, darting away at our approach. Some were big as a man's arm and thick with meat.

Connor retreated to one wall of the canyon and took off her pack. Could we catch one? We would have to chase them with the machetes, and they would be too fast. Connor pulled a small metal rod from her pack, the size of a man's hand, and unfolded it once, twice, over and over until it was as long as I was tall. One end was blunted, but the other—I smiled in spite of myself. A telescoping spear. It was exactly what we needed; of course she had one. A strange thought appeared in my mind. My brothers—who loved to test their skills and sleep under the stars and leave me home safe and sound—would have liked Connor. They might have even admired her. They would have fallen over themselves to try out her telescoping spear.

Connor noticed my smile. "Morra's shops are very interesting," she said. "Much better stocked than you might expect. It's too bad you did not come along."

I wondered briefly how she paid for it—did she even have anything worth selling? But my stomach clenched and growled too much to ask. I did not even want to ask to use the spear. I just wanted to eat.

We hid behind a boulder near the canyon wall to observe our prey—a fat lizard at least a meter long, sunning itself near a group of smaller reptiles. Its dark skin puckered and wrinkled and pebbled over its thick hindquarters, its long tail tapering to a fine whip. Its black eyes were closed. Flies buzzed, touching down on its head, its legs, and lifting off again. Connor crouched, rolling the spear in one hand to grip it correctly. Her legs tensed and quick as a snake she sprang out from behind the boulder, hurling the spear, missing the larger lizard she had been aiming for and piercing a smaller one nearby. The fat lizard and its smaller hoard skittered away and vanished into the crannies and creases of the canyon walls.

Connor swore under her breath, picked up the spear, and put it over her shoulder, leaving the lizard carcass to dangle while we walked. There was no use in waiting. The others would not come out again. I did not say anything, but my stomach felt hollow. There was enough meat for us both, but tomorrow we would have to either catch something bigger or open our ration packets. The canyon walls narrowed and turned sharply up ahead. As the walls closed in, I fell behind Connor, distancing myself from the swinging remains on her spear. I was studying its black, curved claws when Connor stopped so shortly that I almost ran face-first into the carcass.

An old man with a long white beard and a thatch of white hair like dried grass blocked our path. His skin was dark and wrinkled as a dried date, and his dark brown eyes were clouded at the edges. He carried a long stick and wore a ratty tunic with trousers of an indeterminate color. A black scarf was tied at his waist. Tucked into the scarf was a pistol. The old man's right hand rested on its grip. He looked us over and took a step toward Connor.

"Boo," he croaked.

Chapter 24

Strangers meet in the wilderness. What do they say?
"They greet one another. They offer water and food as they can spare."
And then?
"And then, Father?"
Yes, what is next?
"They ask for—"
No, no. Next is shelter and help if they are injured.
"I forgot."
Strangers must show trust to earn trust. You must remember the rules, my Rue. The rules can save your life.

Connor and the old man stared each other down, shoulders tensed, hands clenched and ready to strike. I could not take my eyes away from the hand that rested on the pistol. Was he going to kill us? My mouth opened but my throat had gone dry.

"We…" I tried.

The old man's gaze flicked to me and back to Connor.

I licked my lips. "We have water and food to share."

His eyes darted toward me again.

My hands shook, but I reached up and tried to pull the lizard off the spear to give it to the old man. Connor did not expect this and jumped. The old man cried out, trying to draw the pistol and back away from us at the same time. The pistol sight caught on the scarf. He stumbled and turned in a circle, tugging at the half-drawn pistol.

Connor grabbed the hand still trying to draw the pistol and pulled him backward, pressing one knee into the back of his, making him sit in the dirt.

"God will damn you!" He screeched. The sudden sound bit into my ears. "Kill an old man, and you will be taken by the Devil himself! He will cut out your eyes! He will—"

Connor wrenched his scarf off in one motion and shoved it into his mouth. "Be quiet," she muttered, looking toward the sky.

Though muffled by the scarf, the old man continued to scream. His eyes rolled. He would not stop screaming.

I put my hands on my head covering and pushed down. *The sounds of death bring them closer. The darkness. A wall of sand. The screaming. They will hear us.*

I knelt beside him, took his head in my hands, and forced him to look at me. "Stop, stop, stop," I whispered urgently. "You have to stop. Please stop. We won't hurt you. Please. Please, you mustn't. Please."

He fell quiet and held my gaze.

Connor pulled me back, and I curled into the sand next to the man, holding my body, feeling my breath coming in ragged gasps. *The sounds of death bring them closer. The sounds of death bring them closer. The sounds of death bring them closer.* Connor placed her pack on the ground and angled it over my face, blocking the sky.

She pulled the scarf from the old man's mouth. "I would not have hurt you," he said quietly, looking down at me. "What is wrong with her?" He looked bewildered and sad. A sad old man sitting in the dirt. "I wouldn't. I was not going to hurt you."

Connor said nothing.

"Look! Look." He fumbled with the gun, shaking it. "It's empty. Look, please. I only meant to frighten. Forgive me."

Connor remained silent.

"I can take you to my home. Yes, you can rest there. Please. Then you will know I was not going to hurt you. I was not going to hurt you."

Connor hesitated. To refuse an offer of shelter could be a mistake. I counted the threads of her pack. My breathing slowed. My head felt heavy. "You can have the lizard," I said quietly. "We have food to share."

"The vultures can have the lizard before he will." Connor's voice was like dark clouds before a sandstorm. "We will not be sharing with you."

The man scoffed. "I have better food than lizards. Besides, your little one needs rest."

I did feel very tired. Connor pulled me up and shouldered both our packs.

To the old man, she said, "We accept your offer of food and shelter. But we will not stay. After she has rested, you will show us the way through this canyon." The man started to object, but Connor cut him off. "To make up for trying to frighten us."

His name was Hassan, and he lived alone in a cave in the rocks not far from the mound in the earth we had passed earlier. The mound, he said, was his well. He kept it hidden and guarded it against thieves. Connor was right to keep us away from it—it was death to steal from another's well.

He led us up a path in the rocks that, from the ground, was hidden from view. Skinny and bent thought he was, he climbed and leaped like a goat from one rock to another. He hardly looked behind to see if we were following, and I thought more than once that he hoped we would give up and leave him alone. Connor, with both our packs on her shoulders, walked behind, keeping one eye on me and one eye on the old man ahead of us. My head felt heavy. I wanted to lie down. My feet caught rocks and I stumbled backward into Connor. She braced her legs and took my weight, gently pushing me forward again until I found my pace.

It felt like an age before I finally saw a crease in the rock wall ahead. Hassan motioned for us to hurry. The crease was a crack in the wall as wide as two men standing shoulder to shoulder. A small brown packet lay in the dirt at the entrance, but Hassan snatched it up and stuffed it into the scarf at his waist before I thought to ask him what it was. I had heard of those who lived on the generosity of strangers. Was this how he survived? Donations from passersby? But who would know where to find him? The cave was not visible from the ground.

The small opening in the canyon wall was deceptive. Inside, the rocks expanded outward, making a generous space for the three of us. Hassan had carved a shallow shelf into the walls to hold his meager possessions: a pot for cooking, one knife with a dull blade, a tiny box made of silver, and three spoons. Another shelf held packets of dried meat, dates, and pistachios. A bedroll lay along one wall with a few tattered pillows and a small cup beside it. A circle of stones surrounded a few warm embers. No books or paper.

He pulled the packet from his waist and tucked it into his bedroll.

"What is that?" asked Connor.

Hassan pretended not to have heard her and busied himself with rekindling the fire. He set out some dried meat and dates and motioned for us to eat. He went out again, returning with water from his well, and made tea. He only had two cups, so Connor and I would have to share. He took a pinch of something from the silver box on the shelf and sprinkled it into his cup. Medicine, he said. For his joints. He sat and talked with us, asked us where we were going. We offered him our lie—my father had sent me to be with family out west. He smiled and said I had a good father. Family was important. He asked how we liked Morra and looked to the opening of the cave as I talked. I asked him questions about his life, and he shrugged and would not meet my eyes. Connor asked him nothing. She let me drink most of the tea, her eyes shifting about—back wall, entrance, Hassan, back wall, entrance, Hassan.

Finally, she stood. "Show us the way out of these canyons."

Hassan looked offended. "Are you leaving so soon?"

"Yes. I want to be beyond these canyons by nightfall."

Hassan laughed a wheezing, choking laugh. "That's impossible. It is at least another day to get beyond these walls."

"Then we need to move quickly."

The old man waved a hand. "Out of the question. You will stay here tonight, and I will show you in the morning."

Connor shook her head.

Hassan leaned forward and tilted his head up at her. "You could wander on your own and see how long it takes you. I know the quickest way out, but it's far too late now. I can show you in the morning."

Connor hesitated and then faltered. "At first light."

"Of course."

Connor sat down again, crossing her arms over her legs.

Hassan squinted at her. "What is that?"

Connor looked around, but Hassan pointed at her hands.

"That," he said. "Your ring."

Connor covered her ring with the other hand.

"It's real gold, isn't it? What is that little beast? Is it some sort of god?"

Connor met his gaze and shrugged. "It was a gift."

Hassan thought for a minute. "It must be something. I have not heard a story of a little beast like that. Perhaps it is some sort of snake god. I am sure that is what it is. Little gods are everywhere, you know." This last part he said to me. "They look after things we take for granted. And cause mischief sometimes. Yes, the little gods can be mischievous."

The way he said it—*little gods*—made me wonder. "Who are the big gods?" I asked.

"Oh, there are no big gods anymore. They destroyed each other long ago. This is a fact. I can show you." Hassan looked around at the two of us. He seemed surprised to hear the words come from his own mouth. He examined his teacup, and with one long, dirty finger he wiped the inside of his cup in a long arc, bringing the wet digit to his mouth and sucking thoughtfully. After a moment, he nodded to himself and fixed his dark eyes on me. "Do you want to meet them?"

Chapter 25

All gods are hidden, even the small ones. It takes special eyes to see them. Hassan's gods were big gods, and big gods require big hiding places. A maze of rock. A path worn smooth from travel. I remember the scraping of Hassan's sandals against the ground, the edge of his tunic fluttering as he led us through. Darkness, light, darkness, and then into the sunlight. Sky above and a pit below. Hassan stopped and knelt in the dirt. He dipped one long finger in the dust and touched it to his forehead, leaving a gray circle in the sweat of his brow. Then he stood and invited us to the edge.

Below us lay his gods—a pair—larger than anything I had ever seen. Two arched backs and craning necks. Four pairs of long legs ending in claws that could shred flesh. Two reptilian mouths lined with teeth longer than my hand, forever open in silent screams. Eyes long gone. Blank holes where eyes and noses should have been. Two skeletons, half buried in sand, locked in eternal battle.

"Mightiest of mighties," Hassan called down, clasping his hands together, "I have brought friends to meet you." Hassan turned excitedly to Connor. "Show them your little beast." His mouth stretched into a smile that revealed his half-rotted teeth. She looked at him and then slowly extended her left hand over the pit. Hassan rubbed his hands and gave a small, barking laugh. "They like him." Connor took her hand back and stepped away from the edge. Hassan stood with his toes over the rim, nodding and smiling. "Yes," he said to himself. "Yes, yes."

Beyond the skeletons, in the shadow of the opposite rim, two black vultures eyed us. It was then I noticed the smaller, darker shapes on the floor of the pit—broken bodies of animals, things that had not noticed the edge. I looked at Hassan, the tips of his toes with nothing underneath them but air. I became aware of a strange thought in my brain, and even though I could feel my heart pounding in my chest, I inched forward and lined up the tips of my boots with the rim of the pit. I looked down and felt my stomach drop down into my knees just before Connor ripped me back by my head covering. She looked angry. Hassan was humming to himself and did not notice.

"I have heard," he said, "that when God abandoned the world, He gave us the sky—His greatest gift to us." He glanced at me. "Do you think this is true?"

I shook my head, thinking that was what he wanted.

He smiled. "No. He left us them," he waved a hand over the pit, "in his stead. Many do not see these gods, but they are here. They are with us. That is what we need." He placed a gnarled palm on my shoulder. "We need to be watched over. We need to know someone is with us and guiding our hands. How else would we know what is right?"

He squeezed my shoulder, and I could feel his bones digging into my flesh. He pulled me closer, kneeling down to look directly into my eyes—his with their clouded edges like the scum of a polluted well.

"How could we?" He asked, pulling me closer and speaking more and more urgently. "We are only human. Just flesh. So small. A single rock to the temple. A sickness we cannot even see. That's all it takes. And then we become nothing. Nothing."

From the pit, one vulture screamed at the other, and Connor's hand appeared in front of my face. Hassan's tainted gaze flicked to her ring as he released me.

"Thank you for letting us rest," she said. Her voice, normally hard as stone, was low and flowed like a rolling dune. I looked up. Even her gaze had softened—she looked almost beautiful. "We could not have asked for more generous hospitality," she continued.

Hassan's face relaxed and he took a deep breath, letting her pour praise and flattery into his ear. The longer she spoke, the tighter she gripped my arm. Her fingernails dug into my skin, nearly drawing blood. It was a grip that said, *Listen. To. Me.* Her face betrayed nothing, but I knew to be ready.

Hassan was smiling gently as though standing in the sun on a mild day.

"…and we will remember you as we continue our journey tonight."

"What?" Hassan frowned, his face cracking and hardening. "You are leaving?"

"We could not possibly impose on you further when you have been so kind." The lie spilled from her mouth so easily, like cotton fluff on a gentle breeze, and yet Hassan's face darkened.

"But you do not know the way. I was to show you at first light. You—"

"Will be fine," Connor broke in smoothly. She lifted her left hand. "My little beast protects us. You said yourself the gods like him."

Hassan nodded and glanced back into the pit. "Yes. Yes, that is true."

"Then it is settled. We cannot thank you enough."

"Yes." Hassan's shoulders drooped slightly, seemingly resigned. "But perhaps I could offer you one more cup of tea?"

Connor hesitated. I could feel her searching for the right words—the ones that would both satisfy Hassan and keep us from taking anything else from him.

He cocked his head. "Will you not accept even that? It's only tea. If I am such a good host, surely you would not refuse."

Something inside me sensed a ledge that had nothing to do with the pit behind us. Connor's hand was still on my arm, gripping me so tightly I could feel her pulse. Her face was the picture of grace, but her heart was pounding. She could see as well as I could that Hassan was damaged, broken in a way we could not see before.

She weighed the cost of angering him, and eventually nodded. "Of course. Tea would be very nice."

We should have run.

In the City, some years before, there had been a woman named Lea who lived with her family in a hut near the hunters' campfires. She had two daughters—I can no longer remember their names—and a husband. My father would not let me play with Lea's daughters. There was something about her and her husband he did not like but would not explain. I was a child, so there was no need.

One night, we woke to screams coming from her hut. My father ran out, pushing us back inside when we tried to follow. There had been a fire, my father told us later. The whole family except Lea had suffocated from the smoke.

The hunters helped rebuild her hut, but after that, we did not see Lea anymore. If she still lived there, we did not know, and no one would go inside to look. Lea and her family had kept to themselves. No one could say they knew them well. After the fire, some tried to help her, give her food, talk to her, but eventually they stopped. Life had to go on.

One night she appeared at the community fires. She stood away, almost out of the light, watching. She was thinner, her eyes sunken and dark, lips cracked and pale. Someone called for her to join them, but she walked away. The next night she appeared again, watching us for a little longer this time, and again the night after that. Each night she stayed a little longer, always retreating before anyone could get near her, like a wild animal.

And then children went missing.

How many or who, I could not say. I had not been friends with any of the missing ones. I only know what I heard through the walls, from the people arguing outside my window. My father put me in bed with Cal and Vargas and sat up all night on the bedroom floor with a knife. It was the first time I felt hunted, and the first time I saw murder on another person's face. My father would kill anyone who walked into that room—I did not doubt it for one moment. And so

I stayed in the nest of my brothers' arms and did not make a sound. Outside our home, we heard voices, shouts, and women screaming.

A neighbor came at dawn to tell my father what had happened. There was no one else to take the blame. Hunters had gone to Lea's house and dragged her out. Some held her while others searched her hut, the one they had helped her rebuild after the fire. What they found—my father hushed him. I heard very little, but the small fragment I did hear made my stomach turn. The children—the ones who had been stolen—were dead. Outside her home, Lea had been manic, first weeping her daughters' names into the sand, and next staring into the darkened hut with eyes that were bright and dry. What the people saw inside her hut made them want to beat her, to kill her. Not just kill but rend the flesh from her body and feed it to her, gouge out her eyes, and peel every nail from her murdering fingers. They wanted a slow death for what she did.

They did beat her. But in the end, they could not kill her. Her mind had left her in the fire, followed the smoke that had smothered her children and husband, and now it was gone. In the most gruesome and horrible way possible, she had been trying to replace those she had lost. The hunters' hearts broke even further, knowing revenge for their children was not possible.

But this sickness could not stay in the City. Lea was taken out into the open desert and released far from any village or town. She was given nothing—not food, water, or even a blanket to protect her from the sun. They abandoned her in the wasteland, where she would die alone and not harm anyone else.

My father cried with relief that Lea was dead and his children were still alive. I cried for Lea, for her broken mind, for the ones she murdered. I remembered her sunken eyes shining in the light of the community fires. Her madness had been there for everyone to see.

We just had not wanted to.

═══════

Now I thought I heard an echo of Lea in Hassan's voice, his gestures, and his step as he led us back, back through the maze of rock to the cave.

I tried to keep control of my thoughts. One cup and then we could leave. *He has a gun.* He would be happy and then we could leave. *Will he shoot us as soon as we set foot out of his cave?* Just one cup. *Please let us leave.*

I tried to remember the way down the jagged cliffside; the way we had been going before. It would be dark soon. If we could get another few kilometers before setting up camp, we would be all right. *He will follow us.* I shook my head and moved closer to Connor, pressing my side against hers, but she moved away. I wrapped my arms around my stomach and tried to slow my breathing as we entered his cave.

Hassan's back was to us, pulling the dried tea leaves down from their shelf. The gun lay on the bedroll with the grip toward him. All he had to do was reach out and grab it. I tried to tell myself it was empty. He had no bullets. He had told us so earlier. *No one living alone in the wilderness would keep an unloaded gun.* He had to have bullets somewhere. Had he loaded the gun when we were not looking? Had we watched him the entire time?

I stole a glance at Connor. She was looking at the gun as well and had one hand on her machete. Was she thinking the same thing I was? Connor was strong and fast—faster than Hassan. She could protect us. I repeated the thought over and over in my head.

For his part, Hassan hummed away to himself, either oblivious to our fear or ignoring it. "I hope you like this tea," he said. "It is different from the blend you tried before. This one I got from a trader just last year. It is strong but very nice." He turned and handed a cup to Connor before taking a seat with his own. He sat away from the cave opening and poked at the fire, his gun now out of reach. "You would be surprised," he continued, "at the number of traders who use these canyons as a shortcut to Morra. It seems very treacherous to me—every wall looks the same, and paths can end without warning—but still, they come."

Connor quietly sniffed the tea in her cup before taking a sip. I saw her hold the liquid in her mouth for a brief moment before swallowing and passing the cup to me. I sniffed the cup as well before taking a sip. The taste was delicate at first and then swelled into a heady perfume that made me feel nauseous. I took another sip so that Hassan would not think I was rude and then passed the cup back to Connor, not wanting any more.

"It is too much for her," Hassan said, laughing his short, barking laugh. "It has a floral taste, don't you think? He said it was very expensive."

Connor took a longer sip and grimaced. I was grateful that she was attempting to empty the cup as soon as possible. "Do traders often leave you expensive gifts like this?" she asked.

Hassan ran his dirty fingers through his beard. "At times, yes. Or in trade for something else."

I looked around and could not imagine what Hassan possibly had to trade. I was impatient to leave. The smell of the tea was too strong. I felt sick to my stomach and longed for a breeze from the cave opening to clear the air.

"This though," Hassan held his cup aloft. His voice sounded different— stronger, more confident. "This was given to me as caretaker of the gods. I have been here for over fifty years with only them and the occasional traveler to keep me company. It can be lonely, but there is no higher honor than to tend the gods. They were much different when I found them—half-buried and forgotten. I was much different, too. I cleared the dust so they could breathe once again. *I* tended to them every day. *I* reminded people who they were and made them bow down. In return, the gods ensure I am honored properly."

I thought of getting up and putting my face out into the fresh air. The smell was starting to make my head hurt. I pressed my fingers to my brow. I heard Connor's boots shift against the cave floor and I felt relief. She was preparing for us to leave. But Hassan was still talking.

"Tending the gods can be difficult. They ask for much, and who am I to deny them? I am a servant. They guide my hand and I do their bidding." He paused for a moment before continuing in a deeper, quieter tone. "Do you know why this tea has become my favorite?"

I heard Connor sigh and looked over as her cup dropped from her fingers and broke into three pieces on the ground. Without another sound, she pitched forward onto the cave floor and lay still.

A strong hand grabbed my chin and jerked my head around, sending a rush of nausea into my brain and shadows blooming in my eyes. I could just make out Hassan's tainted gaze close to my face in the semi-darkness. He stared down at me hungrily.

Before everything went black, he grinned. "It makes it so much easier to carry you."

Chapter 26

Cal? Vargas? Help me.

Shadows. The dunes roll gently away from me like clouds pushed by wind, like mighty breath exhaling across the whole landscape. There are no clouds, no moon, only stars. A sky filled with jewels that wink and dance. A sound like loneliness calls out from the darkness. I am being watched. Something moves in the night. Not a shadow. From the center of the horizon, a shape breaks the line between land and sky and rolls toward me—a dune.

A cave.

A cave where a small man sits in the dark. His features shift and change as though he were made of soft sand. One moment he is ancient and the next he is young. Two eyes, sometimes one; sometimes so many that his nose and mouth are pushed to the side. A roll of cloth in his lap that he tears with long, even strokes. He is looking at me but also at the cloth that he tears.

Sssshhhhhh…..sssssshhhhhhhh

There is a glow behind his head, but there is nothing there.

"What is that?" I ask, pointing to the cloth.

Sssshhhhhh…..sssssshhhhhhhh

Smiling, he shows me. "Do you want to help?" His voice is dry as paper.

It is not cloth he holds but skin—human skin with a face and a scar over one eye.

"You may as well," he rasps. "It must be finished eventually."

Sssshhhhhh…..sssssshhhhhhhh

The skin's empty fingers jerk.

"Cal? Vargas?"

The little man nods. "Already done."

A shadow writhes on the floor. This is not a cave but a mouth.

Shadows loom up the wall. Bulbous heads and the whisper of long limbs scraping against rocks.

Sssshhhhhh.…..sssssshhhhhhhh

The sounds of death bring them closer.

A shape spreads high above me—a man's head—but it is swallowed back into darkness. And again, he comes and is covered in darkness. Perhaps my eyes are not working. My head is a cloud, and my feet are so far below me, so far down they are scraping the earth. Where are my arms?

Sssshhhhhh.…..sssssshhhhhhhh

I am being dragged. The realization comes upon me slowly, and I try again to open my eyes. Sleep reaches for me, but I shake it away. *No, I must see.*

My head hits something hard, but I barely feel it. There is a wall in my brain; pain can only shout from the other side. My mind pulls at my eyelids, but nothing happens.

"Stop moving," hisses a snake with a man's voice.

My head is weightless again. My side aches.

Sssshhhhhh.…..sssssshhhhhhhh

Sleep reaches for me again, and this time I let it take me. But someone is pinching me. A slap knocks my head to one side and I can open my eyes. A hand, strong around my jaw, forces my head up. Hassan is looking down at me, his eyes wild with excitement. He lowers his face until his polluted eyes fill my vision.

"There you are," he whispers. "Not too alive. They do not like a challenge." His breath is hot and rancid, and I feel pressure around my torso. "No, not too dead either I see." He is kneeling on my chest. I try to raise my arms, to push him away, but nothing happens. If they are at my sides, I cannot feel them. The pressure in my chest increases, and I cough. Hassan laughs—that strange bark of a noise—and the pressure on my chest goes away. I turn my head to the side, away from him. *Where am I?*

Connor lies on her side a meter away, her head thrown back, her eyes closed, the angle of her limbs unnatural, like a dropped doll. She is so still. Is she breathing?

Hassan forces me to look at him again but does not speak to me. He stares deeply into my eyes, as though looking for something. My pain? My fear? Whatever he sees satisfies him. He stands and speaks to the night sky, throwing his arms wide.

"Mightiest of mighties! I am your humble servant. Guided by your hands, I have prepared this girl and this woman for you."

Blood rushes to my head. My heart pounds in my chest.

"You have granted me a long life. Accept these as a sign of my loyalty and worship, that I may live another year."

Every force inside me wills my body to move. My fingers jump and twitch, and nausea quickly follows. I cannot lie here. *Move!*

"Bless me, mighty ones. All gifts for you!"

Hassan looms over me, flames in his eyes like the Devil himself. With one push, he rolls me down into the pit.

Chapter 27

I tumbled down, down, falling end over end, striking the sloped sides and finally slamming hard into the dirt at the bottom. I landed flat on my back, my head bouncing off the ground, sending stars flying in front of my eyes. The wind was knocked from my body, and I gasped to bring it back. I rolled my head and saw I lay centimeters from the claws of one of Hassan's small gods. I had narrowly missed being impaled on a talon so long it would have punched through the front of my skull.

Above me, Hassan's head and shoulders were just visible over the rim. He was looking down at me, his face in shadow. I had survived the fall and now my death would be slow, and he would watch. I drew another breath and felt knives in my chest. My fingers twitched.

Suddenly, Hassan's head jerked to the left and disappeared. Something was happening up there. I could hear muffled shouts, a yell, and Hassan's head reappeared at the edge of the rim briefly before being jerked back. I heard boots scraping in the dirt and grunts. Hassan's arms flopped over the side of the rim—he was on his back—and Connor appeared above him, hair wild and flying. She raised her arms—something was clenched in her hands—and drove them down over and over again until Hassan stopped trying to push her away and lay still. Connor disappeared. I heard her retching into the dirt and then nothing else for a long time.

I tried to move one arm. My fingers twitched and my hand lifted a little. I tried to wiggle my toes and felt them moving in my boots. I tried to lift my head until a sharp stab in my ribs stopped me. I could not get up.

"Are you alive?" Connor's head had appeared at the side of the rim. She was lying in the dirt, possibly on her side, looking down at me.

My throat worked. "Hhh—" I stopped and swallowed to try again. "I'm alive." I could not take a deep breath.

Connor sighed. "Can you move?"

Tears stung my eyes. "No."

Connor did not answer for a long time. Panic weaved its way into my brain. She could leave me here. She could say there was nothing she could do and walk away. It was impossible to get me out of this pit. I swallowed the lump forming in my throat. *Please don't leave me here.*

But she did not move. Her breathing was coming in gasps and she lay very still. She was injured.

"Connor?" No answer, and I could not yell.

I took a few shallow breaths. Hassan's lifeless arms hung over the side of the rim next to Connor. A dark liquid fell from his fingertips in slow drops.

I did not feel sorry for him.

Connor did not move. We lay—one above and one below—both injured and useless to help the other, and yet my feeling of panic gradually gave way to calm. She was still there. I was not alone, and I would not die because she was still there.

Above us, the stars blanketed the sky. The galaxy cluster stretched overhead like a ribbon. It was strange to feel so much pain and yet see something so beautiful. The stars that night looked down on two travelers and a dead man, but what else did they see? What other hopelessness, what other suffering was within their view? Was there joy, happiness, laughter?

Cold crept into my body, and my fingers and toes went numb. I watched the stars and searched the sky for Orion's belt. *Just one familiar sight.* The largest star in the sky winked once, its light slowly fading and reappearing, as though something had passed between my body and that point in the sky. I wondered how long it would be before something found our bodies and ate them away.

The dark liquid dripping from Hassan's fingers slowed to a stop before darkness took me, and I fell into unconsciousness.

Chapter 28

When I opened my eyes again, the sun was well over the edge of the rim, and I could hear movement in the dirt above me. Hassan was still there, his arms stained red, but Connor was not. I took a deep breath and immediately regretted moving so quickly. I shuddered and tried to wiggle my fingers and toes, feeling a response in my boots and in each hand. I tried next to make a fist and flex my feet, which hurt less than I expected, so I tried more. My elbows could bend, though they were stiff, and if I moved very slowly, I could bend my knees. Every movement was met with a knife-sharp answer from my ribs, but it was small compared to my relief at finding I was not paralyzed.

When I tried to roll onto my side, I keened like a wounded animal. Stars sparked in my eyes, and I rolled back, noticing for the first time that Connor's head had appeared over the edge of the pit, followed shortly by the end of a rope being tossed down to me. It stopped almost a meter from the ground and seemed to be made from clothes and blankets.

"Come on." Her voice sounded raw and weak.

I tried to roll on my side again and make a grab for the end of the rope, but my body refused with a violence that left my hands shaking. I would not roll back and lose what little progress I had made, so I lay on my side, breathing as shallowly as I could. My head was pounding and my stomach heaved—I prayed I would not vomit.

"Come on," she repeated.

I could not answer her.

"Get up," she growled.

I tried to pull myself closer to the end of the rope, tried to reach for it, every part of my body screaming at me to stop. I pressed my cheek against the side of the pit and gave up. It was useless. I could not do this. Even if I could stand, it was impossible to pull myself out of the pit. The pain would be too much, and I would fall long before reaching the top. There was nothing I could do.

I shifted as much as I could so that I could sit with my back against the side of the pit and look up. Connor's face was gone. Before me, the skeletons of Hassan's gods lay half buried in the hard-packed dirt and rock. I saw the talon I had almost landed on sticking up out of the ground. All of that, and I had moved less than three meters.

The edge of the rope jerked and pebbles scattered down over the rim. I looked up. Connor was climbing down. She landed shakily and looked down at me.

She looked terrible—blood and dirt matted her hair and skin, and she had stripped down to a long-sleeved tunic that fell past her knees. I realized that the rest of her clothes made up part of the rope she had just climbed down. She leaned against the wall, breathing heavily. Her calves were covered in dark marks, and an ugly bruise encircled her throat.

"Here," she said, making a move toward me, "get on my back." She took another step and stumbled, catching herself on the wall and lowering herself down beside me. She shook her head. She could no more carry me than I could get on her back. "Pathetic," she grunted.

"What do we do?" I asked.

She thought for a moment before responding. Her left brow, where the scar split the hair, was puffy and an angry purple. Seeing her scar, I remembered my dream of the small man in the cave and wondered if I should tell her about it.

"We will have to stay here," she said eventually. "I will go back up, get some supplies, and come back down. This place is hidden. No one will find us—we are safe here."

I wanted to ask what she planned to do with Hassan but thought better of it. Did it really matter what she did with him?

It took time for Connor to climb back up over the edge. She moved clumsily, her limbs lifting as though rocks were tied to them, and she was out of breath quickly. When she finally made it over, I watched Hassan's arms slowly retreat from the rim—she was dragging him away. Then I heard nothing at all except the wind making its way through the rock walls above me.

Eventually, she returned, tossing down heavy bags and blankets before climbing down herself. After a short rest, she built a crude shelter, stringing blankets up to keep the sun off our bodies. She had raided Hassan's cave, taken everything she thought might be useful, as well as all of the food and water she could find. Digging through one bag, she withdrew a small, square box and held it up for me to see.

"What is that?" I asked.

She opened the box. A heady perfume hit my nostrils and made my stomach lurch. She stood and walked shakily over to the skeletons, where their jaws met in silent rage. Crouching, she sprinkled the loose tea leaves over their skulls. She came back under the shelter and sat down against the wall next to me.

"His gods can have their poison back," she said, watching the breeze lift the dry bits and carry them away.

On the opposite rim, two vultures landed on a craggy outcrop and eyed us. I turned my head to see if Connor was going to chase them away, but she was fast asleep.

A week passed. We slept most of the time, waking for only a few hours a day for food and water. The days and nights were quiet, the only sounds being the wind and the occasional squawk from the vultures, who were growing bolder. It was a shame we could not eat them.

By the fifth day, Connor felt well enough to climb out of the pit for more supplies. When it seemed as though she had been gone a long time, I started to fear she had left me and could not sleep again until I heard her climbing back down the rope.

On the seventh day, she thought it was time I try to get onto her back. We padded my body as much as possible, and then slowly, carefully, I climbed onto her back and held tight. Even with the padding, I had to clench my teeth and bury my face in her back as she climbed. It was nearly impossible. I felt Connor's hands slip several times and was sure we would both fall. Near the top, I could feel her muscles starting to give way, and the moment I could reach the rim, she instructed me to grab the rope and hoist myself the rest of the way. I grabbed the rope and heaved myself over the top, gritting my teeth. Weak from the effort, Connor had slipped further down the rope and had to lower herself back to the ground.

I wanted to laugh. We had switched places from where we were a week ago. How could we do this? The world was too big and too perilous, and we were too small. It seemed hopeless.

Connor waited until she had her breath back before hauling herself up the rope and over the top. Once out of the pit, she made to stand and then sat back down again, exhausted. Her bruises had faded to a sickly color, and her brow was no longer swollen. She was beginning to look like herself again.

We stayed in Hassan's cave for weeks before moving on—waiting until I could breathe and move normally again. Now that we knew this was a trade route, Connor left the cave to hunt only when necessary, returning with lizards, snakes, and hares. One lean week, she could find nothing but rats, which I refused to eat after she accidentally filled the cave with the smell of singed fur. She became angry when I pushed it away because it meant she had to leave to hunt or else let me starve. She waited me out for a day before hunting again, but there really was nothing else in the canyon. I gave in and ate the rat.

One night, we saw light from a trade caravan, and Connor remained on edge for a full day afterward, jumping at every sound outside the walls. The caravan had been so loud, I told her, surely we would know if it was coming back. Nothing I said helped. I wondered if she imagined a scout spotting the cave from below and coming to investigate.

I remembered the packet left for Hassan when we first came with him and asked Connor if she had found it. She nodded and said she had.

"Well?" I asked. "What was in it?"

She fixed her eyes on me. "Bullets."

"Who would leave bullets for him?"

She did not answer and instead went back to watching the cave opening. She spent most of her time watching, listening for intruders.

For my part, I could do very little. Connor thought I had broken a few ribs, which meant time—time spent in one place waiting for me to heal. I wondered if she had ever spent so long in one place. Even while guarding the entrance, she was constantly moving. Her hands mended clothes while her eyes searched the canyon outside, or she drew maps in the dust of the cave floor while her ears listened for movement beyond the cave. At night she paced until she was tired and could lay down to sleep. Even when she slept, she tossed and turned. I thought she must feel confined, and I hoped she would soon settle. She never did, and I could do nothing to help except wait for my bones to knit back together.

While Connor hunted and paced, I studied my blue book or read *The Land of Magic*—my gift from Asha—every day. I still could not decipher the blue book, and I never would, but the pictures within were often the last thing I saw before I closed my eyes at the end of the day. Connor occasionally stopped moving long enough to glance at a page over my shoulder, but she never asked about either of the books.

We had been in the canyon a month before I could stand and carry my own pack. On that day, Connor decided it was time to move on. Our last hours in the cave were spent stripping it of every useful object: cups, food, knives, water bags, bed rolls, fl int. We took everything, including the gun and the few bullets that had been left for Hassan. It would only be useful for so long—we could not know where or when we would find more bullets—but we could use it to scare away anyone who would hurt us. Connor did not seem so sure, but she refused to leave behind anything that could help us on our way. What she wanted more than anything was a map of the area, but she could not find one. We would have to find a way on our own.

The next morning, I waited until we had walked far enough and could no longer see the cave behind us before asking what she had done with Hassan's body.

She was quiet for a while before answering. "I don't know that there would be anything left of him by now."

I did not ask her anything else, and we fell into an easy silence for the rest of the morning. Connor walked ahead of me, looking for signs of which way would lead us out of the canyons. She quickly found the caravan trail, but she avoided it. Wherever the traders were coming from, she did not want to follow. Instead, we moved through the canyon without a sound, carving our own way, far from other people. We did this for days, and I feared we would wake up one morning to find we had gone in a circle. At night, Connor marked the line of the galaxy in the sky and followed its path during the day, until we finally turned a corner and the canyon spat us out into the open.

Before us lay a vast expanse I had only heard of in stories—the rolling badlands that had swallowed soldiers and explorers alike.

We had stepped out into the Red.

Chapter 29

There is no end to the Red. The fine, dust-like soil colors everything it touches, letting dangers hide in plain sight. We tried to travel at night, but that only made things worse. The blood-colored ground and inky dark sky mingled, making it impossible for us to find our way. During the day, the sand blinded us to what was really there. White lizards appeared blue; a tawny hawk looked purple. It was the haze of the Red, Connor said. Our eyes could not adjust quickly enough to see something as it really was.

But the worst was the heat. It radiated off the ground in sheets that wrapped themselves around our necks and covered our faces like it wanted to smother us where we stood. We could not know when we would find water again, and so Connor rationed us to just a few mouthfuls a day, supplementing that with as much cactus as we could find. It was never enough. I craved moisture, relief, but it never came. When the sun sank below the horizon, cold crept into our bones, and we shivered ourselves awake in the middle of the night.

We tried resting during the hottest part of the day. We pitched our crude tent with its walls open to catch any breeze that might come through, lying under its canopy in pools of our own sweat. I felt sure we were losing more moisture than we were taking in.

Connor was quieter than usual. This was not how she wanted to travel. She did not know the Red and had not been able to prepare. I understood, but I wanted her to talk to me. I needed something to take my mind away, but my questions were met with stony silence or one-word responses, and I was too tired to keep trying.

We saw no one else, and no animal larger than a kit fox until we stumbled upon a pack of dogs tearing at a headless carcass. We kept our distance and made our way around them. A spotted dog with a black face kept watch, making sure we did not come near the pack's meal. Dogs are not pets out here.

Days and nights passed without much to differentiate one from another. Eventually, I lost track of how long we had been in the Red. When I mentioned it to Connor, that I could no longer remember how long we had been there, she seemed surprised that I had been trying to remember at all.

"How do you keep track of time?" I asked.

She shrugged. "I don't." It did not matter to her.

How could it not matter to her? How could she not want to know how long we had been traveling?

She thought for a while. "I cannot know how long it will be until I find what I am looking for."

We, I thought. *What* we *are looking for.*

I tried to mark time in *The Land of Magic.* I found a pebble that would leave its color when scraped across a page, and so used to keep a tally of days. Every morning when we got up, I drew a short line on a blank page in the book. Connor watched me but did not say anything.

She had started doing something she had never done before. Connor had started drawing maps. As we walked during the day, she would study the landscape and then draw what she could remember on blank sheets she had taken from Hassan's cave. She sometimes asked me questions then. Could I remember if there were four peaks or three ahead? Did the Red seem to be changing? Perhaps it would be rockier tomorrow or the next day. I enjoyed her questions and liked knowing what she would be looking for the next day. I pointed out rock formations, or strange breaks in the sand, hoping one of them would become part of her map.

Looking over her shoulder one evening—something she hated—I wondered aloud about her maps. These were pictures of where we had been, not where we were going, so what use were they? She did not keep track of the days—how long we had been walking—so why draw what had already happened?

She smudged a line with her finger to soften it. "We could trade these later."

"Who would want a map of the Red?"

She shrugged. "I have traded things that seemed useless to me before. Did you notice the black line of rocks at the horizon today? We should make it to them by tomorrow."

She rotated her pebble to a softer side and made arcs of color to show the dunes we had traversed earlier. She knitted her brows, concentrating on the movement, and I thought maybe what she said was only half true. We could trade maps later, but she enjoyed this. She liked puzzling out the landscape on a piece of paper, putting it somewhere she could contain it and make sense of it. I left her to her maps and read *The Land of Magic* until I fell asleep.

Chapter 30

Three crows followed us today.

I noticed them in the sky in the morning and saw them again when we stopped to rest at midday. They had taken shelter in the shade of a boulder—two picking at the ground while one perched on the rock above, their jet-black feathers glistening in the sunlight. They were something not colored, coated, or tricked by the Red. The black of their bodies was deep and true and defied the touch of the sand. I knew what I was seeing.

The crows cocked their heads at us, the strange, dust-covered women huddled under a canopy. I knew I was covered in grit and grime, but what color my skin was I could not tell anymore. The Red tricks you into seeing only itself.

One crow pulled a lizard from a crevice and took to the sky, the two following close behind, and I did not see them again until evening. We had not reached the line of black rocks as Connor thought we would—those were still a day away. They made me uneasy, standing just short of the horizon like a row of soldiers guarding whatever lay beyond. Connor insisted we would reach them tomorrow, but they seemed no closer than they had been the day before.

The crows landed one, two, three on a rock just outside the circle of light cast by our campfire. I could see their feathers shining, and their bright eyes when they turned their heads. Connor noticed them as well.

"Do you think they are hungry?" I asked.

Annoyed, Connor told me not to feed them, but I was not going to. I knew better than to feed any animal that strayed near a campfire or approached in the wilderness. My brothers and I had been taught as much from a very young age. Cal liked dogs, and my parents had been afraid he would try to feed a stray and would be bitten. My mother and father told us over and over again what could happen, hoping to frighten us enough to keep us safe. They had good reason. I had seen the marks a dog's bite could leave on human skin. A crow would not bite me, but feeding them would only make them follow us longer and pick through our rations to steal what they wanted.

I thought Connor might try to frighten the crows away, but she left them alone. They watched us for a long time, long after the land had grown cold, before taking to the sky again. *A murder. A group of crows is called a murder. What if there are only three?*

<hr>

Connor was right. We did reach the line of black rocks the next day, but when we did, we found that we could not go on.

The line thrust out of the Red over seven meters into the sky. Each stone was over two meters thick at the bottom, but millions of years of being blasted by sand and wind had winnowed the rising peaks to fine, thorn-like points. They were arranged in an almost straight line, retreating away to the left and right of where we stood. In some places, the rocks came together and were impassable, and in others, there was enough space for a whole caravan. But there were no canyons beyond, as would be expected. The landscape should change, but it did not. We could see the sand continue on the other side.

Connor pitched the tent, leaving the sides open, and sat down to think. I crawled in beside her and faced the line of rocks.

"What do you think it is?" I asked.

Of course, she did not answer, but I was getting used to that. Though the bruises on her face and neck had faded a while ago, I knew where they had been. She looked like herself, but I could see her past faces as well. The battered face that had come to Asha's home, the bloodied and bruised one that had looked at me over the edge of the pit after she had killed Hassan.

I looked away from her, wondering what she had looked like when she had gotten her scar—the one mark that had never gone away.

"They look like teeth," I said of the rocks. *Fangs.*

Three black shapes fluttered down and landed in the dirt just between two of the rocks. The crows looked at us, and the way they stood made the opening behind them look like a path. *Why were they still following us?* Crows were curious but we could not be that interesting. One dipped its head low and cawed once. I felt like it expected us to follow. Despite the heat, I shivered, drawing my knees into my chest and folding my arms over them.

Connor still had not said anything. She kept her eyes fixed on a point just beyond the line of rocks. It wasn't the rocks that worried her or the way the landscape refused to change. We had been in the Red so long it seemed nothing could make it be anything except dust. She did not even mind the crows. What worried her stood just beyond the line of black rocks. Embedded in the sand as if it had grown out of the ground, was a figure five meters high—a hand carved from one of the black rocks, reaching, as though in supplication, towards us.

"I know what that is," Connor said quietly, her voice tight. "That's the Devil's Palm."

Chapter 31

Twenty years ago, James Afshes disappeared into the wilderness, never to be heard from again. He was gone—no longer the priest and father his family and city had known and loved—and he had taken others with him. They were people with jobs and families. They were loved, not wayward or lost, and none of them were ever seen again. But where had they gone? What had become of them?

Those are questions for the Dybbuk.

The city sent scouts in all directions to find James and the others. Most came back, some did not, and one returned having met the Dybbuk.

James Afshes was a handsome man—too handsome for a priest, it could be said—with an intense gaze and a way of getting what he wanted. Until the moment he disappeared, many would have said that never would have happened. They knew him better than that. But how well does one person really know another? James Afshes was a master of masks, putting a pleasing visage up for everyone to see while the real one waited in the shadows—that is one story. James Afshes was a psychopath, incapable of feeling anything for anyone but himself, who craved power and control—that is another story. All anyone really knows is that James Afshes—priest, husband, and father—disappeared along with forty-three others, and never came back. The rest is a matter of opinion.

One man, the lone scout, saw what became of James Afshes and the others, but his story has been retold over and over so many times by so many people that it's possible no part of may be true anymore. Only one person knows for sure.

In the wilderness, the lone scout met a man who looked very familiar. The man wore a red tunic that blended in with the sand around him. He smiled at the scout and invited him to dinner. The man did not know James Afshes, but he could offer the scout food, water, and a bed for the night.

The man and the scout passed a border of fang-shaped rocks and into a small community. The people there wore red tunics just like the one the man wore. They were all very friendly and welcomed the scout—who saw enough familiar faces to know he had stumbled upon the missing people from his city. He tried to explain that their families were anxious to hear from them. Why had they left? The people were confused. They did not seem to remember their lives before they had left.

The scout did not press them and only asked to be taken to James Afshes, which he came to regret. The priest had ceased to be. He had removed whatever had made him James Afshes, shedding that skin like a snake. The man who stood before the lone scout was not a man. He was a monster. He was the Dybbuk.

The scout brought back stories of torture, blood, and terror. Whether the scout escaped or was let go, no one really knows, but his story was enough. His words blotted out the name James Afshes and the names of every other who left with him. No one ever went looking for them again.

And that was the last anyone heard of the Cult of the Devil's Palm.

Connor rubbed her hands over her face. "We cannot go through there," she said finally.

"You said yourself it was twenty years ago. How many of them could be left?"

"That is assuming too much."

I crossed my ankles and put my head in my hands. I don't know why I said it. I did not want to go through either. One member of the Devil's Palm was too many. Hassan's face flickered through my mind. There was no way to know what they would do to us.

Connor's gaze followed the border of sharp rocks from left to right. It ran until disappearing into the Red. "We go around," she said, standing.

Crack

A puff of white smoke soared into the air on the other side of the border. The crude flare reached its apex and arced back toward the ground. Its origin was a man standing just behind the line of black rocks—one arm outstretched, a shock of white hair stood out from his head. He wore a dark red tunic that matched the sand around him, and so did the four other men who were advancing toward us.

Connor wasted no time. She snatched Hassan's gun from her pack, pointed it at the men, sighted down her arms, and pulled the trigger. I clapped my hands over my ears just as the sound exploded the air around us. The sand at the men's feet jumped and they fell to the ground, covering their heads. She fired again, narrowly missing the white-haired man. Connor adjusted her aim and pulled the trigger again. A *click*, and nothing else. The white-haired man glared at us and got to his feet. He motioned for the other men to stand, and they advanced on us again. Connor pulled the trigger; the gun misfired again. She threw it down and drew her machete, but then slowly re-sheathed it. "Let me be the one to speak," she hissed to me through gritted teeth. "Look down and say nothing."

Our hands were tied, and we were taken to the center of the Cult of the Devil's Palm. Two of the men carried our packs while the other two gripped our arms and pulled us forward. The man with the wild white hair led the procession. His forehead was smooth, but his cheeks were weathered and deeply creased. His nose was long and straight. His lips were set in a grim line. He wore sandals instead of boots, and his toenails were thick and long. He wore his tunic without a belt and layers of long skirts instead of trousers. When the wind caught the fabric, it ballooned, and he appeared as a small dune moving over the sand.

I was made to walk in front of Connor so that I could not see her. I tried to look behind me once but the man at my arm jerked me forward.

We were led over a kind of path in the sand, compacted by many feet over many years, for what felt like hours, until we reached a group of huts arranged in a series of circles around a central clearing. In the middle of the clearing stood an obelisk made from a single shard of obsidian over four meters high. Its sheared sides ended in edges sharp as blades, and the base was covered in strange carvings.

A group of people stood in the center near the obelisk. They all wore the same blood-red tunics and trousers. They had come out of the huts to look at us. Some were old, some fairly young, and there were even children. The Cult of the Devil's Palm was not dying out. They were growing their numbers.

We were taken to one of the huts—one that was completely empty. Our hands were untied, and bracelets of heavy iron were locked around our ankles and attached by a chain to the wall of the hut. The men left, taking our packs with them.

In the cool air, I swallowed the knot that was rising in my throat. Across the hut, Connor sat with her back against the wall, her head tilted back. She was taking long, measured breaths, gripping her knees, digging in her fingernails. Her throat worked, and I realized she might be afraid. I leaned my back against the wall, tilted my head, and took a deep breath. I matched her pace so that we were breathing together. In, two, three; out, two, three, four. My heart slowed and I let my eyes close. My blood stopped pounding in my ears, and I could hear myself think again.

When I opened my eyes, Connor was looking right at me. Her hard gaze softened slightly, and she nodded. I nodded back but did not say anything. There wasn't anything to say. If she had a plan, she would say so. We could not escape, and if we did there was nowhere to run. For now, there was nothing to do but wait.

I looked around. The hut only had one room, and it did not look as though anyone had ever lived there. The walls and floor were bare, there was no furniture, no clothes, no bedroll tucked away anywhere. The room itself was very small. We were on opposite sides, but if I tried very hard, I could probably touch my foot to Connor's. There were no windows. The only opening was at the front, but it did not have a door. Outside, I could see the obelisk framed perfectly in the doorway. The man with the wild hair was standing beside it, watching us. Connor noticed him and matched his gaze. Unlike most, the man with the wild hair did not look away. I looked away for a moment, and when I looked back, he was gone.

I could not hear any noise outside of the hut. It was as if the people who had come out to see us had suddenly melted away. Even as the hours went by and the light dimmed, I heard nothing until the sun disappeared and night fell. Then a peal of voices went up from the huts, followed by the light of fires. Community fires? I could not see them from the doorway, only the flicker of light from seemingly every direction. The voices rose and fell in rhythm punctuated by a high-pitched wail. They were singing.

The man with the wild hair appeared in the doorway. He had painted his face with a thick, dark liquid that made his hair look even whiter. He stood to one side to make way for a shadow to slip by him and enter the hut.

It could have been a man, that thing that stood before us. A man burned in a fire and then made to stand and walk like it was still alive. Its hairless skin was blackened and charred, and when it moved, flakes of ash broke free and floated around in lazy swirls. It was thin as a skeleton and made none of the sounds of life that people make. No breath, no effort, no living sound. It smelled acrid, not like a being at all. Its limbs were long and ended in tapered fingers and toes with no nails. Its hipbones protruded like carved wood, and between them nothing at all. Its face was heavy, the chin jutting out like a sheer cliff, its cheekbones sharp as knives under the tissue-thin burned flesh. Its eyes were small and black as its skin. The pupils had swallowed the rest, and only darkness looked back. It stared around the room with an intensity that frightened me.

I was looking at the Dybbuk.

"Who are you?" it asked in a voice like burnt paper. Ash fell from its mouth, and the charred flesh cracked with each movement of its jaw.

"Travelers," answered Connor. Her voice was calm and gentle. I recognized that voice immediately. *Not worth the trouble,* that voice said. *Not worth the time.*

The man with the wild hair entered the hut behind the thing and crouched in a corner, never taking his eyes off the creature.

The Dybbuk regarded her for a moment. "In a way, yes, you are. In a way, no, you are not."

The faintest crease wrinkled Connor's brow. What was happening?

It approached her slowly and crouched down so that it could look her in the eye. Its charred back was to me, the flesh crackling and stretching over its bones.

It reached out. With one skeletal finger, it traced the scar that split her scalp and brow, then fell to her left hand, pointing to her ring.

"Connor," it whispered, "Fadi."

Connor's eyes went wide, and she pulled back against the wall.

The thing gave a wheezing laugh and looked at his companion. "I was right." A crack opened at its neck, revealing something red and wet. The man with the wild hair nodded and left the hut. Outside, a cry went up that was followed by more shouts and singing.

The Dybbuk looked back at Connor. It stood slowly, holding her gaze for a moment before leaving us alone in the hut.

Chapter 32

"Who—" I swallowed and tried again. "How does it know you?"

Connor shook her head and rubbed furiously at the spot on her forehead and hand where the thing had touched her.

"What was that?" I whispered, panic rising in my voice.

Connor covered her mouth and shook her head. "I don't know," she whispered back.

"How does it know who you are?"

"I don't know."

Her eyes were wide, her composure gone. The black smudge at her brow stayed where it was, smeared with sweat. She looked terrified. It wasn't that the Dybbuk had frightened her—it had named her.

Outside, the obelisk shimmered in the firelight. Shouts and cries went up from the people outside—the rest of the Devil's Palm. A shadow fell over the doorway and the man with the wild hair reappeared.

"Connor Fadi," he said quietly. "I pictured you differently. The madwoman combing the desert for a miracle. Do I have that right?"

Connor, her jaw set like iron, stood to face the man.

"I see," the man said, and then pointed at me. "Is this your daughter?"

Connor stared him down.

"Your ring," the man continued. "Give it to me."

"You will have to take it," Connor spat.

The man lunged at her and she swung, her fist catching him under the chin. He stumbled back, steadying himself against the wall near me. He tried to grab at my arm, but I squirmed away.

"Connor Fadi gives nothing.," said a voice like old paper. The Dybbuk stood in the doorway, calmly surveying the struggle inside. "She only takes."

"How do you know me?"

The Dybbuk's mouth creased in something like a frown. "Arrogance. I do not know you. One of my children told me a story of a woman in the desert. A woman looking for something no one has seen before. A woman with a scarred face. A woman wearing a ring bearing a creature not of this earth. And here you are." The Dybbuk frowned harder. "He has told many about you."

Connor shook her head. "No one in the Devil's Palm knows who I am."

The Dybbuk held up its arms, ash streaming away from them. "And yet I just told you." It stepped away from the hut, a sharp, almost chemical smell following behind. "They would like to meet you. I give my children what they want."

Two men entered and unchained Connor, dragging her out into the firelight. The man with the wild hair grabbed my arm and made me look at him. "Behave," he growled before unchaining me and dragging me out after her.

They surrounded the obelisk—faces lit by torches on high pikes in a circle around them. There were children even younger than me held by their parents, their small faces alive with curiosity. Adjacent to the obelisk was a table made of rock, its surface dark and splattered with stains. A knife with a long blade lay to one side. Behind the table on a raised dais sat a chair of carved obsidian that shone in the light of the fires. Before the chair stood the Dybbuk. I dug my heels into the dirt and the man with the wild hair wrenched me forward until I stood next to Connor.

The Dybbuk eyed us both, then raised its arms. "My children! We gather on a hallowed night. The first star of the new horizon is upon us, and the Master has blessed our family with new generations and a new light into the future of our family. Our crop has been plentiful, our hunt has brought new blood, and we have raised our voices in prayer to him every night. I am his servant. I am yours. I am but his mouth that he may pour out his words and guide us. To the Master go our thanks."

"We praise thee! We praise thee!" answered the people around us.

"The lord Master sees you, my children. He sees your work and your suffering. Know that he suffers with you. You are not alone. When one of us falls, the Master weeps. Join me in praising the Master for his gifts and for our suffering, that we may know him better."

"We thank the Master! We praise thee!"

"My children, the Master has blessed us again this night. A truly wonderful gift. The Master has sent us a prophet of his own," it pointed to Connor, "that we may know our path is righteous."

The crowd murmured in awe. Faces turned toward us—dark moons with round open mouths that whispered to one another. They pointed at Connor, at her scar, and strained to see her hands. Connor stood still and did not look at them.

The Dybbuk continued, "Connor Fadi brings blessings from the Master to us. She has told me many tales of her journey. There are dangers still in the wilderness, and the people persecute her for her devotion to the Master. The

Master has blessed her by bringing her to us, that we may see his love."

"We thank the Master! We praise thee!"

"See how the Master has blessed us? He has chosen us of all the people in the world to share in his glory. The Master has blessed your houses and your hearts on this night and asks very little of our family. On this hallowed night, only the most loyal will be rewarded and will join him in sacrifice."

"Bless us, O Master!"

"The Master has chosen one of us." The Dybbuk raised a finger, and a flurry of whispers went through the crowd. "He has told me that only one is worthy to join him. Kesh, my child."

The crowd gasped and pressed forward as a young man, naked from the waist up, was brought out from the crowd by two men. He was bound and gagged, a gash across his forehead spilling dark blood down his chest. His eyes were only slightly open, staring at nothing.

Connor tensed beside me.

The man with the wild hair released my arm and approached the dais, taking up a bowl of liquid from the foot of the obsidian chair and holding it up for the Dybbuk to drink. The Dybbuk dipped its head low, draining the bowl of every last drop.

The men laid the younger one on the table, positioning his head toward the obelisk. They lashed his arms and legs to the stone with strips of leather and then disappeared into the people again.

Excitement rolled through the crowd, building to a repetition I could not make out.

On the dais, the Dybbuk arched its body, chanting in a language I did not understand. It threw its head back to the night sky and screamed at the stars, "I am death! I am destruction! I am the flame that licks the sky! I am the power that commands the snake to bite and the poison that drains the spark from every living thing! I am the laugh of the wild dog and the lion that crushes the skulls of men! I am the Devil himself!"

The Dybbuk sprang down from the dais, snatched up the knife, and sliced it across Kesh's throat. Hot blood spurted from the wound, covering the Dybbuk and the stone table. Kesh's mouth opened and closed and then stopped. With a cry, the Dybbuk raised its arms again and plunged the knife into the young man's chest. The roar from the crowd was deafening. They cheered and surged forward, pushing past us to touch the blood that had fallen on the ground. They smeared it on their faces and on the obelisk, raising their hands in praise.

I squeezed my eye shut as tight as I could. *This is not real. This is not real.* When I opened them again, I only saw the blood painted across the smooth surface of the obelisk, the carvings at the base coated in thick grime. The noise— the calls of triumph from the crowd, of gratitude for this grisly gift—I clapped my hands over my ears. *The sounds of death bring them closer.* My head buzzed and everything began to sound very far away. Behind the dais, a long-limbed figure with a bulbous head stood with one hand on the Dybbuk's shoulder. I squeezed my eyes shut again. *This is not real. This is not real.* A woman grabbed my shoulders, laughing with glee. Her face was painted with blood. I shoved her away and took two steps before the man with the wild hair grabbed me and dragged me from the crowd, up to the dais where the Dybbuk sat watching its children bathe in blood. The figure was gone.

Small chairs were brought for Connor and me. I sat, clutching my knees, staring at the hell below. *None of this is real.*

"My children are wonderful, are they not?" The Dybbuk smiled down at them, its charred skin cracking. Its hands were slick with blood that mingled with ash and dripped from its tapered fingers onto the obsidian chair on which it sat. "They would do anything for me. There is nothing quite like that kind of utter devotion. If I told them to kill, they would." It turned to Connor. "Do we understand each other?"

Connor nodded stiffly.

"You live as long as I say," the Dybbuk continued. "I am their father, not you."

The Dybbuk's skin stretched over its bony knuckles as it gripped the chair. Its body smelled like sharp chemicals again. I knew that smell. At its neck was a crease, the same one I had seen before. Inside was something red and wet like blood. *Like blood, but not blood.*

"I don't want your family," replied Connor in a low voice.

"You could not have them if you did," the Dybbuk snapped.

The man with the wild hair stood behind the table in front of the dais with his back to us. He kept the followers away by carving off Kesh's fingers one by one and tossing them into the crowd. My stomach turned.

"We would like to leave," I heard Connor say.

The Dybbuk drummed a finger on the arm of his chair. "You cannot leave until morning. It would not look right."

Connor nodded. "Morning is soon enough."

The Dybbuk jerked its head toward her. "You exist at my pleasure, Connor Fadi. If you so much as glance at my children, you will find yourself in a more unfortunate position at our next celebration."

Below us, Kesh's lifeless body jerked as the man with the wild hair removed the last finger.

Connor pressed her lips together and said nothing. Pleased, the Dybbuk sat back and watched its children.

"Who was he?" I managed to ask.

The Dybbuk glanced over, surprised to hear me speak. "A storyteller." It waved a hand dismissively. "Well, he is nobody anymore."

Its hand, positioned on the arm of the chair, was very close to my face. The arm was slick with blood up to the elbow, and a long, nail-less forefinger tapped the obsidian chair. A gob of ash and blood gathered at the forearm and dripped onto the dais with a wet *smack*, leaving a long gap where no char clung to the fascia. The flesh it revealed was covered in blood, but the hairless membrane underneath was skin as real and normal as my own.

My eyes traveled the Dybbuk's body, and I knew what the chemical smell was—paint. The more I looked, the more I could see this creature for what it was—flesh and blood as real as anyone else. This was no demon in the shape of man, spit up from the pit of Hell. This was a man made into the shape of a demon. For a brief, horrible moment I saw a glimmer of just what James Afshes had done to become the Dybbuk, and how he had earned his family.

The man with the wild hair returned us to the hut later that night, after the followers had tired themselves out and dispersed. He locked the irons around our ankles again so that we would not run off and left us without another word. Outside, the firelight died slowly, and four men came to take what was left of Kesh away.

I felt like a ragdoll robbed of its stuffing. Slumped against the wall, I rested my cheek on its cool surface. I glanced across the hut at the woman I had followed all these months. Connor looked drained of whatever steel she normally had within her. If the Dybbuk decided not to let us go, there was no hope. She would not be able to save us this time. My throat tightened slightly. I wanted her to look at me. I wanted to push her. I needed to hear her voice, to see her strength.

"Why did you bring me with you?" It was the first thought that came to my head, but it worked. It had been so quiet that the sound of my voice startled her.

"Bring you?" She looked almost insulted. "I did not bring you anywhere."

"No?"

"No." She massaged the thumb of her left hand gently.

I felt her retreating into herself. "Why did you *let me* come with you?" I asked.

"I did not think you would. You looked determined that night in your city, but—" she spread her hands. "How much could that mean?" She leaned her head against the wall and looked up at the ceiling. "I thought you would go home that first day. But you didn't. And then the day after, but you did not. I thought you would stay with Asha. You could have."

I hugged my knees to my chest. When I looked up, her eyes were fixed on me. When she spoke again, her voice was quiet but strong. "You walk the same path I do."

She reclined against the wall, turning her ring around and around her finger. She had retreated into herself, and this time I let her go.

We sat in silence, neither of us sleeping or moving again until dawn.

The Dybbuk made us wait another day, just to show us he could. We could hear the man with the wild hair telling the followers outside of how the prophet Connor Fadi had come to the Devil's Palm to beg wisdom from the Dybbuk. No one came near the hut, and we did not make a sound to contradict what we heard. This was the Dybbuk's family. Their minds belonged to him, and he was very right about one thing—we existed as long as he let us do so.

That night, the followers gathered at the obelisk, but this time it was the man with the wild hair who presided over the congregation. He prayed with them and led them in a song we could not understand, but there was no sacrifice that night. The Dybbuk did not show himself, and we did not see him again. He was finished with us.

The moment the sky lightened to a rosy pink, we were taken quickly to the other side of their territory. Our machetes and packs were returned to us, but not Hassan's gun. It was too rare, too valuable, to let go.

We were abandoned in the Red, far from the borders of the Cult of the Devil's Palm.

Chapter 33

We continued on, putting as much distance between ourselves and the Devil's Palm as we could before nightfall. We traveled in silence, lost in our thoughts. I thought of the Dybbuk, of what he had done. I wondered how many people had been sacrificed before Kesh. The noise, the shouting and singing every night. Did he not fear witches? Or perhaps witches feared the Dybbuk. My stomach turned.

Connor walked a little ahead of me, as always, but now the long tail of her head covering was wrapped across her nose and mouth so that only her eyes were visible. I did the same, hiding my face from anyone who might be watching. We had thought the wilderness was empty, but if they had known who Connor was, how long before they knew who I was as well? It was unnerving to imagine finding a stranger in the middle of nowhere who already knew me. It would be as though a part of myself did not belong to me anymore.

Connor never looked back. That night, she sat with her back to the fire, looking out into the night and up at the stars. Eventually, I crawled into the tent without her and lay staring at the canopy above my head, listening to the breeze rustle the fabric.

The next day, the landscape changed, at first spotted with a few stones, and then rocks and pebbles that slid and crumbled underfoot. Our feet were sore, and we risked twisting an ankle with every step. By midday, I was exhausted and ready to rest. We sat under the canopy and Connor bound cloth around our ankles to better support them as we walked.

The way was slow, and the heat never relented. Our supplies were running low, and I watched Connor's face when she realized we would need to stop at the next settlement we came to. I felt anxiety rising in my chest at the thought of walking into another town, and I wondered if Connor would let me stay behind in the tent. Looking at her face, though, it would not be right to leave her alone. She had retreated into herself since the Devil's Palm, and I did not know how else to help her.

That night, neither of us could sleep. Our bedrolls had grown thin over the journey, and the terrain refused to lay flat. We cleared the sharp-edged rocks from the campsite, layered every blanket in our packs on the ground, and still, we could not sleep. The ground itself was puckered and pointed and dug into our bodies so that we tossed and turned until morning.

The days and nights dragged on without rest or respite. While the sun was in the sky, we walked, stumbling every few meters, and sliding on the unstable ground. When night rose, we turned and paced and could not close our eyes for more than a few hours. I stopped counting the days in *The Land of Magic*. I stopped reading altogether. Connor tried to draw her maps at night, but more often stared into the fire, her papers forgotten in her hands. After days of little or no sleep, she stopped talking to me entirely. Sometimes I did not know if she was even aware of me—she started if I dropped a tool or rolled over too quickly in the tent.

I tried to let her sleep by staying later and later by the fire at night. Perhaps she could fall asleep better if I were not there, but it was no use. Little by little, I stopped going into the tent, preferring to watch the fire dwindle into orange coals and gradually die into ash. It made me think of the Dybbuk's skin, the mottled one he had created for himself. I did not like to think of the Devil's Palm, but it crept up to me in the dead of night when sleep refused to take me.

Shadows came to me after the fire died away—faces I knew and some I did not. One night I saw a flicker in the fire and thought the crows were following us still, but when I turned my head, nothing was there. Sometimes I thought I saw lights on the horizon, but when I woke Connor, she saw only darkness. She looked at me askance, as though I were losing my mind, but I knew she saw things, too. I had seen her staring at the space opposite the fire at night, as though someone was sitting there. I had seen her twisting and turning her head at a line of rock, following the movement of something that only she could see.

My body began to ache, my joints throbbing constantly, and my head thundered at all hours. Sleep ran round and round my brain but never touched my body. I thought of the bed at Zazi and Cyril's—large enough that I could spread my arms and barely touch each side. I thought of the pillow-covered floor at Asha's and the furry warmth of Mow. I thought of clouds of fleece and rabbit-skin blankets, of sinking into a nest of cotton fluff, but when I lay my head down all I felt was the immovable point of a stone in my side.

And so, I sat by the fire and waited for my body to exhaust itself. I would sleep eventually, no matter what the terrain. My brain would shut down and nothing would be able to wake me until I was well and truly rested. I must sleep or—

"Or else you will die."

I jerked my head in the direction of the voice. Nothing but cold darkness. But there had been someone, hadn't there? Someone sitting across the fire? I gritted my teeth at the empty space and pulled my knees up to my chin. My mind was playing tricks on me, making me hear things that were not there. Even so, I kept my eyes open, scanning the campsite for signs that we were not alone. At dawn, Connor appeared, and we silently packed our things and moved on.

That night, I retreated to the tent after we ate and pulled the blankets over my head. I drew my knees up and huddled in the darkness, curled around *The Land of Magic*, and cried as quietly as I could.

There is a cave. The mouth of a cave. An opening into the deep, wet earth.

The man sits in the dark and performs his task. There is a light behind him, but not behind him. He is looking at me, but not at me.

There is a shadow. There is a darkness within the darkness. Long limbs reach for me in the night.

The sounds of death bring them closer.

I jerked awake and stared wildly into the canopy above me, then around the tent and at Connor lying next to me tucked tight in her bedroll. I clutched my hand to my heart and took a deep breath. *I was asleep.* Relief flooded my brain. *I was asleep. I slept.* Running my hands over my face, I threw the blankets over my head again and searched for a quiet spot in my mind that would allow me to sleep again.

Something is outside.

I held my breath and listened. There was something there. Or maybe a stick had shifted in the fire. Did Connor not put it out? I twitched back a corner of the blanket. The light had turned grey, signaling the approach of dawn. A shadow grew against the side of the tent, near the fire, and my heart stopped beating.

Long limbs and a bulbous head stood just on the other side of the thin fabric. A strange ticking reached my ears and a whisper of skeletal feet over dirt.

I could not move, could not scream, could not breathe. My mind opened and drank me down and I saw nothing but the shadow on the wall of the tent. My ears filled with the maniacal laughter of hyenas and the rush of a sandstorm. I smelled the blood and remembered the weight of the thing on top of me as it stripped the bodies clean with its long fingers. I remembered my chest aching for air and the sound of its feet on the ground.

Shuf…shuf

The shadow dipped, emaciated limbs disappearing and reappearing, the bulbous head turning this way and that. It was picking through our campsite, looking for something.

Cal grabbing my hand, Vargas staring at us with an open mouth, trying to make us run faster, and then they were gone.

Beside me, Connor's body tensed. She was awake. I could see the top of her head moving, tracking the creature's shadow from wall to wall. Very slowly, she inched her head back toward me. Her gaze met mine, and she raised a finger to her lips. Slowly, oh so slowly, Connor freed one arm and reached for the machete on the far side of the tent. Her fingers brushed the sheath, but it was too far away.

Outside, the noises faded and then were gone. We lay still, listening for any sign it might still be there, and then Connor snatched up her machete and parted the tent opening. She waited, but nothing happened. Throwing back the flap, she jumped out, machete drawn. There was nothing there.

My breath was coming hard and fast, too fast. I could not slow it down. My heart was pounding in my chest, and I could not stop shaking. I wrapped my arms around my body and buried my face in the blankets. There was nothing but silence.

Connor let me lie there a moment before coaxing me out of the tent. In the grey light, we found cookware strewn over the ground, the crumbled wood from last night's fire scattered everywhere, along with one or two of Connor's maps. Our food was gone.

We gathered our things, looking between rocks for any scrap of food the thing might have missed, but there was nothing left. Connor sat back on her heels.

"We've gotten sloppy, you and I."

I nodded. There should have been nothing for the creature or any other scavenger to find. If we had been able to think clearly, we would have kept a better campsite. We were starting to make mistakes. We needed sleep.

But the Red went on and on.

Every day, Connor looked for signs that it would end soon. She saw hope in every new feature of the landscape, every bird and animal we had not seen before. She hunted as we walked, always keeping her spear out. She had become quite a shot, able to take a lizard from six meters. Hares were a different story, but I did not mind the lizard meat.

Hoping to feel more useful, I kept an eye out for cacti and plants that might be full of water or could at least sustain us if Connor did not catch anything. The plants in the Red were strange, and its haze still obscured colors, making it difficult to tell what could be eaten and what was poisonous.

Sleep still did not come, but after the witch had appeared in our camp, neither of us could close our eyes for very long. Connor kept lists in her head, running through them over and over, checking and rechecking the campsite every evening. I saw she even kept her machete within arm's reach now. She did not want to be surprised again.

I asked her if she had ever seen a witch come into a campsite like that before, but she only shook her head and told me to stop calling them witches. I knew no other name. What did she want me to say? She ignored me for the rest of the day. Lack of sleep had done little to improve our tolerance for each other. We coped as best we could, but she began walking a little further away from me during the day, often running out of earshot in search of a lizard only she had seen.

I wondered again how long she had been alone in the wilderness, how far she had gone, and what she had seen. I knew I irritated her, but she could have left me behind long ago. I wondered who she had been before, when she had not been searching—then again, why had she begun?

The Red rolled on and on, like the terrain of another world, and I started to think there would be no end, that we would one day walk around the entire Earth and wake up to find the low dunes of my homeland and the spire of my City.

I spent nights in the tent, refusing to sit by the fire for very long after dark. Shapes haunted me, things I thought I saw outside, sounds that were there one minute and gone the next. Connor sat outside long into the night, drawing the landscape—where we had come from—looking for signs it was almost over.

And then one morning, far in the distance, a sliver shimmered at the edge of the horizon.

It was white.

Fearing a mirage, our hearts were in our throats, but it grew and spread itself across our view as we walked. It was real. We traveled carefully, packed and unpacked each campsite with superstitious diligence, afraid that if we made a mistake the line would disappear. But it didn't. It was there every morning and our guiding star throughout the day.

By the third day, we could see rolling dunes, and by the fourth, we stood at the line where red sand touched white. I smudged the place where the two met and laughed—it was pink.

I looked behind us, at the rocky, blood-colored landscape that had dogged our every waking moment and robbed our nights of rest, then to the dunes before me like clouds come to earth. The uneven, crumbling land ended as suddenly as it had begun. I sank to my knees, powdery sand burning my skin as I pushed my hands into its softness, and I did not care. Behind me, Connor pitched the tent, and we sank into a deep sleep that lasted all day and all night.

Chapter 34

We rested again the next day, allowing ourselves to be lazy for just little longer. Connor drew a line through her map to show where the Red ended, then put the paper aside and barely moved for the rest of the day. We ate dried lizard meat and looked out over the rolling white dunes, talking about what came next. Our rations were nearly gone, and our water was running low. There were more worries ahead if we did not find water. We both wondered at the possibility of a well somewhere, but that could also mean trouble. Wells were fiercely protected, and we did not know the territory. If we found a road, we could get to a settlement, but we had very little to trade.

Sleep had done much to improve our outlook. It had lifted us—my body no longer ached, and my head had stopped pounding. Connor spoke more than she had in weeks, reclining against her bedroll, lying on her side like a Bedouin queen. I sat at the edge of the canopy sifting the white sand through my fingers. It left trails of shiny grit on my palms, and I relished the feel of it in my hands.

Once we set out again, our path was clear—find water and conserve what we had as much as possible. We kept an eye out for signs of a settlement, looking for depressions or flat areas that would indicate a road, but there was nothing. The camel-backed dunes rolled high, and we climbed one for a better look at the horizon. It was beautiful country—soft sand as far as the eye could see dimpling the landscape in every direction ahead. The wind pulled a string of sand into the sky, a white wisp that arced and spread into the blue above. My heart followed it.

As a witch hunter, I had never really seen the world around me. I was not supposed to get distracted, as Cal had often told me. *Cal.* I wondered if he would have loved this place or any of the places we had been before now. Would his practical eyes have seen or merely observed? It was an unkind thought, and I brushed it aside. I knew better than anyone the deep, rushing soul that had lain beneath. Vargas' brash, haughty nature had run unchecked, and when I joined the line Cal had to put away his heart and his far-reaching thoughts to keep me safe, to teach me how to be a hunter. *And a poor hunter I am.* What shame comes with knowing you have failed someone and can never make it right.

The wind whistled around me, and I reached out a hand, turning my palm upward. I offered my guilt, my sorrow to the wind. It tasted my fingers, ran over the flesh, but my heart still ached. I would have to carry my burden on my own.

Dropping my hand, I gazed out over the landscape and felt it settle into my bones. The longer we traveled, the more I felt the pull of the open land, the clean horizon unbroken by settlements or cities. There was beauty in every place, in the ancient craggy rocks, winding canyons, and cloudy peaks of dunes. Even the Red had been beautiful in its own, bewitching way. Viewed from above, it would have seemed to be a stain, a drop of wine in a cup of cream, a puckered seam in a ream of cloth. It was the disruption, the departure from the vast stretch of sameness that drew you into its spell. I wondered if that's what the crows had seen. Had they been pulled in? Or were they sirens of the Red itself, leading cursed souls to their doom as punishment for their curiosity? There was a story in *The Land of Magic* of three murderers who were hanged and their souls rebirthed as crows, made to wander the earth until the last star faded from the sky.

I followed the curves of the dunes and looked until I could see it even with my eyes closed. I wanted to remember this view forever.

"Do you see that?" Connor was pointing slightly south of where we stood.

I squinted. "What?"

She stood close so that I could sight down her arm—my father used to show me the stars that way. *Do you see, little one?*

"There." Connor's voice brought me back.

The barest stroke of a line broke the horizon at the ridge of a far dune—the slightest band of gray.

"What is that?" I asked.

Connor stuck her thumbs under the straps of her pack and chewed her lip thoughtfully. "People," she answered.

"Do we go that way then?"

She crouched and drew in the sand, tracing lines with her forefinger, watching the horizon. I stood back and let her think. There was no use asking her questions until she was ready. *Vargas is Vargas. You just have to wait.* I paused and tapped my collarbone absentmindedly. My father was with me today. The last time I saw him he was saying goodbye, letting his last remaining child leave him. I had not even stayed long enough for us to share our grief.

Connor swiped sand over the lines she had drawn, obliterating them. "Yes." She straightened and tightened the straps of her pack.

I did the same and followed her, hoping my father would walk with me for a little longer.

Chapter 35

“Is it a spear?”

"For what? A giant?”

"What else could it be?”

"Something to protect against the weather? Maybe the storms are rough here.”

"For lightning? Like a…”

"A lightning rod? It could be.”

We were sheltered behind the ridge of a dune, peering at the next peak. We had followed the strange line we had seen on the horizon. It had taken two and a half days to reach the origin—the way was easy, but we had not built a fire when stopping for the day. Connor wanted the chance to see what we were up against, and she did not want a scouting party to find us first.

Huddled behind the ridge, we saw it was some sort of gray pole sticking out of the rounded top of a dune that was slightly smaller than the others.

Connor had actually smiled when she saw it. I tried to remember if I had ever seen her smile before—it was disarming.

"That is very clever,” she said.

"What is it?” I asked.

Connor shrugged. "I do not know what the staff is, but *that* is a shelter.” She nodded at the dune. "Someone lives there.”

How many people, she could not say, and as the day wore on none of our questions were any closer to being answered. We saw no one—the land was silent except for the hum of a slight breeze.

Connor rolled a pinch of sand between her fingers. "It's not military, or there would be a patrol.”

"What if it is another Devil's Palm?”

Connor shook her head. "Too quiet.”

"Or—” I swallowed. "What if they're like Hassan?”

Connor looked up at the sky and thought for a while. "They could be," she admitted. "Do you want to stay here?"

"While you go?"

She nodded.

"No." I shook my head hard. *Do not leave me.*

She scratched her nose and thought some more, pouring sand from one hand to the other. "Give me your machete," she said finally.

"Why?"

"Because I'm faster with it. Stay behind me and keep your eyes open."

She strapped my machete to her other leg and after one more look over the ridge, climbed over and started for the dune. She held her head high and walked with long, confident strides, while I trailed behind. The closer we came, the more the dune revealed itself to be exactly what Connor said. We could now make out rounded shades of sand for a door and two windows. A few tools lay near the entrance. The domed top looked solid, like stone, and sand had gathered and crept up the sides so that the entire home almost completely disappeared into the land around it.

Connor stopped a few meters from the door and called out, announcing our presence. We did not want to surprise someone by walking into their territory, but there was no answer. Connor kept her distance and tried again.

"Is anyone here?"

A hulking figure in black robes suddenly appeared, filling the doorway. It jabbed a black rod, almost like a long gun, in our direction. "Stop there!"

Connor raised her hands and backed away a few steps. "We will not hurt you. We need water and food. We were hoping to trade." I raised my arms as well.

"Back away!" yelled the figure, jabbing the gun at us again.

Connor nodded and stepped further back. "Yes, we are leaving. We will leave you alone."

"Get out of here!"

"We're going!" I cried.

The figure faltered, looking around Connor at me. It lowered its gun slightly. "Is that your daughter?"

Connor continued to back away. "Don't worry, we're leaving."

"How old is she?"

"Don't worry about it. We will leave you alone."

"Wait."

Connor stopped, and the figure lowered its weapon. "What you need?" it asked.

"Food and water," she answered. "We can trade."

The figure hesitated, then reached up and pushed the top of its head covering back, revealing the tiny head of a woman nestled in layers and layers of clothing. Her eyes were very large, and her black hair was streaked with gray. The woman herself was half the height of the figure we had first seen and peered at us with bright curiosity. She raised one comically large arm and waved tentatively. "Call me Min."

Chapter 36

The dome opened itself to us, and we stepped into a brightly lit space filled with shining things I had never seen before. At the center, a tower of gray metal spiked by short branches of brass. It hummed softly to itself, filling the chamber with a life of its own.

Behind me, Min shed the layers of clothing down, down until a pebble of a woman remained. She stood barely a meter and a half tall and was thin as a rail. Connor could have picked her up with one hand. Her tunic and trousers clung to her slight body. Her hair was short, and she had pulled it back and tied it in place so that she could look at us. Her large and expressive eyes flicked between the two of us. The flat plain of her face was interrupted by a brief point of a nose. Her mouth smiled readily and was full of shiny round teeth.

She approached to examine our faces. Connor was not tall, but she had to look straight down to meet Min's gaze. After a moment, Min smiled a warm and open smile that reached all the way up. It crinkled the corners of her eyes into swooping lines that left echoes of themselves even after she had stopped. I liked her immediately.

She shrugged and wiggled the hand still holding the long gun, which we now saw was only a metal rod with a tapered end. "Sorry," Min said, somewhat guiltily. "Can't be too careful." She must have seen the machetes strapped to Connor's legs, but she did not mention them.

Connor nodded and swung her pack down. "We do not have much, but we can arrange an acceptable trade."

Min cocked her head. "Sure," she answered, "but you want something to eat first?"

Connor looked around. This was not how trade worked. I recognized the code immediately but hesitated, thinking it was too good to be trusted.

"I mean," Min went on, "you hungry, right?"

She had an odd way of speaking—words would burst out of her tiny body one moment, and the next she would casually lay them out, dropping a word or two like they meant nothing to her. Min's eyes roved over Connor, taking in her boots, her tunic, her scar. Min rolled her lips to one side and waited.

Connor glanced at me and then nodded. Yes, we were hungry.

We sat on the ground with our backs against the wall, and Min set out an ewer of water and served us bowls of spicy stew made from lizard meat. She ate with us, passing a round of flatbread for us to share, watching us over her bowl.

"Where you two from?" she asked finally.

Connor shrugged. "Do you not get many visitors?"

Min rocked her head from side to side. "A few." Connor looked up, but Min smirked. "No, course not. Who comes out here?" She gestured around with her spoon. "Besides you two, I mean."

"We are only passing through," said Connor, taking the bread from me and tearing it in half.

"No, you don't look like settlers. But you don't look like you kill me either, so we're friends."

Connor paused, her spoon over her bowl. "No, we won't hurt you."

"I said kill," Min responded, pointing her spoon at Connor. "You never told me your names."

"No, I didn't."

Min smiled. "Oh, it's like that, huh?" Her eyes flicked between the two of us. "None of my business, I guess, but I don't do business with people I don't know."

"Our names would not change that."

I set my bowl down, annoyed. "My name is Rue. This is Connor."

Connor closed her eyes in frustration, and Min grinned. She eagerly scooted toward me and sat back on her heels, looking into my face with owlish eyes. "You two related?"

I shook my head. "No."

"Where you from?"

"East of here."

"Far?"

"Yes."

"How you know this one?" She cocked her head at Connor.

"She saved my life."

"Where you going?"

"I have family west of here. Connor is taking me to them."

"Ooh!" Min pointed at me. "That one was a lie! Where you really going?"

"Enough." Connor broke in, setting her bowl down firmly. "Trade with us, or don't."

Min rocked back to lean against the wall. "She's no fun." This she said to me, winking impishly.

I bit back a smile. I could feel Connor glaring at me, but I ignored her. Min wasn't dangerous. She could know us a little.

"Now!" Min clapped her hands once, crossed her legs in front of her, leaned forward, and fixed Connor with a serious stare. "Trade. What you got?"

It took time. We did not have much that Min wanted. Connor pulled items from her pack one after the other, but Min waved them away saying, "I got that already, but better." Connor glanced at me once, and my hand tightened over my pack, over the square lumps that were the blue book and *The Land of Magic*. I set my jaw. She could not have them.

Chin in her hand, Min watched Connor bring out knives, blankets, even her telescoping spear, but she shook her head at all of it. In the end, what Min liked were Connor's maps of the Red. She fingered the pages, turning the drawings this way and that. Connor showed her the route we had taken, tracing it with her forefinger.

Min sighed. "If this all you got, I take it." She turned one of the pages upside down. "Not great, but I like the color." She stowed the pages somewhere behind the metal tower before fiddling with one of the brass pieces branching off from the base.

"What is that?" I asked.

Min poked her head around the tower to look at me. "Oh, this?" She asked with mock innocence. She gauged us for a moment and then rubbed her hands together with a sly grin. "I call it a water generator."

Connor stood. "A generator?"

"A *water* generator," Min corrected her, rolling her eyes at me. "I made it myself. It pulls moisture from the air and from the ground, then stores it. I get four liters a day, just from this thing."

Connor's eyes widened. "And this is how you survive here?"

Min put a hand on her hip and nodded. "Fifteen years next month."

"You have been out here for fifteen years?" I asked. "Alone?"

Min shrugged. "Why not?"

I tried to imagine being alone for that long, of no sound except the land and your own voice, of no faces but your own for a decade and a half. It was longer than I had been alive.

Connor was pensive. I wondered again how long she had wandered alone before me. My gaze involuntarily flicked to the ring on her left hand.

Min busied herself at the tower, touching one or two pieces, and listening to its hum. "It's not easy," she continued. "Requires a lot of maintenance. It broke down once, eight years ago. I was almost a goner." She grinned at us.

Goner. I rolled the word around in my mouth—I liked it. It sounded exactly like its meaning, and my mind formed a picture of Min's tiny body on the ground of the dome, dried and mummified.

Connor approached the tower, running a tentative hand along one of the brass arms as if it were alive. Min picked a tool from a pile on the ground and held it out to her. "You want to help?" She did, and Min talked animatedly in between showing Connor what to do.

Eighteen years ago, Min had worked as a metallurgist in a settlement a week or so away. She lived alone, did not have many friends, and made no effort to make any. Other people were not that interesting. She went to work and then straight home every day, working in her own forge in the evenings. But something tugged at her. She felt the string of her life slowly fraying and wondered how she had never noticed before. Was this all her life could be?

Min found herself daydreaming about bigger ideas, trickier problems to solve. One day a seed planted itself in her brain—how long could a person live in the wilderness alone? The thought burrowed in and grew. On days she did not go to work, she looked for a place to build. One day, she did not go to work at all. She packed her things, left her home, and never came back. There were hardships, of course, difficult years and new problems she had never anticipated, but never regret.

That night, when she threw open the doors and we stepped out into the darkness, I understood why. The moon was so bright it caused the sand to glow blue, and the rolling dunes were visible for what seemed like tens of kilometers. Stars blanketed the sky, and the galaxy shone with its own brilliance. We wrapped ourselves in blankets and sat looking up at them. They seemed so close tonight, as if all we had to do was reach out and we could touch them.

I searched for the familiar sight of Orion's belt but found it had moved in the sky. I tried to think where it had been the last time I looked, but I could not remember. It would seem I was not the only one on a journey.

Min insisted we stay in the dome that night, and she and Connor worked on the tower until late. I watched them for a while, but could not understand what they were doing, so I retreated to a dark patch of floor away from them. Huddled in my bedroll, I held *The Land of Magic* to my chest and dreamed of Asha.

Chapter 37

We lingered at the dome, Connor pulling every ounce of information from Min that she could. They talked of the landscape, locations of various settlements, and where trouble lay. Min drew maps in the dirt, telling Connor which settlements to avoid and which would be friendly. The settlements, including the one Min left all those years ago, were all clustered to the north of the dome.

"This one." Min drew a circle to indicate another settlement to the northeast. "Don't go there. Not with her." She pointed at me.

Connor examined the map and tapped the empty space to the west. "What about here?"

Min scoffed. "Nothing there."

"There must be something."

Min shook her head. "Wasteland."

Connor's brows knitted together. "For how far?"

Min shrugged. "I don't know. No one goes there."

Connor rocked back on her heels, draping her arms over her knees. "What if we did?"

Min scoffed again. "Just kill yourselves now and get it over with."

"What would we do? How could we carry enough water?"

"You can't. No way to know how far until you find more."

Connor stood up without a word and went to the doorway, strapping her machete to her leg and grabbing her spear on her way out.

Min glanced at me. I shrugged. I had no explanation for Connor—I rarely did.

Connor stayed away the rest of the day, hunting in the dunes. When the high sky started to fade and the horizon grew red, I looked out and saw her on a nearby ridge. She stood with her back to the dome, looking toward the setting sun.

When the light sank and darkness pulled itself over the landscape, Connor had still not returned. I thought I could see her still on the same ridge but could not be sure.

She returned long after the sand had given its heat back to the sky, tan lizards with spiked heads slung down her back. She dropped the lizards by Min and crawled into her bedroll without a word, pulling the blankets over her head.

Min ignored her, pouring two cups of tea and handing one of them to me. "Come on," she said, leading me outside.

In the night air, I wrapped a blanket around my shoulders. Min did the same and took a deep breath, sucking the cold air into her lungs. She had left her boots inside, her small feet encased in only a thin pair of socks. "She don't know what she's asking," Min grumbled. "Can't be mad if she don't like the answer. Why she so mad?" This she said to me, wrinkling her tiny nose.

I shrugged and held my face over the cup of tea, letting its warmth seep into my pores. I did not think Connor was angry, but Min did not really seem to want me to answer her. I sat quietly and listened.

Min kicked at the dirt, looking up at the sky. "You ever wonder how many are up there?" She gestured to the stars with her cup. "Or what they are? Oh, I know. Balls of gas. Just words. So boring. What if you could be up there with them, right next to one? What if you could really see up close? Without dying. What would that be like?" She paused, her face tilted back, her socked feet taking her in a slow circle. "People don't know something real if they can't touch it, you know? Really real. Sometimes I'm that way with them." She gestured to the stars again. "Which one you go to?" she asked, looking at me. "If you could."

I looked up only to point it out in the sky. I already knew where I would go. "There," I said. "Orion's belt."

Min turned her face toward the constellation. "Oh? He a friend of yours?"

I smiled. "Orion was the first constellation my father taught me."

Min traced the outline of the bow with her finger. "The hunter," she said quietly.

I swallowed the lump in my throat and nodded. "Yes, the hunter."

Min fixed her owlish eyes on me and took a sip of her tea.

I shifted. "Which one would you go to?"

After a moment, Min traced a small circle with her finger in the sky. "Seven Sisters." She folded her arms over herself. "I would sit in the middle of them so that anywhere I look, I see one of them. Then I reach out like this—" she spread her arms and lifted one leg, "and touch them at the same time." She smiled. "That's what I do."

We regarded the sky, the shivering balls of fire above us, the haze of the galaxy, the spaces in between.

"So, what's wrong with her?" Min tipped her cup toward the dome.

I shook my head. "There is nothing wrong with her."

"Sorry. I know you two are friends."

Friends. I searched for the right words but nothing came. *Was Connor my friend?* Min's owl eyes were on me again; I had a feeling I was being puzzled out. "She is looking for something. She has been for a long time. And then—well, now I'm looking with her."

Min frowned. "For what?"

I hesitated, but only briefly. What did it matter if one person—someone in the middle of nowhere—knew? "Something else. Something no one has seen before." *How to say it? How to explain?*

"What?" Min's voice intensified. I could almost smell her curiosity.

"A miracle," I said simply.

A slight breeze caught the tail of steam from Min's cup and twirled it until it disappeared into the air. The tower hummed, filling the silence that lay between us. My fingers tensed, holding me together, gripping the edge of my blanket and the cup of tea, its heat barely reaching me.

I opened my mouth, but no other words came. I could not explain what I said, and I could not take it back. The two words hung in the air like birds catching thermals, looking for roost.

Min's brows drew together, the skin between puckering. Her owl eyes crinkled, probing mine for something—a joke, a lie, a delusion. The corners of her mouth turned slightly downward, contained by the deep creases on either side.

Inside the dome, the tower shuddered twice and then hummed along again. Min looked toward the open doorway, its warm light spilling across the night blue sand. "I should see what that's about," she said quietly, not meeting my gaze.

I watched her go, standing alone in the dark, wondering if I had just made a horrible mistake.

Chapter 38

"Could we generate more?"

Min looked up from her drawing table. Connor was standing across, staring at her intently.

It had been a full day since any of us had spoken to one another. Min had not moved us along or asked us to leave. Instead, she had withdrawn to her forge, pulling metal and pounding it into submission, her face covered with a heavy mask to protect her skin. Connor and I had eaten separately—she had taken her bowl outside to eat in the open air. I left a bowl for Min near the forge door but returned later to find it untouched.

When night fell, Min sat at her drawing table, sketching intermittently and then staring into space, her shoulders slumped and her hands in her lap. She had not even looked at me.

Now, Connor's voice startled both of us. It was the first human sound we had heard all day, and I stood apart from them, apprehensive. Connor did not know what I had told Min the night before. I had wanted to tell her but could not bring myself to break the silence.

"Could we generate more?" Connor asked again. "Water. In the wasteland. Like that?" she nodded toward the tower.

Min squinted at her. "You still want to go there?" She glanced at me and then back at Connor. She shook her head and picked up her pencil, resuming her sketch.

Connor placed a hand on the table, gently, just at the edge. "You made something. Before, no one would have said it could be done. You did this."

Min eyed her. "Flattery. That's cheap."

Connor scoffed and spread her arms to take in the dome. "You made the solution—it came from you. There must be a way."

Min's eyes took on a faraway look. She shook her head, then slid her thumb between her teeth and chewed the nail. "You would have to be able to collect and process your body water. You know, what you lose. But even then, it would not be enough."

"How do we survive?"

"Why you want to go there?" Min asked quietly, trying to catch Connor's eye.

I crept forward, waiting for Connor to say something. Min did not look my way.

"It would be safer," said Connor at last, "If you did not know."

Min stared at her for a moment before bursting into laughter, her mouth stretched wide to make way for the sound, her round teeth shining in the light. Startled, Connor took a step back. I folded my arms over my stomach against the noise, gripping my elbows.

Still laughing, Min leaned over her desk toward Connor. "Who you think you are?" She threw her head back and cackled.

Connor did not move, her shoulders remained square, her back solid. She waited.

Min wiped her eyes, the last few chuckles bubbling up and dying away.

"Yes," said Connor quietly, "I know how it sounds."

Min chuckled and nodded. "Crazy."

Connor nodded sadly. "Madness."

Min smiled and shook her head. "You—you don't know what you asking from me. Help you survive for who knows how long?" She crossed her arms and sat back in her chair. "You know what that takes?"

Connor looked askance. "What does it take?"

Min shrugged. "Look around. You talking to someone who lives alone in the middle of nowhere. You the first people I've seen in months, maybe years, who knows?" She folded her hands behind her head, an impish twinkle in her eye. "You want my help? I want a story."

Connor hesitated, casting a brief glance my way.

Min raised her eyebrows. "Who am I going to tell?"

I edged forward again, feeling the deep well in Connor beginning to open. There was so much I wanted to hear. I desperately wanted Connor to say something, to tell me more than I already knew.

Connor held her hands in front of her, twisting her ring, considering, then removed it and placed it on Min's sketch on the drawing table. Min snatched it up, and Connor let her, the flesh of her naked finger indented and shades lighter than the rest of her skin. She stood casually, but I saw one hand resting on the handle of her machete. My pulse quickened as I realized she was prepared to take the ring back, if she had to, even from Min.

Min did not see this. She was holding the ring up to the light, turning it this way and that. She scratched at the surface with her nail, then hefted it in her hand. "Real gold." She sounded impressed. She rotated the ring in her fingers, bringing it close to her eyes, running them over the creature, what Hassan had called Connor's "little god."

"What's this?" she asked.

Connor swallowed. "Have you ever seen it before?"

Min frowned. "I never see anything like that before."

"I have not either. It's a clue."

"Of what?"

"Look at it. Nothing like that can live. It does not exist."

Min shrugged. "Right."

"So, what is it?"

Min rolled her eyes. "An ancient animal? Folklore?"

Connor shook her head. "I do not think so."

"This is what you looking for?"

Connor put both hands on the drawing table. "I am looking for where it lives."

Min cocked an eyebrow at her. "And you think it lives out in the wasteland?"

"Perhaps. Or perhaps further."

Min sat back, turning the ring in her fingers. "Further? There's nothing out there, no settlements, nobody." She turned the ring in her fingers and held the creature close to her face so that she had to cross her eyes to look at it. "You know," she said, setting the ring back down on the drawing table, "I seen jewelers make all kinds of things."

"You said yourself this is something you have never seen before."

"True."

"Neither have I."

Min leaned forward. "Well, you bought it from someone, right?"

Connor hesitated. "It was a gift."

Min frowned. "Where they get it? No, forget that. You should be looking for the jeweler. You know, the one who made it. Maybe they could tell you what it is."

Connor gently took the ring and slipped it back on her finger, the gold sliding into place where the flesh was indented. "I have done that already," she said quietly.

"What did the jeweler say?"

"He's dead."

Min chewed her thumbnail. "That's a problem. There anyone else?"

Connor shook her head. "No one knows what this is but him. I think he *saw* this creature. I think he saw it with his own eyes and made the ring in its image. I have not found anyone who can tell me what it is, so there is nothing left except to find the thing itself and where it comes from."

Min shrugged. "Or go home."

Connor stood very still, her eyes turned away. She rotated the ring on her finger.

Min sat up. "Oh. Sorry." She glanced at me, then back at Connor. "I didn't know."

Connor did not look at her. "There is something out there no one else has ever seen before. Something that lives in a way we do not understand. If you thought you could find a miracle, would you?"

"How you even know you can find it?"

"I don't, but I am willing to try."

Min wrinkled her lips and was quiet for a moment. "What's so dangerous? You say it safer for me if you don't talk about it."

"For you?" Connor exhaled sharply, then untied the belt at her waist. "I have tried it both ways," she said in a dark voice. She pulled each hand into the cuffs of her tunic, then slipped the garment up her back and over her head so that she stood in her trousers and underthings. "One has served me better than the other."

A cold pit opened in my stomach. A strip of cloth was bound tightly over her chest and shoulders, her bare stomach and arms gleaming in the light. Tracks of pink, raised flesh traveled her forearms and biceps, disappearing under the cloth, falling into circular divots that were scattered over her torso. There, the fascia had been dug into, scooped out so that it would never heal—a lesson that would forever follow her. She had been marked.

Min circled her slowly, examining the scars. She reached out as though to touch one on Connor's back but stopped, her hand hovering above the skin. "What does this say?" she asked quietly.

Connor's shoulders tensed and pulled together. "I have never seen it. I do not know." She swallowed, her breath coming a little faster.

Min rolled her lips into her mouth and nodded, coming back to stand in front of her. Connor looked her full in the face, unashamed. I wondered if anyone else had seen her skin since it happened; if she had shown herself before.

"So," Min said, raising her eyebrows, "you not afraid I tell someone about you two?"

Connor's gaze went flat. She inhaled, rolling her shoulders back, bringing herself to her full height. Her skin stretched and shone in the light, lines of muscle just visible beneath the scars. In my mind, I saw Hassan's arms hanging motionless over the edge of the pit, dark liquid dripping down his fingers.

The impish twinkle in Min's eye disappeared. "All right." She sniffed and slid her hands into her pockets. "I got an idea."

Chapter 39

They took time to design, longer to create, and even longer still to perfect. Connor camped outside for weeks at a time to test them, Min fiddling with pieces and taking notes. I helped where I could, carrying Min's forging tools across dunes so she would know how much weight I could handle. Whenever she finished a design, I dropped it off the top of the dome while she stood below, retrieving the bits and taking them to her forge to make something stronger. She moved with speed and intensity as though burning from within. She did not completely understand Connor, or why I wanted to go with her, but we had given her a problem to solve—something that had never been done before.

No one had ever traveled the deep wastelands before. With the rise and development of cities and the mass settlement of the outer desert, the time of explorers had ended long ago. Even they had not started a journey without teams of men and slaves to carry surplus water, without animals that could be released as supplies dried up, without the wealth of a country behind them. I heard it said that astronomers had mapped more of the stars in the sky than anyone had of the earth beneath. Magellan had left a trail of death in his wake, but he had been the only one to try to circle the globe. What else was out there? Connor was right. There could be something no one had ever seen before.

We spoke often, the three of us gathering together or going out to Connor's campsite throughout the day. There were still long periods of silence, all of us lost in thought, but our voices were heard more in that time than any other. I came to know their voices well, their pitches, tones, moods, and sometimes what they did not say. I came to feel the two of them as though we were neighboring stones of the same rock outcrop. I often chose to sit with Connor at her campsite during the day, if Min did not need me.

I became ravenous for knowledge, for things that could help me survive. Connor taught me to use the telescoping spear, which was difficult to master. Lizards escaped my throw more often than not. I was better with the machete, and Connor showed me where animals like to burrow and how to find snakes in the sand, how to spot the head and avoid a bite. She taught me how to dress wounds, how to treat infection, and how to judge direction from the position of the sun. Min taught me how to care for the tower so that she could work in the forge, how to recognize different types of metal, and even how to prepare a lizard and make her spicy soup. She would not let me into her forge—that was my only forbidden place. She did not want me underfoot.

I took the things they taught me, these morsels, and put them away for when they would be needed, as a fox buries scraps for lean times. I also left pieces of myself behind. I drew in the corners of Min's sketches that she left on the drawing table—hands, faces, suns, crows—whatever I could think of, hoping she would see them after we had gone, and remember us.

There were the inevitable frustrations, anger, and impatience—the kind that welled up in the worst moments, burst, scattered us to separate places, and then drained away to let us drift together again. If I were not the source of them, I came to sense the tension that preceded those moments and retreat. When the moment came, Min would explode and throw anything within arm's reach—tools, pieces of metal—venting her anger in one shower of shrapnel and curses. Connor burned slowly, turning on her heel and melting into the dunes, leaving the other person to shout impotently at her from the open doorway. I preferred Min's way to Connor's.

One morning, I woke while the sky was still gray, and the light was just beginning to float below the horizon, and decided to go out and greet the rising sun. Wrapping a blanket around myself, I boiled the water and steeped the leaves, careful not to disturb Min. Connor was sleeping at her campsite, testing the latest version of Min's device, so I was able to take my cup of tea and steal out onto the dunes without waking anyone.

The sand was cold and slightly firmer underfoot than at midday, chilling my soles with every step. I had left my socks and boots inside, preferring to wander about in bare feet. Cresting the ridge of the nearest dune, I cradled the hot cup of tea in both hands, curling and uncurling my toes until I had sunk to my ankles, enjoying the brisk sensation creeping up my shins. I held my face over the cup, letting the steam warm my nose and cheeks. Ahead, a sliver of orange fire peeked over the horizon. I closed my eyes, letting the rising light wash over me. But the glow did not come—the dawn did not reach me. I opened my eyes, but the sun was not there.

A dark line had appeared where the sun was supposed to be, snaking from north to south as far as the eye could see. The breeze shifted.

Oh no.

I threw my tea into the sand and raced to Connor's campsite, hitting the walls of her tent to wake her before fleeing back to the dome to wake Min as fast as my legs could carry me.

The Khamaseens had arrived.

The fifty-day winds had come early this year, a full two weeks sooner than they had the year before, throwing us in all directions to pack the campsite and seal the forge and the dome before it was too late. Min threw open a panel in the floor and pulled up a bundle of fabric, leaving me to seal the windows while she took care of the forge. I secured cloth over the windows, stuffing it into every nook and cranny. I jumped down and threw open the door—they were almost here. Connor appeared at the ridge, her churning feet sending sand into the air behind her, caught in the rising wind. I waved my hand, shouting at her to run faster. The moment she skidded into the dome, I slammed the door, and the two of us scrambled to seal the space where it met the floor.

The Khamaseens came. The leading edge hurtled over the dunes, carrying sand and dust from thousands of kilometers away and slamming it into the dome. We were trapped while the wind raged beyond the door, the air a thick, brown haze that could fill the lungs. Anyone who wandered outside unprotected would die within hours.

Without her forge, Min could not work. There was nothing to do but wait. Particles found their way in, building piles in the corners of the windows and scattering over our bedrolls. We woke every morning covered in a fine veil of dust. We resealed the windows and door, but it still found its way in. Eventually, we gave up and resigned ourselves to gritty meals and silt in our tea.

Connor and I took turns helping Min keep the tower. It had to be cleaned with brushes every day to keep the sand out of its machinery. If the particles accumulated, the tower would die, and soon after, so would we.

Before the Khamaseen winds, we argued freely, without fear. Now, an odd sort of civility descended, and we spoke to each other in overly polite tones, instantly forgiving the smallest of slights. Even so, we gave each other as much room as possible. Min sat at her drawing table, sketching silently, while Connor and I huddled on opposite ends of the dome, Connor fiddling with her gear or sitting quietly while I read. We even moved our bedrolls as far from each other as possible, staking out our respective areas and keeping to them. We came together for meals, but we did not have much to say.

Boredom was the only real threat. The worst days were when Connor could no longer sit still and jogged about, stopping to perform pushups to release her energy. Min and I shared looks and tolerated it as best we could, but one day Min lost her temper and pitched a cup at Connor's legs as she jogged around the dome. After that, Connor contented herself with bracing her forearms on the floor and kicking her legs up the dome wall, remaining upside down as long as she could.

On the fifty-third day, we awoke to blissful, deafening silence. We unsealed the windows and looked out onto a bright, clear day and four meters of sand piled over the door. Connor and I stepped out of the window, dug out the entrance, and then the forge. Min seemed glad to have the help this year.

"Normally this take two days!"

She wasted no time, retreating to her forge once it was clean and ready. Connor took the latest device and headed into the desert to set up camp once again, leaving me alone in the dome. I boiled water, steeped the leaves, and poured a cup of tea that was free of silt and grime. I then took my cup to the door and leaned against the frame, looking out over the changed landscape. The dunes had shifted, pushed by the Khamaseens, their ridges now high peaks instead of gentle rolls.

Crisp, fresh air filled my lungs. The days would be cooler for a little while, and I thought of the last time the winds had come. My father and brothers and I had hunkered down in our hut, telling stories, playing games—the fire throwing shadows on our faces, our laughing mouths. Hunting in the few days after the Khamaseens died down had been easier, the sun did not plague us so much. Looking at the sky, I wondered who hunted witches outside the City now. Who protected us? *Us.* The thought surprised me. Was I still a part of that place?

Min's hammer rang out from the forge three times. I sipped my tea and turned, closing the door behind me.

One day, I noticed the hem of my trousers no longer tucked into my boots, and my tunics had grown tight under the arms. My joints ached sometimes. I could now lean an arm across the top of Min's head, which she did not like, but made Connor smile. They showed me how to rip seams and sew together fabric to make my clothes larger. Min braided my hair in one long rope, just like Connor's. When my blood came for the first time, Min poured homemade wine and the three of us toasted the occasion, howling at the moon like wolves. We slept under the stars that night, huddled in a row, Connor and Min on either side of me. I held Min's hand and once I was sure Connor was asleep, I rested the other on her back, feeling the deep, steady rise and fall against my palm.

Chapter 40

And then it was done.

We sat together, contemplating the black compilations of metal and tubes in front of us.

Connor broke the silence. "We will not be able to carry much else."

Min nodded, her chin in her hand, forefinger over her mouth. "I can fix that," she answered, her lips moving around her finger. "You can carry a little."

"What if they break?" I asked, the horrible possibilities opening up before me.

Min looked sidelong at me. "If they break and you can't fix them?"

I nodded.

"You die. Don't break them."

I swallowed and nodded again.

Connor stood and placed a hand on one of them. "We need to know what could go wrong."

"We tested these same as the others," said Min, looking up at Connor without moving her head. Her eyebrows pushed the skin of her forehead into ridges.

"No new parts?"

Min took a breath. "One. That one kill you if you don't know how to fix it. I show you."

Connor stooped and swung one of them onto her back, fixing the tubes and straps into place. I did the same, but my hands were sweating and slipped on the rough surface of the metal—Min had treated the surface so that it would not glint in the light and attract trouble. Connor waited. I had to know how to put it on without her. I had to know how every centimeter of it worked. We did not know what awaited us in the wasteland. Though we traveled together, I had to know how to survive alone until I could make it back to Min. She was our last outpost.

Min threw a waterbag over her shoulder, and we trekked out past Connor's campsite. Once the dome dipped below the horizon, Min put us through our paces, unscrewing tubes and showing us how to clean the sand out and reattach them. She had us remove the packs and throw them as far as we could, then retrieve them, clean them out, and test the function.

The packs hung from our shoulders, with various pads connected to tubes that gathered most of the water our bodies excreted as sweat, processed it, and stored it in small sacks so that we made our own drinking water. It was not much, but it was enough for survival. We would carry minimal rations and rely on hunting for food and plants for additional fluids. We would have to carry supplements to ward off the effects of extreme malnourishment and loss of body salt, and we would have to clean the packs every night to get as much sand out of the machinery as possible. The supplements would come from Min's storehouse of emergency supplies, which she kept under the dome.

"What about you?" Connor asked.

Min waved a hand. "I have more. Besides, I only needed them once in fifteen years."

I shared Connor's concern, hoping Min was not putting herself in danger for us.

"I got more than you think," insisted Min. "You don't know. Now," she continued, taking my pack and tossing it over the side of a dune, "go get it."

We ran through drills the rest of the afternoon and most of the following day. In between, Min waited until we were not looking and sabotaged the packs to keep us on our toes. She wanted us to know the devices inside and out, for us to know by sound alone if something was not right, to be able to fix a problem without hesitation.

As a final test, she sent us on an extended hike with only our packs, a little food, and our tent. We traveled in a wide circle around the dome for several days before returning. When we came back, we found her waiting for us, arms crossed over her tiny frame, owl eyes wide and round. She questioned us—were they too heavy, did we remember to clean them every night, did anything go wrong—and took the packs from us to test they were still working. She picked, looking for something that could be made better, but the truth was the packs were a wonder. We had not suffered.

Eventually, she sat back on her heels and pressed her lips together. There was only the final test—the wasteland. We ate together that night, talking little, avoiding each other's eyes. The inevitable was fast approaching—it would be time to move on very soon.

Chapter 41

We delayed—packing, repacking, and adjusting the loads we would carry. The packs were heavy; we could not carry much else. Min added several attachments so we could carry the tent, rations, supplements, wound and infection supplies, blankets, two sets of clothing with patches and thread, small pots of aloe, fire igniters, brushes and cloths to clean the packs, and a small set of tools. Connor carried the tent so that I had room for my books. We both carried half of the rations. Min made another attachment for Connor's spear, and we strapped our machetes to our legs.

But something was wrong. Most evenings, I caught Min standing just out of my eyeline, owl eyes darting away the moment I noticed her, shifting to cover the shadow I had seen on her face. There were other things. A cup of tea would appear near my bedroll in the mornings, steam mingling with the morning light from the window. I received an extra helping of food at dinner. My daily water allowance slightly increased. She had stopped working in her forge during the day, sitting with me long after we had tended to the tower, but not speaking. I started taking long walks, relishing the flex and pull of my muscles as I climbed dunes made steeper by the Khamaseens, and the way my breath came faster with the effort. Each time I reached the last ridge on the way back, I saw Min's tiny form leaning against the doorway of the dome, waiting for me.

I thought of asking her what was wrong, but annoyance choked the words before they left my mouth. I chafed at her kindness, the niceties she offered. It felt like deceit—why could she not say what she wanted?

A box appeared on my bedroll one day after I returned from my walk. Min stood nearby with her hands clasped over her heart while I reluctantly opened it. A metal face the size of my hand grinned up at me from the depths. It was in the shape of a cat. I did not take it out.

"What is this?" I asked her, holding the box out with one hand.

"You like it?"

"How am I supposed to carry this?" Heat crept to my cheeks.

Min's face fell. "It was a present."

"Why?"

She shrugged and would not meet my eyes. "I thought you might like it."

"Why?" It was a ridiculous, absurd thing to give, and she knew it. Even if it could fit in the pack, it was heavier than both my books combined. She had pushed her designs and improved every pack she made, testing and retesting. She had spent months in her forge to create something that would keep us alive. She was brilliant and practical and had already given us something no one else could. I tossed the box down, letting the cat face clatter onto the floor, and pushed past her.

The sun was brushing the crests of the dunes, which glowed orange with its touch. I climbed the nearest one and sat with my back to the dome, looking out over the land. A short while later, crunching footsteps made their way up the dune and stopped behind me.

"What do you want?" I asked, wanting her to go away.

The footsteps came nearer. Min plopped into the sand beside me, wrapping her arms around her legs, and resting her chin on her knees.

"I'm sorry," she said after a moment.

"Why did you do that?" I asked, shaking my head.

Min shrugged. "You have your books. I thought I should give you something to remind you of me."

I thought of the pack in the dome that would gather my body water, the pack I would have to clean every evening and remember how to fix if something went wrong. I wrapped my arms around myself against the lie. "If you will not tell me the truth, leave me alone."

Min covered her face and then ran her hands through her hair. "People die in the open every day. Out there," she gestured west, "who knows what could happen?" She paused, rubbing her lips with her fingers. "Why you going with her?"

I tried but I could not explain it—the pull, the feeling that I was looking at the world through a pinhole, the ever-present belief in *more*.

Min pulled her legs closer to her chest. "What if you die out there because I don't say you making a mistake?" Her voice cracked. "What if my stupid machine kills you?"

I looked at her in surprise. Min was afraid. And then I laughed. "Why me? What about Connor?"

Huge tears tracked down her cheeks and dripped onto her knees. She waved a hand and sniffled, wiping trails of snot onto her sleeve. "She stupid already. No stopping her."

I chuckled and put my arms around her, wrapping her up while she choked out a few more sobs. Her bones felt delicate and slight. She folded herself into a tight ball and leaned into me. I rested my cheek on the top of her head and rocked her back and forth. "It will be all right," I murmured, watching the sun sink below the horizon. "It will be all right."

Chapter 42

Connor spent the evenings going over lists, looking for the gap, searching for the mistake that would kill us. Min grew quieter and quieter, but she had stopped showing me any special treatment. My water and food rations returned to normal, there were no more cups of tea by my bedroll, and she stopped waiting for me to come back to the dome from my walks. The cat face had disappeared, most likely melted down in her forge. We did not speak of it again. She was quiet but did not look drawn and sleepless as she had before. Her energy was renewed, and she set aside time for additional drills outside. She produced a third pack and beat it with metal tools, pulled out tubes, contaminated the water sacks, and directed us to fix it. When we did, she kicked it over the side of a dune and made us do it again until she was satisfied.

In the evenings, we both left Connor to draw in the sand and look for what was missing. The night she stopped and sat looking up at the stars, we knew she was ready.

Resigned, Min took a bottle of homemade wine and three cups outside. I followed with blankets, draping one over my shoulders and handing the others to Connor and Min.

"So," said Min, dropping to the ground and pouring wine into each of our cups, "When you leaving?"

Connor took her cup and passed the other to me. "The day after tomorrow."

Min nodded, owl eyes glancing from me to Connor. She looked very serious, and I felt sad to leave her. She had done so much for us, and the three of us had grown close.

"Min—" I started, but she waved a hand dismissively and raised her cup.

"None of that. I hope you find what you looking for. To the journey."

"To the journey," we echoed, raising our cups.

"And to me!" she laughed. "You lucky you know a genius."

I laughed with her. "To Min!"

We drank and talked and looked at the stars until the bottle was empty.

Min turned it upside down and let the last drop fall onto the sand, then fetched another bottle to refill her and Connor's cups.

"How many of those do you have?" asked Connor, shaking her head.

"Let's just say I won't run out any time soon."

Connor downed her cup and held it out for Min to pour her another before settling back on her elbows to contemplate the sky. Min glanced at me across Connor's outstretched body.

"What's in those books you always reading?" she asked me.

Connor tipped her head back to look upside down at the stars behind us. Min nudged her and she looked up.

"You going to hurt yourself," chided Min. Connor took another sip of wine and Min shook her head at me. "So? What's in them?"

I shrugged. "I can read one of them, but not the other. The one I can read is full of stories."

"Oh, I saw the other one. I can't read that either, but it's pretty."

I smiled and nodded. "It is pretty."

"That why you keep it?"

Connor glanced at me, and I shook my head. I was not sure. "Maybe because it's the first thing I found. When Connor and I started traveling."

Min thought about this and nodded. "What about the other one?"

"*The Land of Magic*," I said, taking a sip of wine. "Gods and goddesses, sorcerers and kings, witches and queens."

Min made a noise of approval "I like that. Where you get that one?"

Asha's face rose in my mind. "A friend."

Connor looked away. I thought of how she had walked ahead to let me cry on the road out of Morra.

Min glanced from one of us to the other and decided to let it go. "Friends are good. Not many friends out there, you know."

No, the enemies have them outnumbered.

Min put her cup down on the sand with a decisive *plop*, sending wine sloshing over the rim and staining the sand. "I want to hear one."

Connor looked up. "One of what?"

"A story!" Min chirped, rolling her eyes at Connor. "Last night, last chance. I want to hear a story. Come on, Rue, tell us one."

"I don't really— "

But Min was on her feet, scurrying into the dome, calling out as she went, "No! It's time for a story!"

I glanced at Connor, but she only shrugged. "I like stories."

Min scampered out, her shadow playing in and out of the warm light spilling across the sand. She was carrying *The Land of Magic* in one hand and another bottle of wine in the other, handing one to me and slapping Connor's hand away from the other. "Finish the other one first," she scolded. "This for later. I'm not getting up again."

I opened the cover, running my hand over the first page, feeling slightly drunk. "What do you want to hear?" I asked.

Min took a deep breath and thought for a minute, then turned her face upward. "I want to hear about them. I want to hear a story about stars."

Connor smiled faintly, which I took for agreement. I checked the page number and turned to the middle of the book. I already knew which story Min would enjoy most.

I cleared my throat and placed my finger on the first line, following with words across the page. On the opposite page was an illustration of a woman dressed in black, flanked by an aura of clouds.

"*The Sorcerer and the Dragon Slayer.* This story begins, as all the best stories do, in the traditional way."

Once upon a time, in a faraway land, there lived a young girl. From birth, her mother and father knew she was different. After a long and difficult labor, she emerged from her mother's womb with eyes fully open and a head of wild, raven black curls. She looked at the midwife with dark, serious eyes and let out a yell so powerful that the midwife fled the house immediately. Her father named her Alala, after the sound.

She was strong and fearless. One night, while she slept in her cradle, a serpent made the mistake of crawling in, seeking to bite the child. When Alala's mother came in the next morning, she was shocked to find the animal coiled belly-side up, its spine snapped just behind the skull, and her daughter sleeping soundly.

She was fast. As soon as she learned to run, she was swifter than all of her brothers and sisters, easily beating them in footraces. When she sought out other children in the village, they refused to race her, saying it was no fun to lose outright. Alala invited them to tie stones to her waist to slow her down, but even with the added weight, she still beat them. The children were angry and refused to play with her. Alala was sad and played alone at the outskirts of the village. Looking out into the wilderness, she wondered what the world held for a girl like her. Little by little, she stepped beyond the bounds of the village, tempted by the emptiness beyond.

Seeing this, her father grew worried. If the village could not hold his daughter, he wanted to be sure she could protect herself beyond its walls. He gave her a sword and taught her to fight, showing her how to carry and care for the weapon, and how to make it do what she wanted.

At the same time, in another kingdom, there lived a boy, who was equally unloved by the people of his village. From birth, his parents knew he was different. After a long and difficult labor, he emerged from his mother's womb with eyes fully open. He looked from his mother to his father, and their hearts sank. His eyes were blue, and therefore he was discarded at an early age, taken to priests and left in their care. His parents had not bothered to name him, and so the priests called him Horus. They fashioned tinted goggles for him to prevent blindness. His eyesight would not last, but the priests hoped their invention would allow Horus' eyes to remain unclouded until his fortieth year.

He was watchful. The priests instructed him in daily chores, and he was made to accompany them on trips to the well to gather water. Once, on the way to the well, Horus noticed a yellow pompom pod had fallen from a nearby sweet acacia and was lying in the dust. Ants had covered the yellow pod to gather its nectar before the sun dried it out. Fascinated, Horus sat in the dust and observed the ants for hours and could not be called from his reverie.

He felt the flow of the world around him and saw into the beyond. Horus described things he could not know and related conversations he had had with people who had been dead for years. The priests listened and looked at each other and said nothing.

One day, a strange man appeared at the well and offered to take Horus. The stranger was dressed in unusual garments and wore no head covering, despite the immense heat. The stranger was Magys, the king's magician and sorcerer who lived in a high mountain that overlooked the village. The priests relented, perhaps a little too quickly, and Horus was taken to the mountain. There, Magys trained him in the ways of the unseen world.

In those ancient, primeval days, the gods delighted in meddling in the affairs of mankind, playing with them as a hyena would a doomed rat. The gods were not kind. Their seat of power was the land of Krakum, inside an ever-burning well. There, they gathered around the eternal flames to watch the beings they had created and devise misfortunes to test them.

They saw the birth of Alala and Horus—these children who sprang from the womb with eyes wide open—and they felt it was an omen of terrible things to come.

They summoned Fate, who appeared cloaked in a garment of mist. When she opened her mouth, her voice crackled like a funeral pyre. "What do you ask of me?"

Tartarus spoke first. "Two children have been born of the mortal world with open eyes. They are Alala and Horus. What future do you see for them?"

Fate did not answer immediately, taking her time and looking them each in the eye. "You will not like the answer," she said coyly.

Winged Thanatos raised his head. "Go on," he commanded.

Fate wrapped her mists closer around herself. "Their joining will mean death for one in power. Horus and Alala are willful children, the worst of your creations. They will not be stopped. There will be undoing."

Chaos came forward. "One in power?"

Fate smiled. "Yes."

"Undoing?" asked Hypnos.

Fate shrouded herself in mists and faded out of sight. Her words had thrown the gods into a panic.

"They must be stopped," demanded Ananke.

But what was to be done? They argued amongst themselves. Only Chronos, the god of time, remained silent. When the others asked his opinion, the god merely gestured to Thanatos and said, "Death comes for all, in time."

Achlys, older than Chronos himself and the goddess of poisons and misery, shouted him down. His answer was laughable, she said, and declared the two children be killed before they could do any harm. Once awakened, her bloodlust must be quenched, and so she called the titans Crius and Theia to her.

"Crius, titan of the constellations, use the stars to search the night for these two mortals. Theia, titan of sight and the clear sky, search the day for these two children. Kill them and bring the heads to us. No mortal defies the gods."

The titans obeyed and searched the whole of the world for Horus and Alala, traveling the skies both day and night, their eyes turned toward the dunes. No human escaped their gaze.

But Nyx, goddess of the night, had other ideas. She had watched Alala and admired her strength. A plan formed in her mind. She instructed Pallas, god of warcraft, to construct a shield and a breastplate. Pallas did as he was told and fashioned them from an ore known only to the gods, stronger than any mortal weapon. He gave them to Nyx, who painted them with the ether of darkness.

She emerged from the ever-burning well and traveled to the wilderness, where she waited. Soon, she spied Alala hunting lions under the cover of night, stalking a pride from the high ground of a cliff. A child to no one but those as old as the gods, Alala had grown into a strong, able young woman. She had proved herself in many battles, fighting alongside her father and brothers. There was no one who could best her in combat.

Nyx threw up a cover of darkness to hide her deed from Crius and revealed herself to Alala.

Surrounded by clouds and crowned in starlight, Nyx held her hand out to the mortal girl. "Do you know me?"

Alala faced the goddess, clear-eyed and unafraid. "I do. You are Nyx, goddess of the night."

Nyx was pleased. "You are in danger. The gods have marked you and another for death."

Alala was taken aback. "How have I displeased them?"

"One day, your joining with another of power will bring death to one of us. It is written. And so, you must die."

"I know of no other like me."

"He is near."

"What do you ask of me, Goddess?"

Nyx presented the shield and breastplate. "I give you these so that you may conceal yourself from the eyes of the gods. They have been cloaked in magic and will hide you from any immortal who means you harm."

But Alala did not take them from Nyx's hands. "What do you ask in return?"

Nyx felt a prick of anger. "You reject my gift to you?" The clouds around her darkened.

Alala held up a hand. "No, goddess. I ask only what you would have of me, your servant."

Nyx pretended to think. "Remember my kindness," she said at last. "If you are destined to slay a god, I would like the choice to be mine."

"Which god do you choose?"

"In time." Nyx held out the breastplate and shield.

Alala took them and slipped the breastplate over her head. It settled over her and molded itself to fit her body. She slid the shield over her arm and admired the way the metal seemed to swallow any light that touched its surface. When she looked up, the goddess was gone, and the pride had moved on. She looked out over the land and knew she had to find the other like her.

But there was one who had seen Nyx's act—Selene, titan of the moon and sister to Crius. Selene had no love for her brother and did not think to tell him of what she had witnessed. Instead, she came to rest on a mountaintop in a nearby kingdom and appeared to the young sorcerer who dwelled within.

Horus had finished his lessons with Magys for the day and was sitting alone in his chamber, reading by candlelight, when Selene materialized. He blinked in the sudden glow, for Selene was cloaked in the brilliance of the moon.

"Do you know who I am?" asked Selene, her voice like the tinkle of a small bell.

Horus thought for a moment. "No," he said carefully. "But I imagine you are a goddess."

Selene preened at the compliment—a goddess! "Why yes," she answered. "I am Nyx, goddess of the night."

Horus knew this was untrue, but he was curious. "Welcome, goddess. Your servant awaits your bidding."

Selene studied Horus' blue eyes, finding him a very unusual mortal. But then, all sorcerers were odd. They had the habit of looking not quite at you, but at someone just behind you. She had seen this with Magys, the older sorcerer who lived in the mountain.

"You are in danger, mortal."

"Am I, goddess?"

"The gods fear you, for you and another are destined to destroy one of them."

"How is that possible, goddess?"

"The future remains in shadow. Crius and Theia have been sent to seek you

out and kill you, and I have instructed Selene, titan of the moon, to turn her face away from this dwelling so that Crius will be blind to you."

"That is kind, goddess. And Theia?"

"I can only protect you from Crius."

"I understand."

"In return for my protection, I ask that when the time comes, you allow Selene to choose the god who will be destroyed."

"Selene, goddess? You do not wish the choice to go to you?"

"No. Selene is wise and will choose best."

Horus paused. "Yes, goddess. I imagine there are advantages to a titan choosing the fate of a god that I would know nothing about."

Selene narrowed her eyes. "You will let Selene choose."

"Yes, goddess. This other I am meant to find…"

"The other is like you."

"A sorcerer?"

Selene thought but could not picture Alala as one of magic. "No, but she is near. She too has my protection."

"Thank you, goddess."

"Remember, you must find a way to protect yourself from Theia."

A peculiar glint flickered in Horus' eyes. "I will."

Selene returned to the sky and turned her face away from the mountain to conceal Horus from her brother.

Horus was no fool. He went to his tutor's chambers. Magys, having sensed the presence of an immortal in his home, was already awake and waiting. Horus told him of what had passed, and Magys fell into deep contemplation.

"I concur with your instincts," Magys said at last. "No goddess has been in this house. But an immortal masquerading as a god is trouble. They seek to trick you."

Horus nodded. "I sensed a deception, but of what I am not sure."

Magys held up a finger. "There is one truth in what the immortal told you. You have been marked for death by the gods." He gestured in the space above Horus. "I see a shadow over your head that was not there before. You have angered them somehow."

"The immortal spoke of another—a woman similarly marked."

"I have seen her."

Horus was surprised. "You have?"

Magys closed his eyes. "She comes to me in visions. She is strong and wild—a warrior born as you were, with eyes wide open. Before, she was only a mist, but as years have passed, I see her more and more clearly."

"Why did you not tell me?"

Magys considered his answer. "Visions are not like looking into clear water. They come unbidden to my mind, make little sense, and are a constant nuisance to me. One thing is clear, your destiny rises to meet you, Horus. You must find this woman."

"I must protect myself from Theia first."

Magys waved a hand. "She is dangerous but, like the human eye, easily fooled. I will show you how."

In the days that followed, Magys fashioned a cloak for Horus and bewitched it so that no light would reflect back to Theia as she passed. She would not see Horus, only the things around him.

Many revolutions passed. The titans searched for their prey while Horus and Alala looked for each other. Crius and Theia grew angry at their failure and fearful of Achlys' anger, should she find out. They tore through the sky and screamed their rage down on the world. Their cries shook the ground, opening cracks to another, much older existence below, disturbing a monster more terrible than either of them, awakening Draco, the world serpent.

At the beginning of the world, a great volcano erupted, spewing ash and fire, bleeding lava onto the land below. The lava and ash hardened, forming solid earth, but still, the volcano bled. Touched by Chaos, the lava ran together, coiling and squirming, pulling itself into the shape of a gigantic serpent. Its surface puckered into spines to cover the volcanic fascia underneath, and four lizard-like limbs sprang from its body. Talons of obsidian slashed the new earth, fire erupted from jaws like the maw of Hell, and Chaos brought Draco into being.

These were the days of fire. Cursed with an eternal hunger, Draco devoured every being that sprang from the minds of the gods. They cast spells to protect their new creations, but still, Draco came. Indiscriminately violent and cruel, Draco was ungovernable. The gods implored Chaos to destroy this abomination, but Chaos refused. What did it care for the world its fellow gods were trying to build? And so, Draco ran unchecked over the earth.

But Gaia could not wait for the others to act. The soon-to-be mother of the titans felt her time drawing near and foresaw the death of her many children. She lay down and gave birth to one, who she named Tethys. The infant titan's cries drew the eye of Draco, who signaled his coming with a breath of fire. Knowing she could not save her child, Gaia put her hands into the sand and opened a cave that led to the center of the Earth. There she placed Tethys and returned to the surface alone. She concealed herself in a stone and waited for Draco's approach.

It did not take long. The world serpent had detected the scent of new life and was eager to take it. He rushed into the cave without a thought, tunneling further and further, until only the tip of his tail remained above the earth, when Gaia sprang from the stone and commanded the earth to close. The world sealed shut, severing Draco's tail, and imprisoning him inside. Gaia fell to the ground and gratefully allowed the rest of her children to be born.

But Chaos was angry. Its child had been tricked; Gaia could not be allowed to go unpunished. Chaos demanded retribution, but the others refused. It was Chaos' own fault for creating such a monster.

Chaos decided to teach the other gods a lesson. It returned to the spot where the earth had swallowed Draco and retrieved its offspring's severed tail. As it held the tail in its hand, the remnant dissolved into lava and spilled onto the sand, splitting into millions of serpents. Chaos filled each one with poison powerful enough to destroy living beings and scattered the serpents over the whole of the world. Satisfied that it would have its revenge, Chaos returned to the pit of eternal fire.

Now the son had returned, awakened by foolish Crius and Theia. As the ground trembled from their screams of rage, a fissure—the old scar of Gaia's making—split the Earth to its very core, forming a gateway for Draco's escape. Smoke billowed from the crag, and a fetid stench followed close behind—the smell of rotting flesh. In the pit of eternal fire, Chaos lifted its head as though awakening from a deep sleep. Draco was coming.

Theia was the first to see the crack in the earth. Remembering the stories Gaia had told her, she fled to the furthest end of the sky, shrieking, "Draco has awakened! Draco has awakened!" as she tore across the atmosphere. On the other side of the world, Crius heard his sister's cries and fell back, concealing himself among the stars.

Midst the ever-burning flames, the gods cast glances in Chaos' direction, but it ignored them, leaving the pit to observe its offspring. Chaos liked to be present in times of destruction.

The world fell silent for one brief moment before a column of fire barreled out of the fissure and into the sky. Talons of obsidian gouged the earth as the world serpent hauled himself out of his prison and into the daylight. For the first time in millennia, Draco's lungs pulled in fresh, clean air and he gleefully expelled fire with every exhalation. Extending himself fully, Draco stretched and blinked in the sunlight, relishing the heat on his spiny flesh. The world had changed since he last beheld it—the gods had been allowed to fill the land and sky with all manner of beings. Deep inside his body, Draco's stomach twisted, and he felt his hunger quicken.

He fell upon the earth and began his reign of slaughter. The first to die were the inhabitants of a small, nearby village. Draco razed the buildings and consumed every last inhabitant, turning next to the cattle and livestock, then the beasts of the wild. But nothing slaked his hunger.

Chaos transformed itself into a fly and lazily buzzed around Draco's massive head. "Did you get enough to eat, venerable one?"

Draco snapped his jaws at the fly but missed.

"I thought not," said Chaos. "Look to the east. There is a kingdom nestled *at the base of a mountain. Do you know what a kingdom is, world serpent?"*

Draco cast its gaze to the east but did not understand.

"A kingdom is a big collection of boxes positively stuffed with humans—the little hairless beings—and animals of all shapes and sizes. Enough to satisfy even one so hungry as yourself. Go there and see for yourself."

Draco had heard enough. His talons tearing deep furrows in the earth, Draco traveled toward the kingdom in the east, annihilating everything in his path. Satisfied with itself, Chaos decided to wander the Earth for a little while longer. After all, it had been so long since it had had a chance to stretch its legs.

Alala had been searching for the other like her for some time, going from village to village, asking for a man born with eyes wide open, but she had not found him. She was preparing to travel to the neighboring kingdom when word of Draco's escape reached her. He had destroyed a village and was making for the nearest kingdom—the one at the base of the mountain—and no one had been able to stop him. An army had been raised to put an end to him—a line of soldiers was already on the march and would pass her village soon. Alala, with her magic breastplate and shield, ran to join them. The other she sought would have to wait.

For his part, Horus already knew who he was looking for. He too had visited village after village, asking for one born with eyes already open. No one had heard of such a woman, but when Horus said he was looking for a female warrior, the one name he heard time and again was Alala. Old soldiers spoke of her skill and strength, of her bravery in battle, of how she could not be beaten. The more Horus heard of Alala, the more he believed she was the one he was looking for. But the old soldiers knew little else about her, and could not tell him where she lived. Then, on the day he saw a line of soldiers in the distance marching to stop Draco from entering the kingdom, Horus chased after them. Alala would surely be one of their number.

Magys was fearful and warned Horus to take care. His pupil was a skilled sorcerer, but Draco was an immortal monster and would not be stopped by any army. Magys watched Horus run straight into danger, then retreated into the mountain, sealing the entrance behind him.

Far ahead, Draco had spotted the coming fighters. Before they had a chance to see him, the world serpent reared back, slamming his claws into a soft area of sand and forcing his way in. He burrowed just under the surface until the sand covered his body and he appeared as an innocent dune. He waited patiently for the army to approach.

The line of fighters came nearer, hesitating and cautious, sensing a trap. Alala was near the end of the line, her sword already drawn and shield at the ready. She thought she heard someone call her name, but before she could turn, the ground in front of her exploded.

Black jaws lined with razor-sharp teeth burst from the earth, split the horizon, and erupted into the sky. Half the line of fighters disappeared down the enormous gullet, their screams drowned out by the blast. Alala froze, transfixed in horror. A hand grabbed her arm and she turned to face a strange man wearing tinted goggles and gray robes. The man yelled at her to run and she kicked him squarely in the chest, sending him head over heels into the dirt. Turning, she lifted her voice in a terrifying war cry and charged at the world serpent.

Horus lay in the dirt, clutching his chest and gasping for breath. Alala was headed for certain death, but he could not speak to cast the simplest spell. As he struggled to his knees, he cursed himself for being so impetuous. After all he had heard about her, what other response had he expected?

By the time Alala came within striking distance of Draco, she was the only soldier left. The world serpent had eaten the rest. She raised her sword and stabbed the monster's spiny flank. The metal shattered like glass and Draco turned, swiping a talon in Alala's direction. She tumbled out of the way and faced the creature, her shield in front of her in case Draco decided to spit fire. Still struggling to stand, Horus felt a rising panic. She would be killed.

But nothing happened. Though Alala stood in front of him, Draco bobbed his head from side to side, looking in all directions. He lowered his head closer to the ground and tasted the air with his forked tongue. Realizing the beast could smell her but not see her, she kept the shield up and started to back away, planning to return with stronger weapons.

Draco jerked his head in Horus' direction and lunged forward. Alala broke into a sprint, grabbing Horus by the arm and yanking him out of Draco's path, but the monster did not slow down. He seemed to decide Horus was too small a snack and was heading for the kingdom at the base of the mountain.

Deep in the pit of eternal flame, the gods were in a frenzy, shouting and fighting over who was responsible for Draco's escape. Only one god remained silent and apart from the uproar. Watching the world serpent make his way across the land, Nyx narrowed her eyes. "Death for one in power," she muttered. Smiling grimly, she turned her attention to the two mortals.

Alala helped Horus up from the ground and then turned to run after Draco.

"Wait!" Horus cried.

Alala slowed, giving him time to catch up. "I must stop that monster!"

Horus gasped for breath. "Were you by any chance born with eyes open?"

Alala stopped and stared at him. The only other people who knew that were her parents and the midwife who had fled the house. Then she understood. "Were you?"

Horus nodded. "Yes. I think we are destined to find each other."

Alala snorted. "Destiny is for lazy cows. I spent months looking for you."

"Well, so did I."

"I do not feel anything."

"Sorry?"

Alala shook her limbs. "The goddess Nyx told me our joining would mean death for one in power. That is why we are marked for death. I thought when we met, something would happen." She gestured to the sky. "Lightning, maybe."

"Are you sure it was Nyx who came to you?"

"I am a night hunter. I know Nyx when I see her." Alala showed Horus her breastplate and shield. "She gave me these. I think they are why Draco could not see me. They will help me defeat him."

The magic of the shield and breastplate sent a faint echo through the magic that dwelled within his body. Horus swallowed. She truly had been blessed by Nyx. "I can help."

"You can fight?" She looked him over doubtfully.

"Not as such. I am Horus, the sorcerer."

Alala nodded. "We will need magic. Follow me."

The two headed after Draco, who by this time had reached the walls of the kingdom and was tearing them down.

Within the mountain, Magys heard the falling outer walls and was wracked with guilt. Unsealing the mountain entrance, he looked down on the kingdom below. Draco had coiled himself over the ruins of the outer wall and was devouring the guards of the watch. Their struggling bodies slid down his throat whole to be digested in the burning lava that lay within.

Magys cast fire and called winds to drive Draco away, but even his strongest spells were not enough. They fell harmlessly on the world serpent's spiny flesh and did not even slow him down. Magys fled back into the mountain, sealing the entrance shut again. He fell on his altar and prayed to the gods for mercy. Only Nyx, who was preparing for her nightly journey across the sky, heard his plea.

By the time Horus and Alala reached the kingdom, Draco was well inside the walls, devouring every human and animal in his path and clawing buildings to the ground. Alala struck the monster with the edge of her shield. Horus conjured a sand spout and drew it over Draco's head. The world serpent ignored them both. Alala grabbed weapons left behind by devoured guards and jumped on the creature's back, grabbing the spiny skin and pulling herself toward Draco's head as dusk fell.

Helplessness crept over Horus. His spells were useless. Draco was too powerful for him. Horus clasped his head and looked up at the sky—darkness was spreading. Remembering how she had favored Alala, he fell to his knees and cried out to Nyx. The goddess saw who called her, but more importantly to her, she saw Alala making her way to Draco's head. She was struck with sudden inspiration and appeared before the sorcerer.

"Horus, sorcerer of the mountain, why do you call me?"

"Why do the gods plague us with this beast?"

Nyx, surrounded by clouds of night, glanced at the world serpent as if just noticing it. "I had no hand in this. What would you have me do?"

"We are creations of the gods. Help us! Draco will destroy all of us and the world if he is not stopped."

Above them, Alala brought a spear down into the left eye of the monster. Draco screamed fire, throwing her down to the ground. He twisted his head, trying to see his attacker, molten matter pouring from his now empty eye socket. Alala snatched up another spear and threw it, narrowly missing Draco's remaining eye. She found one last spear and prepared to climb the creature again.

Nyx knew she had to work quickly. She saw the possibility of Alala killing Draco and fulfilling Fate's prophecy. But, if she herself were the one to rid the world of Draco, she would become most beloved of all the gods and defeat Fate at the same time. However, she still wanted one more thing.

"I have already helped one of you. I bestowed gifts and received nothing but a broken promise in return. Why should I help further?"

Horus squared his shoulders. "What do you want?"

"The death of an immortal comes with too heavy a price. However, there is an alternative."

"What do you ask in return?"

Nyx took her time. "I will remove the world serpent to a place where he can never harm another living being."

Above them, Alala lunged, stabbing Draco just under his right eye. The giant reared back, scrabbling at his face with his claws, gouging his own skin. Alala dropped to the ground just before Draco let loose a torrent of fire, engulfing nearby buildings in flames.

Horus turned back to Nyx. "Yes! Do it!" he shouted at the goddess.

Nyx raised a brow in pleasure. He was getting desperate. "In return for my generosity, I want one to serve me."

"Serve you?"

"My servant. For all eternity. You or her—I do not care which, but the choice is yours."

"Eternal life?"

Nyx chuckled. "No. No mortal can follow a god and live."

Horus hesitated. Existence between life and death for all eternity—a kind of damnation from which there would be no escape.

But Horus was watchful. He felt the flow of the world around him and saw into the beyond. When he looked at Alala, he saw more than a soldier. She was born like he was, but her strength was boundless. He saw a hero, perhaps even a future queen with the power to raise armies. Even now, in the present, she had done more damage to Draco than he had managed with his magic. The world needed her. It did not need him.

"I will go with you," said Horus quietly.

Nyx looked surprised but accepted his answer. The world grew very dark. Nyx shielded the stars and commanded the moon not to shine, bringing a deep night to the kingdom. Almost blind and still in pain, Draco clawed at the sky. He raised his mighty body, coiling himself into knots, searching for the horizon. In the darkness, Draco became bewitched. He could not tell top from bottom, up from down, sky from land, and in his panic he allowed himself to be pulled into the sky. The world serpent stretched himself across the bowl of the night, becoming tangled and hopelessly trapped in the stars. Crius stretched out his hand and marked them, making Draco a part of the night sky itself. He was doomed to endure his unending hunger, watching his prey from above, but could never come down.

Alala, her eyes on the night sky, turned to where Horus had been standing, but Nyx had already taken her payment, leaving only a husk. She fell beside his lifeless body and mourned him as she would a fallen soldier, when the cry of many voices rose up from the kingdom. The people were cheering Alala—their warrior.

Horus was taken up and his shade forced to follow Nyx and never rest. She paraded him in front of the other gods as her prize for ridding the world of Draco, but she had sorely miscalculated. When Selene realized she would not get her reward, she told the gods of Nyx's treachery, and they turned their backs on her. Nyx was banished from the eternal flames and made to live a solitary existence. She blamed this on Horus and delighted in tormenting him. His shade was bound to her but was not as swift. Her favorite game was to shoot back and forth across the world, knowing he would be forced to follow, but would never be able to catch up.

However, Horus had been very right about Alala's future.

Alala was strong.

Alala was brave.

And Alala was shrewd.

She allowed victory over Draco to be laid at her feet. She spoke Horus' name but never that of the goddess Nyx, or indeed any other god. She was granted land and built a kingdom of her own, placing herself at the head as queen. She commanded her people to build a statue to commemorate her slaying of the world serpent. She led her soldiers in battle and won many victories. Her name was their war cry. She was a mighty queen, and most infuriating of all to Nyx, Alala was beloved. The people worshipped her. Gods were creatures of mystery and half-truth. Alala's people could see her deeds, victories, and defeats with their own eyes. She fought alongside them and mourned their dead with them. She absorbed other kingdoms into her own, building a strong and prosperous empire, and her people loved her beyond any god.

Alala conveniently forgot to order the building of temples, and the people never built any on their own. Nyx was enraged but could do nothing. She had underestimated Alala, and now she and the other gods were fading, less relied upon by one generation, and forgotten by the next. Eventually, there would be nothing left but crumbling stone, and it was all Alala's doing.

As the gods faded from memory, so did Nyx's hold over what remained of Horus. One day, his shade found the bond had broken, and it could finally lie down and rest.

When she could no longer swing a sword, Alala hung the enchanted breastplate and shield behind her throne where all could see them. By then, they held no more of Nyx's magic. Instead, they had become a symbol of the queen herself—of her mortal power.

Though she privately wished she could have died in battle, Alala would rule her empire for fifty years before quietly passing away in her sleep at a venerable age.

At sundown on the night she died, Alala asked her servants to prepare a bed on the balcony adjoining her chamber and pile it with furs to keep out the cold air. When it was ready, she climbed in, wrapped herself up, and waited. The light bled from the sky and darkness grew. She fixed her eyes on the heavens. One by one, points of light appeared, more and more, until it seemed the sky would burst and the galaxy would spill down onto the world below. But there was one group of stars that, to Alala, shone brighter than the rest—a string that coiled across the bowl of the sky, once held there by Crius' hand, and now forever a part of the night. Alala looked deeply into the star that marked Draco's one remaining eye and, smiling, closed her eyes forever.

The death of Alala was mourned by the entire empire and beyond. Her funeral was attended by royalty from kingdoms far and wide. As a memorial, a new constellation was named—formed by a small cluster of stars above Draco's head—the Dragon Slayer.

I fell silent and looked over at Min and Connor. Their faces, shadowed in the blue light of the moon, were turned toward to sky. A gentle breeze touched the tops of the dunes.

"You know," Min said softly, "I don't like a lot of people. But I like you people." She looked at us with her owl eyes. "So don't die." She turned her face upward, back to the sky.

"Min," Connor began, but broke off.

"No." Min waved a hand without looking at either of us. "We just leave it there. You know, as it is."

We lost ourselves in silence, gazing up at the infinite galaxy, as the night breeze played over the sand.

Chapter 43

The night before we were set to leave, I did not sleep. My body thrummed with anticipation—a particular anxiety that had visited me the night before I set out with Connor for the first time. Its familiar hand settled over my stomach and twisted my innards, balanced equally by the pull of the horizon. In my mind's eye, I set my gaze on the beyond, the west, the wastelands. I packed and repacked my things over and over, memorizing their placement, arranging the most important items for easy access. As for Min's device, I knew it down to its component parts. It could explode into individual pieces right here and now, and I could reassemble it in hours. Min had taught us well. I placed it at the edge of my bedroll and lay down flat on my back, looking up into the hollow of the dome and waiting for the word from Connor.

Nearby, her breathing came steady and deep. She was not asleep, but I did not speak to her. I decided she would want me to leave her alone with her thoughts. Min snored soundly, having put herself to sleep with plenty of homemade wine. I hoped our absence would not wear on her. Min had been alone a long time. I comforted myself with that thought. I imagined our journey back—we would visit, of course—and the joy and relief at seeing the dome again. Maybe Min would be waiting. We would tell her all about our adventures, and she would no longer have to worry about us. Yes, we would be back. We would not leave her to wonder what had happened to us.

If we survived.

The hand around my stomach turned to a fist.

I wondered what Cal and Vargas would think of me. How would my father see me now? My mother? I thought of Asha. We would have to stop there as well. I would have to tell her I was all right.

The night seemed to go on forever, and yet I was surprised when the light began to turn gray. Dawn was approaching so quickly. Seized by impulse, I leaped up, wrapped a blanket around my body, and slipped out the door. I climbed the nearest dune, the night-cold sand crunching slightly under my bare feet, my lungs waking up after hours of rest.

I straddled the ridge, one foot on either side, and looked to the east. The light there was pink, deepening to blood red at the horizon. I waited, cold air burning my throat, for the first peek of fire. It came, shining like a coin, peering like an eye across the landscape to the west. I turned to the wasteland, watching the last of the gray night ebb from the sky and become saturated with light.

The energy pulsed in my veins, my heart strong in my chest—the drumbeat of adventure—and my mind chanted to the rhythm of *more, more, more.*

Chapter 44

Connor was waiting for me when I went back inside. She was dressed and ready, her pack already placed and tested. I wondered if my eyes looked like hers. She was positively vibrating with impatient energy, as though the wild in her was reaching for the wild outside the dome. When I realized Min was still asleep, I stopped Connor and pulled her back. She did not know she was supposed to say goodbye.

Min got up to see us off, pulling a blanket over her head and body, partly against the cold and partly against her own feelings. She embraced Connor first, standing on her toes to wrap her arms around the taller woman's neck. To my surprise, Connor pulled Min into a warm hug, patting her back with one hand and nodding in response to Min's muffled reminders to travel safely, to be careful. She told Connor she had packed paper and kohl for her to draw maps of the route we took, which made Connor smile. She eventually released Min, who wiped a tear-soaked trail of mucous across her sleeve before embracing me. She pressed her wet face against my cheek.

"Stay together. Stay safe," she whispered. I nodded.

She released me and watched us go, staying in the doorway even after we reached the nearest ridge. We turned back and waved to her. She waved back and stayed in place, watching us until our steps took us out of sight. We walked on, past Connor's old campsite, past the areas we had used to test our packs. When I eventually did look back, the dome had disappeared, swallowed back into the landscape.

A breeze picked up and cooled our journey throughout the morning and afternoon. The way was easy, and Connor set a quick pace to take advantage of it. We would not always be able to travel so far in one day, and we had to cover as many kilometers as we could. More than half a year had passed since we last traveled, and yet we fell into roles and routines as if we had never stopped. Connor traveled ahead while I lagged a few paces behind. Connor hunted while I looked for plants. We took turns tending campfires.

The packs were the only change, requiring cleaning every night and testing every morning.

The landscape was easy to traverse, but there was little to hunt, and almost no plant life to speak of. Connor refused to use our rations, and I did not press her. They were the last resort—it was too early to use them. The land was also difficult to map. It went on in the same way for weeks with nothing but rising and falling dunes. The color of the sand did not even vary, remaining bone white as far as the eye could see. Connor had to be very careful to not take us in the wrong direction, for every way looked the same. She scribbled on the paper Min had given her every night by the fire, though what she marked I do not know.

We saw no one, no trade caravans, no settlements, nothing. We had not even come across a road. Every day, we realized more and more that we were completely alone, and yet that thought did not frighten me. I was enthralled, exhilarated by the idea that my feet might be falling on land no one had traveled. I felt like a true explorer. Connor was especially full of energy. I took pleasure in watching her. Even laden with a heavy metal pack, I have never seen anyone more a part of the land and sky. She summited dune after dune and never faltered. She hunted snakes and lizards, keeping one eye always on the direction we were headed. She covered kilometer after kilometer with long strides, her back straight and strong. She had stopped hiding her scars from me, openly exposing her arms to let the wind cool her skin. I felt guilty, thinking of how long she had kept herself tightly covered, how miserable she must have been, and how I had not even noticed. I wondered if this change was a sign that she trusted me.

Our packs did not fail us. We still had not touched a drop of our water reserves, able to survive on the moisture of our bodies. I felt almost giddy when I realized how long it had been since I had last tasted fresh water. The packs worked. We did not have to stop to find water or incessantly count every mouthful. All things felt possible.

It was not until the nightmares came to me again that I realized how long they had been gone, how many nights I had slept in peace, untroubled and unvisited by shadows. The nights now found me bathed in a cold sweat, eyes wide and searching. Evil things lurked just out of my eyeline, and I started sleeping by the campfire again, watching the orange flicker shrink and fade to ash.

It was on one of these nights I saw him. Just there, sitting across the fire. He peered at me, bright eyes in a round face, and smiled faintly. I did not speak for fear he would disappear. He did not seem to have anything to say. I waited, longing to ask what he wanted of me. We watched each other for a while, and then he was gone. He disappeared without a flourish, without a word, without a sigh—just gone. Though I knew he was never there to begin with, I felt his absence. The moment of realization, the eye telling the brain there was nothing there—but there had been! *He* had been there. And the stubborn air that refused to acknowledge him, the heartless void that insisted on replacing him, was cruel and cold as any monster of my nightmares.

He returned again the following night, and again I held my breath, wanting him to say something. The moment he disappeared wrenched my heart, as though the force that took him was trying to take me as well.

On the third night I reached out to him, but he was already gone. I touched the sand where he had been sitting, but it was cold. I looked up and saw Connor peering at me from the tent. I sniffed and wiped my eyes on my sleeve. Her face was pensive, and though she seemed ready to close the tent and return to bed, she thought better of it and stepped out into the night air.

She stirred the fire, bringing it back to life, and sat back on her heels. She waited.

"I am being haunted," I said hoarsely, running my sleeve over my eyes again. "My brother." His name rose in my mouth, ready to be spoken, but I faltered.

Connor nodded and held her hands out to warm them. "I am also haunted sometimes." Her voice was quiet, almost reverential, or perhaps she did not want her ghosts to hear her.

"I do not know what he wants. He won't speak."

Connor regarded me for a moment. "Perhaps he only wants to know if you are all right."

I shook my head. "No. I don't know. He follows me—in my dreams, here, ever since he and…"

Connor dropped her gaze and considered the fire. "The living tend to keep a place for the dead. We leave the door open just a little. Were you close?"

I did not want to cry, so I only nodded my head.

"I saw someone once," she continued. "Someone who was not there. Someone I did not want to die. It was hard to see past the face and look at what he really was."

"What was he?"

"An echo. Guilt. My guilt."

I pulled my knees into my chest. "What did you do?"

Connor looked at the fire, not at me. "I let him follow me. I wanted him to. I did not want him to go, but it was no way to live for me. I had to lay him to rest. His echo. My guilt."

"How?"

She shrugged slightly and looked up at the stars. "In my own way."

I sat with this for a while. I knew what he was, but I did not want to let him go. Not yet. I did not want him to leave. When I looked up again, Connor had returned to the tent. I sat for a little longer, listening to the silent night, before crawling into the tent as well.

<h1 style="text-align:right">Chapter 45</h1>

C al appeared again the next night, his round face looking at me from across the campfire. I had to speak. I had to know.

"What do you want from me?" I whispered.

His expression did not change, and in another moment, he was gone. I curled my body around the cold ground where he had been and slept there until morning.

I allowed this to go on for several more nights. I wanted to continue. I wanted to go on for a lifetime of brief moments. It was the absence I could not bear in the end—the moment I realized the spot across the campfire was empty. He did not want to know I was all right. He haunted me. He was an echo of what I felt. He was here because I called him. He was not Cal. He was the part of me that believed I was the reason for his death. He would never speak to me. For all this, I decided to lay him to rest.

The next night, when he appeared, I looked at him for a long while, wondering if this was how he had really looked or if I was somehow remembering him wrong. I decided to tell him a story. And so I did, a little at a time, each night before he disappeared.

I told him the story of a sister and her two brothers. I told him of their adventures, and how one brother protected her and guided her. I told him of the brother who put aside his dreams to help his sister. I told him of the day the brothers died, and how the sister almost died as well. I told him how she was rescued and returned to her city. I told him why she left that safety and journeyed into the wilderness. I told him how much the sister regretted her brothers' deaths. I told him how sorry she was. I told him how sorry I was.

After I finished, I knelt in the sand by the fire and used a piece of ash to draw three figures—a girl and two boys—standing next to each other. I drew a circle around them so that they would always be together. I knew that when I looked up Cal would be gone, so I did not move for a while. I thought of the Khamaseen nights when we could not go out and stayed up late telling stories. I thought of how bitterly Cal and Vargas fought the day before they had died. I thought of how much Vargas wanted to be anything but a witch hunter. I thought of my father's face when I came home.

I touched the figure for Vargas and said his name out loud. I thought of his spirit, how he bucked against what everyone wanted him to be. I touched the figure for Cal and said his name aloud. I thought of his warmth, how whenever I thought of home, I thought of him.

Only then did I look up.

I was alone.

Every night after Connor went to sleep, I drew the figures in the sand, naming my brothers and thinking of them, reminding myself of who they were. New memories came, things I had forgotten, moments of happiness. The sadness did not leave me, but I began to feel like I had room on my insides, as though there was space for something else. Eventually, Cal stopped appearing.

The nightmares still came, but not every night. I could sleep. I was not afraid of sleep. When the nightmares did come, they were always the same, as though the demons inside me had gathered to decide on the form that would do the most damage. When the nightmares came, a dune rose in my mind and gave way to a deep dark cave, where the man with many faces sat at his terrible task, as shadows with long limbs and bulbous heads grew along the walls.

Chapter 46

Time passed and the landscape flattened, stretched taut like a drum over the core of the Earth until it split, sending spiderweb cracks in all directions. Food was plentiful here—lizards and small mammals used the cracks as shelter from the constant heat. All we had to do was prod the spear into a crevice and pull out a meal. Here and there, small clusters of round cacti grew, their blobby, spherical heads filled with water-logged flesh that we could eat straight from the plant. To build up our reserved water supply, we wrapped the flesh in cloth and squeezed the fluid into a water bag. When that was full, we filled a water bag we had kept as a spare part to our packs.

Connor sketched whenever we stopped to rest—every animal we ate, every plant we consumed. There were still no landmarks to put on a map, so she marked the days and direction in which we traveled. Once, she rolled a drawing into a tight tube, tied it with a strip of black cloth from her clothing supply, and slid it into a crack in the ground. She left a length of the cloth exposed, where it fluttered in the breeze. When I asked her who the marker was meant for, she shook her head and pushed some loose dirt against the cloth to better secure it in place. She did not know. She left three more markers over the course of a month. I managed to look over her shoulder at one before she rolled it up. It was a picture of the landscape with our names and the direction we were headed scrawled in the middle. I wondered if she thought Min might come looking for us.

We cleaned our packs every evening, ridding them of sand and dislodging the salt of our bodies from the machinery. The clean water they produced carried a slightly sour taste that we had become used to. Any change in the taste roused suspicion and sent us pawing through the packs' innards, searching for a fault.

Some nights I heard howling in the distance, the sound carried on the back of the wind. On those nights, I would reach one hand outside of the tent and cup my palm to catch the air that carried that voice. The howls never came closer, their owner never ventured into our space. The only sign of it was a lone voice in the night—a call that was never answered.

The weeks rolled one after the other, on and on, as dung beetles endlessly turning their finds over the dirt. No roads crossed the flatlands. No other travelers appeared. The wind that touched the ground and hurtled across the landscape met only the resistance of our two bodies.

We were entirely alone.

Chapter 47

nd then blue shadows appeared low at the horizon. The landscape turned rocky, swelling up in striped layers of dark stone, long fingers pushing out of the earth and reaching into the sky. Some were so tall and broad we could use them as shelter from the sun. Sometimes they stood apart, straight as soldiers, and sometimes they crossed over each other, forming arches we could walk beneath. The round, water-filled cacti were replaced with dry tangles of brush studded with thorns. Animals made burrows in the soft dirt beneath, using the thorns for protection, and we had to take care not to step into them and twist our ankles. We were glad to have a change from lizards and small rodents, but so was another predator. The larger burrowing animals attracted wolves. We could hear them howling in the night, the scream of a rabbit often following close behind. We kept the campfire burning all night and surrounded the tent with cut branches of thorns, but even so, we slept lightly.

The worst problem was the flies, drawn in by the moisture and salt of our bodies. The metal packs chafed against our flesh, leaving the skin raw and ripe for fly larvae. Connor itched at a spot on her back for days before finally allowing me to look, only to find the red, prickled flesh alive with maggots. They had to be washed out with sanitizing solution from the small medical bag; the last few pried from their burrows with the help of thin, needlelike pincers from the toolkit. After that, we kept our skin as clean and dry as possible, watching for lesions that would allow maggots to get inside and poison our blood.

Though Connor had remained quiet as I rid her of the larvae, the experience stayed with her. Whenever we stopped to rest, I saw her shoulder muscles twitch, and she would slap at her skin even if nothing was there. At night, she wrapped herself in blankets and covered her face with a thin fabric to keep the flies away. It was impossible to keep them out of the tent completely, so in the end, I did the same.

The wind picked up the day we entered this new terrain and did not die down again. It whirled through the fingers of rock, weaving between, calling all the way, wearing the stone smooth with each pass. It blew so hard sometimes that it carried the flies away and covered us in dust. When that happened, we had to stop to clean out our packs, shielding each other from the wind as we did. Connor's face was often tight with worry as she hovered over me, urging me to hurry.

One day the air grew cold, the winds blew harder, and a line of darkness appeared at the horizon. We were completely exposed, standing on a rise, surveying the morning route. Dread opened a pit in my stomach, and I pointed at the coming line.

"Come on!" Connor shouted, grabbing my arm and hauling me down to lower ground. We raced through the columns of rock, searching for shelter, when Connor yanked me toward a spot where the columns folded over themselves to form a half-dome.

We had almost reached it when the wall of sand hit, knocking us to our knees. Connor pulled her head covering over her nose and mouth and pulled me forward. She put her face close to mine and yelled something I could not make out. The wind roared over us both, pulling our voices away from each other. Sand filled my mouth and I spat, tiny grains stinging my face and eyes. I pulled my head covering over my face and let her drag me on.

Behind the half-dome, the wind struggled to reach us, and we were able to build the tent. Connor drove sharp-ended tools into the ground to secure our shelter and shoved me inside to seal every cranny and crevice I could find.

Above, the dust and sand blotted out the sun, turning the air brown. We huddled inside for days—waiting. The packs had been damaged, but we could barely see to fix them. Building a fire was impossible. There was nothing to be done. We ate from our stock of rations. The water in our packs was gritty, polluted with sand that had turned to mud, and we could not strain the water from the silt. We drank instead from the water bag we had filled in the flatlands, refusing to touch the spare water bag.

At night, we were completely blind. We could not see each other and could hear nothing but the rush of wind outside. A few hours into the first night, I was seized with a terrible thought and reached out with my hands, groping toward someone I could only hope was still there. Her body jumped away from my touch, and I felt immediate relief.

I leaned in close to where she had been and shouted to be heard over the wind. "What if the Khamaseens have come early again?"

I felt hands on my legs, touching with brief, tentative taps to orient themselves. The hands came to my face and Connor's mouth was hot against my ear. "It is not the Khamaseens."

"How can you be sure?" My throat tightened.

Her hands were on my shoulders, gripping them gently. "Breathe," came the voice in my ear.

I took a few shaky breaths. The hands stayed on my shoulders. I reached out and found her torso, putting my hands on her shoulders. I followed her breath, feeling the rise and fall of her shoulders, focusing on the rhythm and feel of the rough cloth under my fingers. We were all right. I was all right.

On the morning of the fourth day, the winds shouted themselves out, and silence fell. I opened the tent and light spilled in, fresh air flooding the cramped space. We climbed out, finding the rough land covered in fresh powdery sand. The rocks that had protected us were half buried, sand clinging to the cracks in the stone.

We pulled our packs into the light and set about cleaning and repairing them. Sand had invaded every tube and opening in the machinery. It took a full day to get them back in working order, which meant using more food and water rations. As the sun set, Connor looked at me, her hard brown eyes narrowed in a serious gaze.

"We have lost time."

I shrugged. Did it really matter?

"We used too much of our rations," she insisted.

"We can hunt tomorrow and make up the food we used."

"And the water?"

I had no answer for that. We had not seen a water source since the flatlands—too far to go back just to replenish our supplies.

"It would be easier to hunt at night and dry meat during the day," she continued.

A shiver went down my spine, and I shook my head. "The wolves hunt at night, and predators would be attracted to drying meat."

Connor sat back on her heels. I knew she was going to push me. I knew she would get her way. She fixed her eyes on me. "The wolves would have fled the sandstorm. We have to make up the rations and the time we have lost."

I tried to argue with her, tried to convince her it was too dangerous to travel at night, but we had done it before. We had traversed the salt flats in the dark. Still, I did not like it. "We are alone out here," I reminded her. "We should not be taking risks if we don't have to."

"One night," she replied. "We need one night to hunt and replenish our supply of food. We can't know what awaits us—when we will reach poor hunting grounds. Food here is plentiful. We should take advantage."

"And our water?"

Connor shook her head. "Nothing to be done. We can only hope to come upon another water supply. For now, we should take one night to restock our food. Tonight."

I knew she was right. Our prey would be active at night. We could gather as much as possible, dry the meat, and then be on our way again. It made the most sense. It was what we *should* do. Still, a knot coiled itself in my stomach and a tightness wrenched in my chest. But the light was already fading from the sky, and I had no time to sit with that feeling—the creeping dread that we were making the wrong choice.

Chapter 48

Darkness crawled on its belly, sliding across the sky and smothering the light, its tail dragging the cold moon from its sleep below the horizon. In the blue of the moon, the heat seeped from the earth, as warmth leaving a corpse, leaving only coldness and stillness. The fingers of rock became like bones, exposed rib cages curving overhead, while we—the remains—scurried in the dark.

The land came alive with hunters and prey. Long-eared hares dug out their burrows and nibbled new leaves from the thorny bushes, occasionally dashing across our path. White kit foxes clawed at the dirt to dislodge scorpions from hiding. Orange eyes bobbed and glinted in the dark. For the first time, I wished we still had Hassan's gun.

The lantern moon hung over us. I felt too exposed and yet wished its light extended further into the dark. As it was, a halo of blue surrounded us and ended abruptly a few meters away on all sides. Connor walked ahead of me, casting a long shadow to one side, two hares dangling upside down over her shoulder. Their blood fell in slow drops on the sand. Machete in hand, I scanned the darkness for hungry things that would like an easy meal. My mouth was dry—*she needs to hurry.* Sand shifted to my right, and my head snapped in that direction, only to see the tail end of a mouse disappearing into the night.

Sensing my anxiety, Connor whispered, "Two more."

I took a breath and scanned the darkness again. Three pairs of orange eyes shone to the left but tilted and disappeared—the trio had changed direction. I switched the machete to my other hand and shook some life into the free fingers. *Two more. Two more.*

Suddenly, a fat hare appeared at the edge of our vision and dashed in front of us. It came so close we could make out the pupil of its eye and the grain of its fur. Connor fumbled and threw her spear clumsily, missing the animal completely. The hare disappeared into the dark, and Connor's spear landed in the dirt with a *shuk* somewhere outside the ring of blue moonlight.

She sighed. She swung the two dead hares down from her shoulder and dropped them in the sand. Their blood had slowed to a stop, the last drops coloring the sand black. Empty eyes stared up at me, motionless and glassy. I let them lay where they were.

Connor jogged toward the sound of where her spear had fallen. The darkness closed up behind her just as it occurred to me to follow her. I opened my mouth to call her name, to tell her to wait for me. I took one step and was stopped by the horrible sound of Connor screaming.

Chapter 49

She was there and then she wasn't. I saw her face—the circle of flesh caught in the moonlight—on the ground, one hand reaching for me, and then nothing. Her face. My god, her face. Her mouth had been a chasm, her eyes were slashes, her scream from the pit of her insides. She was gone.

Another noise rose in the night, a keening wail coming from my own mouth. The machete dangled uselessly at my side. I had not even seen what had taken her. My feet moved unbidden toward the spot where she had been. I was running. Marks in the sand. Long depressions. Something was dragging her, moving so fast I could not keep up. I could not see. My feet carried me over the dirt, between the shards of stone, through the dark. Where was she?

Further ahead, shadows darted away—two ink blots in the dark, one larger than the other—and I heard Connor's voice. She was shouting, fighting against whatever still had hold of her. The sound froze my brain, commanded me to stop, turn around and run away, and yet my feet changed course and moved in her direction.

The light grew, as though a cloud covering the moon had finally moved away, and for second I saw them. Connor kicking at the thing that dragged her along the ground. It had hold of her pack, dragging her so fast I only saw the glint of moonlight off its bulbous head before it disappeared into a hole in the ground, pulling Connor in with it.

Not a hole in the ground, but an abyss cut into a stone slab welling up from the sand.

A cave.

A cave that rose before me, pitch black and empty and soundless. My feet stopped dead. My ears strained to hear but nothing came back. My breath came in ragged gasps. They were down there. Connor and the creature.

Or more than one. More than one. More than one.

I squeezed my eyes shut and pressed my hands to my head. The ground tilted and I knelt.

Rumbling earth, the terrible laughing of a hundred hyenas made of wind and black sand bearing down on us, hungry jaws snapping, eyes glowing. The unholy fear. Cal grabbing my arm, Vargas staring at us in open-mouthed panic. Cal losing his grip, the earth giving way underneath me, burying me in a shallow pit. My brothers. My brothers. The smell of blood. The long, emaciated legs jutting out over the body on the ground. The small, wet sound from every pluck of long fingers traveling back and forth to that grotesquely bloated head.

A quiet descended, wrapping itself around my mind. I looked up, met the eye of the void in front of me.

I pictured myself walking away. I imagined turning my body. I imagined looking down at my feet and seeing them move, finding the hares that had been left in the sand. I imagined my hand reaching out to open the tent, and then I imagined crawling inside and sealing it shut.

But I could still hear her screaming.

My ghosts rose on either side—the echoes of people I could not have saved—looking down, down into the hole that held the one I could. I thought of Connor. Connor, who believed in something no one else had ever seen. Connor, who made me believe in *more*. Connor, who had saved me from dying alone in the open, saved me from Hassan, saved me from dying a witch hunter.

"I will not let her die here," I whispered.

I looked down into the darkness for a moment, then stepped into the cave.

Chapter 50

The darkness drank me down.

My eyes gaped wide and blind.

The walls slick under my touch.

Toes dragging feet, searching for the way.

My ears deaf to all but the pounding in my chest.

Down, down, down.

A sound. A rushing filled the passage like distant wind. I was breathing too quickly. I pressed my back to a wall dappled with moisture and lay my palms flat against it. I closed my eyes and imagined being far away. The wall was not a wall but the ground. The darkness was the night sky filled with stars. Min was lying next to me, drinking homemade wine. I opened my eyes.

The darkness was still filled with stars.

I blinked.

The walls and stone above were smeared with greenish-blue light, glowing ever so faintly. My hands. I brushed one palm across the wall behind me. The wall went dark but my skin glowed. Ahead, a circle of black curved away from me—the way forward.

A sound.

That sound. The sound of a monster picking its way through dead bodies while I cowered in a pit of sand.

Shuf shuf shuf

A grotesque shadow broke the glow, and I crouched low, waiting.

Shuf shuf shuf

Long, emaciated limbs rose over me, dragging over the walls with a sound like tearing paper.

My hand was on the grip of my machete, pulling it from the sheath bit by bit, the tiniest of movements until it was free.

The shadow bent forward, limbs coming to earth, and then it was gone.

My breath caught in my throat. Where was it? My eyes opened wide, searching the glow for the shadow.

No sound.

A puff of air on my face, like the barest breeze. The glow was all around me, and a crescent of light arced itself into a halo above my face. The breeze came again but the air was foul. The shape outlined in the light just centimeters from my face was that of a bloated head.

And then it lunged.

My skin tore and I felt my collarbone splinter in its jaws. I screamed and lashed out, but it was on top of me, its weight pinning my arms down. I kicked, twisting the machete until it bit flesh. Suddenly, the weight was gone, and I scrambled backward on my hands, kicking and waving the machete wildly in all directions.

I pushed my back to a wall, machete up and ready, but I could not see the thing. I held my breath, listening. Something scratched in the dirt to my right, and I struck. I slashed the machete upward, downward, side to side, but hit nothing. I held my breath again, eyes wide and searching. My lungs felt ready to burst.

Shuf shuf shuf

I struck to the left and was hit from the right with such force that I was knocked to the ground, the side of my head smacking something hard. Stars bloomed in my eyes. Teeth dug into my side, straight down to the bone, and I screamed. I lashed out. This time the blade cut deep, and something hot poured over my legs.

The weight was suddenly gone, but I could hear the thing scrabbling in the dirt. Long fingers grabbed my legs, and I drew back, bringing the machete down hard, over and over and over, until I could no longer hear the creature moving.

Falling back, I rested my head on a wall and tried to get my breath back. I could smell my own blood and something else—a sour odor that choked my lungs. I folded my knees and slid my back up the wall until I could stand. I managed to slide the machete back into its sheath before nausea overtook me and I retched, emptying my stomach against the wall and floor. Shaking, I put one foot in front of the other, leaning heavily against the wall.

"Connor." I coughed and spit. "Connor." My voice was weak, yet still reverberated through the passage.

Suddenly, the wall was gone, and I stumbled to the ground. The glow had changed, bowing outward and soaring high above me. I could feel every bone in my body as though they are all on fire.

"Connor!" My voice echoed, carrying throughout the cave. "Connor!"

"Here," her voice reached me. "I'm here."

I rolled to my side. "Where are you?"

She did not answer.

"Where are you?" I repeated.

"Here."

"Say again." I turned my head toward the sound of her voice. I reached toward it, digging one arm and leg into the dirt, and pulling myself forward. I could hear her labored breathing.

"Stop, Rue."

I paused. "Why? The witch—the thing—is dead. I killed it."

"There will be more. This is a nest. More will come. You have to get away."

Anger rose in my throat, and I held onto it for dear life. "This is not a nest," I snarled at her. "This is *Hell*. And I did not come down here for *nothing*. Get. Up."

Things shifted in the dirt.

"Get up!" I yelled again.

I could hear her moving in the dark, crawling, feeling her way toward my voice. I kept yelling at her, pounding the ground with my hand until hers finally closed over mine. We linked arms, the two of us leaning heavily against each other. She put one arm around my waist for support, but I yelped and bent over, collapsing around my wounded ribs. She drew me back up, putting my arm around her waist, and looping her arm around my hips. Her clothes were wet and sticky.

We made our way slowly back up through the passage, our free arms using either wall to keep us standing. The black bent away, fractured in places from where I had dislodged the glow. Our feet found the body of the creature, still and silent, and we helped each other over it.

Ahead, a cold blue light, a silver disk in the darkness. "The moon!" I cried with relief. "We're nearly there."

"Quiet!" Connor stopped dead. "Do you hear that?"

I strained to find any sound. "No."

Connor jerked me forward. "Hurry." The arm around my hip pressed hard. I grabbed her hand, but she was pulling us toward the moon at the end of the passage. I gasped for breath and clenched my teeth. A shadow darted over the moon. "Hurry," she urged. "Hurry!"

We spilled out of the mouth of the passage and onto the sand, Connor released me, letting me collapse to my knees. I felt her hands at my side, pulling, the weight of my machete suddenly gone. I put my hands on the ground, watching my blood drip onto the moon-blue sand.

And then I looked up.

Shadows in the dark moved and caught the moonlight, pulling them from the inky black around them, separating them into abhorrent shapes with long, emaciated limbs. There were four of them in the dark, only a few meters away. The figures crouched down, distended heads bobbing this way and that.

My stomach dropped. *Too many. There are too many.*

Connor stood next to me. She raised my machete menacingly and swung it in a wide arc. The nearest shape flinched, moving closer to the other three. Connor hesitated, but only for a moment. She nudged me with her boot.

"Scream," she said. "Scream as loudly as you can."

One of the figures lunged toward us, and I screamed with everything I had left in me. Connor joined, our voices rising into the cold night, piercing the deep stillness. She swung the machete toward the charging figure, and it changed direction, dodging away.

Connor dropped her voice, spread her arms wide, and bellowed at the creature like a lion. I opened my mouth wide, mimicking her pitch. She scooped sand up and into the air with long sweeps of her arms, then swung the machete around and around her head. The creatures hesitated, tilting their grotesque heads toward the sky. They were waiting for something, but whatever it was, it was not coming. No bird tore down from the sky. The sand lay still, and the laughter of hyenas did not come. Is this all they were? I was angry. I bellowed louder, and the things backed a few steps away, dragging their bony limbs over the sand, before turning and retreating into the night. We screamed and yelled until we could no longer see them.

Connor's arms dropped to her sides, and she crumpled onto the sand next to me. In the light of the moon, I could see her face and clothes were covered with blood. Her breath came in choking gasps and she spat something dark and wet onto the ground.

We slowly dragged each other through the night, pulling ourselves further away from the cave, away from open sand. Eyes watched us in the dark, orange points bobbing just out of the light. Predators were circling, and Connor swiped the machete in their direction when she felt they were getting too close. We did not stop until we reached the shelter of the stone spires. We stripped cloth from our tunics and packed our wounds as tightly as we could. Our arms and legs were shaking from exertion, and we lay in one place for some time.

I turned my head. Connor lay on her stomach next to me. "What do we do now?" I whispered.

She turned her head, sand packed onto the blood on her face. "We hope to not bleed to death," she gasped. A ghost of a smile passed over her face before she turned her head away and lay still.

For the first time, I noticed her pack was gone.

Chapter 51

I t is a strange thing to become aware of your existence—the presence of your life. To find your heart still pumping blood through your veins when you had seen so much of it spilling from your body hours before. To feel the rush of air in your nostrils, cold and clean, and find your eyes filled with the light of another day when your last thought hours before was of the end.

Some spark fired in my brain. My hands flinched. A flurry and a scrabbling of claws on dirt—a retreating blur, furry, and on all fours.

I'm alive.

I wanted to laugh.

My body smelled strange, and I remembered that not all the blood that covered me was my own. A fly darted across my eyeline, followed by another and another.

I curled my fingers and tried to roll onto my side. My head pounded and nausea threatened from below, but I managed to get my knees underneath me before the ground tilted. I pitched forward to rest on one elbow and cradled my head in my hands. My side and collarbone—where the beast had bitten me—were on fire.

Beast. I frowned, remembering the four of them frightened away by our voices, by Connor whirling my machete overhead like a madwoman. They had not called a sandstorm to ambush us or transformed into birds. They had not conquered us. They had run like animals from a campfire. *Beast. Yes, a beast. An animal.*

Shifting sand close by told me Connor had also survived the night. I rolled my head carefully in her direction.

Her face was mottled with dried blood that cracked as she worked her jaw. "We need to move. To get to the shelter." Her voice rasped.

I lifted my head slowly. The stone spires and thorny bushes all looked the same. "Which way?"

Shaking, Connor pulled herself into a seated position and looked around. She indicated a direction and used the nearest stone to help get her feet under her. I did the same.

The land tilted and swayed. We used each other and the stone fingers to keep ourselves upright, finding our shelter still standing in the protective embrace of the rocks around it.

We collapsed side by side on the floor of the tent, silently watching the light track overhead.

"Give me your water sack," whispered Connor.

"Drink from the spare."

"No. We must save that."

I turned until the pack faced her so that she could unclip the water bag. Metal clicked and the bag slid out. I heard her throat working, gulping the water as fast as she could. Anger surged in me—she was not holding back.

"That's enough," I hissed at her.

She did not stop.

"That's enough!"

Her breath came in gasps. I shifted so that I could see her face. The blood caking her skin was flaking off. She looked like she had that night at the Devil's Palm—cornered, exposed. My anger retreated, but I said nothing. I did not know how to help her.

The look passed quickly, and she slid the water sack back into place.

"Yes," she said, quietly, "we must be careful. There is only one pack now"

"We could go back," I replied. "We could get the other."

Her eyes were dark hollows. "That will never happen."

I knew it would not, but I had felt compelled to say it, to let her deny the option. We would not survive a return to the cave.

We used the last of the sanitizing solution to clean our wounds and tore our remaining set of spare clothes into bandages. We stitched the deeper gashes, holding cloth in our mouths and digging our nails into our flesh to distract ourselves.

Connor's torso had been torn open, the viscera exposed. She had packed it with cloth and dirt to keep from bleeding to death, and it took time to gently extract the fabric and wash out the dirt with sanitizing solution before sewing it closed. Long cuts in her back marked where the metal of her pack had bitten in as it was torn from her. I sewed those as well.

My collarbone was badly broken, the skin around it bruised and swollen. Without the adrenaline of the previous night, I could no longer lift the arm on the broken side. Connor made a sling and helped me slide the arm into place, but she could do nothing else for it. She examined my side and cleaned the dirt and sand out of the ragged wound as best she could before stitching the flaps of skin back together.

We squeezed every last drop of sanitizing solution from its container before letting ourselves rest again. By then, day had given way to night. I thought sleep would evade us, that our minds would be alert and gazing into the dark, that every sound would shake us, that no rest would come. Sleep did come, not with the rush of gentle wings, but with the sudden drop of quicksand. It drew us under and covered us up and did not loosen its hold until the sun was well up the next day.

Chapter 52

Connor wanted to go on.

When she told me, her face was still covered in dried flecks of her own blood. Her hair was matted with it. I had stitched her back together with a needle and thread. Her pack was gone, swallowed up in darkness.

She wanted to go on.

She wore the pack—she was bigger and would generate more water than I could, but she would also have to carry everything else. I could do nothing but walk. And if I wanted to live, I no longer had a choice.

We barely spoke for three days. My wounds throbbed constantly and gave me no peace, even when we stopped for the night. The water from one pack was not enough. Min had never intended for one to keep two alive.

Connor kept the spare water sack away from me, away from herself. I knew she wanted it as much as I did, but she refused to touch it.

"It is our last option," she insisted. I wanted to laugh in her face.

We walked apart. My blood boiled as the days wore on. I could not see the land for my anger anymore. She was killing us. She did not care. She never cared. The only thing that mattered to her was something she could not know even existed. I saved her life, and she did not even care about me. Perhaps I had made a mistake. I should have left her in there. She would have left me.

Finally, anger fired inside me so strongly that I released it.

"Connor!" I closed the gap between us, reached out, and yanked at the pack strapped to her back. I immediately released her, doubling over, trying to cradle my collarbone without touching it.

Connor whirled around, hands raised to push me back, but saw I was not coming for her anymore. "What are you doing?"

I gasped and gritted my teeth. "I'm thirsty."

She furrowed her brow. "There is nothing yet. You just drank it."

"Then give me the spare water sack."

"No." Her voice was flat and hard.

I lunged for her. "Give it to me."

She sidestepped me easily.

"God damn you, Connor!"

She stepped back. I had never sworn before. "What is wrong with you?"

"What is wrong with *you*?" I shouted at her. "I won't let you kill me. Give it to me!"

In one motion she dropped the pack and supplies down onto the sand and squared her shoulders.

I ran at her and she put her arm out, knocking me flat on my backside. I howled, and my body instinctively curled around its wounds.

Connor loomed over me, her hands balled into fists at her side. "Pull yourself together!" she barked.

I kicked at her, and she grabbed my ankles, swinging herself around and sitting on my legs. I tried to scratch her with my free arm, but she stepped on it with her boot. Unable to move, I screamed at the sky. What did it matter if something heard me? Connor made no move to silence me. Pinned under her weight, there was nothing else I could do. I screamed and hollered the anger and thirst into the cloudless atmosphere. I screamed every scream I had wanted to since the journey began. I screamed the fear I had felt in the cave, and the fear I felt now. I screamed and yelled until my throat was raw. I felt ridiculous and selfish, like a toddler, but I did not stop until I was good and ready.

When I did, Connor waited. I did not start again. She cleared her throat. "Do you feel better?"

My voice cracked. "You never thanked me for saving your life."

She raised her eyebrows. "Was I supposed to?"

I regretted it instantly. I had never once thanked her. My cheeks burned. "No," I whispered. It had been the right thing to do.

"You cannot go back now, Rue." Her eyes held mine. "There is no other way."

Something in her expression, a tightness around her mouth, made me feel she was telling this to herself as well.

I nodded, and she stood to help me get up.

Some of the supplies had come free and scattered when she dropped them earlier. She checked the pack and then secured it into place on her back. Stooping with my free hand, I started to gather the rest of the supplies but stopped when I saw the spare water sack half-buried in the sand. I was reaching for it when Connor's shadow fell over me.

"I was not going to drink from it," I said, feeling an echo of shame.

She did not answer and lowered herself to her knees. Bending over the water sack, she gently brushed the sand and dirt away. "What is that?" she whispered.

I looked. Inside, obscured by the clouded material, something moved. Connor whipped her head around to me. "Get a bowl."

I pulled one from the food supply and handed it to her.

She placed it in the sand and curled her hands under the water sack, bringing it up above her head. In the bright light of midday, something wriggled inside.

Connor removed the top of the water sack and gently tipped the contents into the bowl.

There, floating in the clear water, was a creature. Its body was short and slender, and instead of legs or arms, translucent petals undulated against the liquid. Big, round eyes peered up at us above a tiny, toothless mouth that puckered in rhythm with flaps that opened and closed on either side of its head.

I stared down into the bowl, unable to look away from the impossible being in front of me. In the bowl, the round body wagged its petals until it reached the other side of its container. Beside me, Connor slipped off her ring and held it above the bowl. They were the same.

There, in front of us, seemingly from nothing, was an animal that neither crawled on land nor flew in the sky.

Alive.

Chapter 53

I expected Connor to search for an explanation, for a *how* that would unveil the mystery of the creature's appearance, but she did not. She seemed to want there to be no answer. She sat with the bowl in her lap, curled over it with her face hovering just above the surface, shading the water from the sun. She stayed like that for the rest of the day, watching the small animal travel in weightless circles.

When the light faded from the sky, she carefully tipped the water and its inhabitant back into the spare water bag. She pitched the tent and built the fire, the same as she had for the past three days, but every once in a while, she would pause and turn her head toward the spare water sack.

I pulled food rations from the remaining supplies and made her eat. After, she wrapped herself in a blanket and drew the animal on her maps, over and over and over.

"It did not come out," she said quietly. If she had meant for me to hear, she did not look up to see if I was listening. "The whole day. It never came out of the water."

"And yet it is alive," I said.

Her head jerked up. "It breathed. I saw it. I do not know how, but it breathes water." Her lips pulled back into a grin, then opened. She laughed. Connor was laughing. I was so surprised that I laughed as well. She held her hands to her mouth as her laughter became a soundless spasm.

She stood, the edges of her blanket flapping dangerously close to the flames. "But there are more. There have to be. Where did this thing come from? There can only be one answer." She pointed to the west.

My heart echoed with *more, more, more.*

"This is not the end. This is the first sign."

"Of what?"

"That we are on the right path."

I smiled. "So we go on?"

Connor put her hand on my good shoulder. "We go on."

That night, Connor took a tool from the kit and dug it into a rocky finger. She scratched the shape of the animal into the stone, mimicking its curves as best she could. Below it, she carved our names.

The land changed again, sloping gently upward.

The swelling in my collarbone spread to the shoulder, as did the bruising. The skin around my stitches was puffy and oozed foul-smelling pus. I changed the bandages every day, but we had no more sanitizing solution. Yet I felt myself coming alive even as my body bowed to my wounds. For her part, Connor kept herself well covered and did not complain. If her wounds were worsening, I had no way to know.

My flesh suffered, but inside my mind was clear, and my eyes were open. Without my anger, I could see the land around me again and the horizon that never ended. As we walked, the spires of rock thickened and lost their points, merging into each other and forming a gradual incline. Slender cacti and thick brush filled the cracks between. The cacti were in their fruiting season, and we gathered as many of the bulbs as we could, greedily squeezing the moisture from the pulp into our mouths.

Brown birds with triangular beaks were also there for the fruiting season. When not digging into the soft flesh, they watched us calmly from their perches atop the round buds. They were not afraid of us and often would not relinquish their meals unless brushed away.

We spotted wild boar, but after seeing a trio of young following a female, we kept well away from them. A boar's tusks were not worth the trouble.

As the land changed, so did the sky. As we climbed upward, it seemed to be journeying down to meet us. Heavy gray clouds, swollen with moisture, hung low in an unbroken blanket above us. In the mornings, the outside of our tent was slick with water that we could scoop into our mouths with our hands. We had never seen anything like it.

At night, Connor placed the spare water sack between us so that we could watch the shadow of the animal inside. We lay with our faces turned toward it, as though we were flowers following the light in the sky. We did this until we woke one morning to find its petals still, its small body motionless at the surface.

When Connor opened the tent to bury the animal, the air was wet. The sun was still hidden, but despite its filtered light, we could not see very far around us. Droplets of moisture clung to our hair and clothes, but water did not fall from the sky. The air shifted gently as if we were surrounded by smoke made of water.

In death, the animal had blessed us. I ran my fingers across the droplets on my clothes and they disappeared into the fabric. I scooped a handful of water from the top of our tent into my mouth.

"The clouds now touch the earth," said Connor, looking out into the gray.

She set a bowl onto a rock, opened the spare water sack, and emptied the contents into it. The animal's body bobbed gently, its eyes clouded over. Its skin, once dark and shiny, was now dull and gray. Connor took some brush and laid the twigs in a peak around the bowl to keep the birds away.

Taking a tool from the kit, she etched the animal's image into the rock. As before, she carved our names below. Touching her palm to the finished image, she stood quietly for a moment before turning away.

Chapter 54

We moved slowly. Direction did not come easily in the gray smoke, and we found ourselves drifting. Connor took to using the rocks to guide our way, carving lines and shapes into certain ones to mark where we had been. She chose a different symbol each day and kept a list of them on paper. If we went in circles, we would know how far backward we had gone. I struggled to find a use for myself and resorted to gathering the water droplets that collected on the tent every night. Our water supplies were always full.

My fever came on after we entered the land of the clouds. Chills followed soon after that. I could no longer touch the skin around my stitches without disturbing the pus, and I had run out of clean bandages to keep it covered. My collarbone was not healing properly. I could not move the arm on the broken side very well, and the bruises were not fading. The fingers of that hand—the right hand—were dark and tingled as though I had lain on them. I covered all and said nothing to Connor. What could she do for me?

At night, I practiced writing with my left hand. It kept my mind focused. I wrote on the empty pages of the blue book and *The Land of Magic*. I wrote my name over and over. Then I tried Connor's name. I wrote our names next to each other, and then a brief account of our travels. It helped, trying to remember.

Connor worried the time was quickly approaching for the Khamaseens, and she was constantly on the alert. We could not see the horizon, or more than twenty meters in any direction, so she stopped at every sound, straining her ears for the rushing winds. As time went on, we came to know we were traveling in a land untouched by the fifty-day winds—the only land they could not reach.

The terrain that had sloped upward for so long was now flat. It was still rocky, but the stones were quietly being overtaken by scrubby plants and tall, straight cacti that towered high up and disappeared into the white. We could see the wind, for it pushed the clouds around us. I liked when they swallowed me up, and I disappeared into water smoke.

Sometimes my fever ran so hot I could feel the water turning to steam as it touched me. Connor would call to me to stop until the cloud passed and she could see me again, but sometimes her voice sounded far away. It was getting further away all the time.

I stopped looking at my wounds once the skin around my stitches began to pull away. I could no longer feel my right hand. On nights when my body shivered and shook, I could not write. I held myself with my left arm and traced our journey in my head. In the morning, my eyes were slow to open. I did not eat much anymore.

Eventually, I stopped writing altogether.

One morning, as the air shifted the clouds, I heard Connor stumble, then the sound of her vomiting. When the clouds moved and I could see her again, her eyes were sunken and dark. She said she was only sick, but I knew better. Vultures could have found us by smell alone. We were rotting.

A terrible, wonderful lightness had entered my brain.

As clouds blew by, I felt I understood them. I felt I knew what it was to be a cloud, and if I could just lift my arms I would rise and float away with them. If I did not have a dead arm, I could be a cloud. I asked Connor if she would cut it off and she stared at me. I knew she was afraid. She was afraid if she cut off my arm, I would float away and leave her alone, but I would never leave her alone. I told her that even if I was a cloud and floated away, I would never leave her alone.

I promised her.

omething scratching outside the tent woke me—Connor, I supposed, carving the day's symbol into a rock. The light was gray. It must have been the very early morning. I lay still for a while, listening to her moving out there. She was the only sound. The water smoke silenced all else, even the birds that ate the cactus fruit. I thought of the birds, so small and light. The smoke never left, and yet they found their way. They found each other. They ate and nested and laid eggs and grew up in the gray smoke. They had never seen how wide the sky could be, seen the stars spread thick as honey, or the wide belt of the galaxy. I wondered if they had ever seen something like us before.

Something was tickling my left hand.

I turned my head. A little white spider was making her way across my fingers, on her way to the floor. She must have crawled from one side of my body to the other in search of her breakfast. I lifted my hand to get a better look at her. I was not afraid. She was too small to hurt me.

Her body was covered in short, bristled hairs. She was not just white, but white flecked with gray. Her delicate legs were banded with gray at the joints. She rotated and seemed to regard me as I regarded her. I wondered what she saw.

Worried that she would be crushed when Connor packed the tent, I decided to put her outside. The spider waited patiently as I pulled myself up and toed open the entrance. The water smoke brushed my hand, and she lifted her two front legs as though testing the air. I deposited her on a cactus away from the campsite, where Connor would not accidentally step on her.

She tapped her legs on the cactus for a moment and turned to regard me once more. With one little jump, she was gone. If she had ever been there at all.

The gray smoke touched the top of the cactus and then drifted on. Connor's scratching had stopped. Soon she would pack away the campsite and we would continue on. Or maybe we had already begun.

I touched the cactus fruit, breaking a bulb and rolling its round flesh in my hand. I wanted it to be real. I bit into it, the juice filling my mouth and the pulp crunching between my teeth. I was not hungry, but I ate the whole thing, relishing the weight of it in my stomach. I heard Connor's voice somewhere behind me, but I was not ready to be pulled away. The fruit had stained my hand pink. It was real. For a moment, I was where I wanted to be.

Then the smoke came.

It crept in through my mouth, my ears, my nose. It seeped in through the corners of my eyes. It wrapped itself around my brain, taking up the space, muffling my thoughts. It covered me up and hid me away.

And I was gone.

Chapter 56

I no longer felt hunger or thirst. I was aware of my legs moving me over the earth, but that was all. Connor would sometimes speak, and if I really tried, I could hear her. Sometimes I would turn and see on her face that she had been speaking to me, but I had not heard her. What she did not understand was that I was becoming something else. What was the use in talking?

One foot in front of the other, little baby.

"I can't, Mommy."

Just a little further.

If I looked ahead, I could see the water smoke, the cacti towering above me, but there was a darkness at the edges, as if I were looking at the world through a small opening. If I turned my head, the darkness followed.

There were people in the water smoke. People who watched me. My mother was there, but sometimes it was Asha. My father. My brothers. Connor's face appeared in front of me sometimes, but she wanted me to talk to her. I did not want to talk, and so I turned my head so that I could see the people.

But I was not in the smoke, I was inside, in the tent, and the day was gone. Connor was in front of me, holding a light to my face. She was talking. I squeezed my eyes shut and opened them again to hear her.

She opened her mouth but all that came out was the buzzing of flies.

"What?"

A hand shook me gently. "Do you know where you are?"

"Yes, of course."

Connor sat back and dropped the light from my face. She looked sad. "We are so close. We have to be."

My mind wanders freely if I let it.

I have lost all sense of time.

I stopped walking for a moment and felt a tug at my waist. A length of twine there, the other end tied to Connor. I touch the knot at my stomach, but when I look up, we are in the tent. Again, a light is held to my face. Fingers on my collarbone, but I don't feel them.

"Do you know where you are?"

"Of course."

"Can you"—*hear me?*

Vargas is grinning in my face. *Wake up, lizard.*

"Do not call me that."

Vargas laughs. *Come along, lazy lizard. Don't want to be late, do you?*

"Late for what?"

"What?"

The light is too bright. I turn my head and close my eyes.

"Rue."

Connor was sitting back on her heels. Her eyes were sunken and sad. Her mouth was turned down. My vision suddenly became very clear.

"What is happening?" I asked.

Connor grabbed my chin, looked into my eyes. "You're here." I heard her sigh with something like relief, and she sat back again. Her face was bathed in sweat. How long had she looked so terrible?

"It has been a while since you looked at me," she said quietly. Her voice sounded different, like it was trapped deep inside her body.

Something was missing inside the tent, but it made my head hurt to think of what was gone. I dragged my good hand over the floor. I was sitting on my bedroll. Connor was sitting on hers. There was no fire outside. The air was always too wet now for fire.

Suddenly it hit me. "Where is the pack?"

Connor looked at me for a long while. "You do not know? You have been gone longer than I thought."

"I am here." I insisted. "I'm always here."

Connor's jaw worked, testing the weight of her words before she let them out. "The pack failed weeks ago."

I tried to hold myself here, tried to listen to her, though I felt the pull of something else. *My books.* I looked around the tent.

"What is it?"

"I can't find them," I muttered. "Did we lose them?"

I pulled uselessly at the corner of my bedroll, patting the fabric, feeling for them.

"The packs are gone."

I slapped the bedroll with my good hand. "My books!" My throat tightened. My breath came faster. *No. They were just here.* I slapped the bedroll again.

Connor grabbed my wrist and held it firmly. My head drooped. We couldn't have lost them. Connor laid me back gently onto my bedroll, then she pressed my hand to my stomach, against two hard rectangles tucked into the waistband of my trousers. I pulled up my tunic and removed them. The sight of their familiar covers eased me. I had filled every blank space of the blue book, so I opened *The Land of Magic.*

I heard Connor sigh and looked over at her. I gripped *The Land of Magic* to my chest as though it were my tether to this world.

"I tried to fix it." Connor said quietly. I did not know if she meant the pack or something else. She gently tilted her body down onto her bedroll. She moved with care, as though full of the thinnest glass. "But it had gone on as long as it could. There were no more spare parts. There was nothing left, and I could not carry a useless object any further." She looked at me.

I felt the word *useless* clinging to me, painted onto my skin. "What can I do?"

She took a breath. "Stay here for as long as you can."

I looked down at the page I had turned to in *The Land of Magic*. The last of the blank pages. There was just enough room for one more thought. I wrote it down and then closed the book, knowing I would never open it again. There was nothing left.

My tether had been cut. But I tried to stay. I tried.

Chapter 57

I opened my eyes to what I hoped was the next morning. The interior of the tent was lit with the weak gray light of dawn—a light that in the land of clouds would only brighten slightly during the day. The pinks and reds of dawns past were well behind us. I had not seen the sky in a very long time.

Connor shifted and I could sense her looking at me.

"I am here," I whispered. "Don't tell me how long it has been."

"Are you hungry?"

I shook my head.

"Neither am I."

We harvested the moisture from the outside of the tent, guiding it down into the water bags Connor had saved from the failed pack before dismantling it. We had camped near a gently sloping ridge of rock and low scrub, the top of which disappeared into the cloud smoke. There, a ghostly figure watched us—a white goat crowned with curled horns. It watched us solemnly for a moment before turning and vanishing into the smoke. I touched my waistband—the blue book and *The Land of Magic* were there.

Connor secured one of the water bags to my hip. It seemed strange to be surrounded by water and to still need more. But then, I could not remember the last time I felt thirsty.

I felt a tug at my waist and realized Connor was knotting us together with twine again. I plucked the taut line between us. Connor looked back, and I tried to smile. Her face looked different than I remembered—sharper. Her chin and jaw were heavy and exposed, her cheeks sunken, eyes hidden in shadow.

She no longer moved with ease over the land. She had once climbed through canyons and plowed her way through soft sand unhindered, as though she were made of the very fabric of the desert. Now, she moved cautiously. Her legs shook, and she picked her way over the rocks as though her boots were filled with lead.

The vapor rose and fell over us, leaving droplets on the plants and making the rocks slick underfoot. I thought of how easy it would be to lie down. It was nice here. We could just stop for a while. I touched the twine and thought of tugging it to let Connor know we should stop and rest, but looking at her, I could not do it.

Let her go on. Just for a little while longer.

Faces appeared in the mist. I tried to tell them to go away, to let me stay here. I tried, and I hoped they had let me stay. I hoped the foot I placed on the ground was continuing a movement from moments before, and not days or weeks. I had no way to know, and I was too afraid to ask.

The land tilted upward again, and as the air lifted, we could see the line of a ridge ahead.

A sound.

Something far away.

A high and low sound, continuously running. Like wind.

"Do you hear that?" I called.

Ahead of me, Connor stopped. She turned her head this way and that, then held herself very still.

My heart pounded in my chest. The Khamaseens?

I cast about for shelter, for a crevice of rock, for an outcrop that could protect us until Connor could put up the tent. Our supplies, our water, there would not be enough to outlast the winds.

I tugged the line between us, tried to pull her back toward me, but she would not move.

"Listen!" she called to me.

I closed my eyes and strained to hear what she did. The wind sound did not howl like the Khamaseens. It did not hurtle through the air toward us like a meteor as Khamaseens would. These wind sounds lifted and fell, called and faded, over and over, in a kind of rhythm.

I opened my eyes and Connor was coming toward me.

"Do you hear it?" she asked.

"I have never heard winds like that. What is it?"

She shook her head and looked around. "Have you noticed we can hear it, but it does not move the clouds?"

The water smoke around us, the low-hanging clouds, floated as gently as they had since we first came here. This was wind that moved nothing.

We eyed the rocky ridge that lay in heavy mist up ahead. The sound was coming from just behind it.

At that moment, the mist lifted from the ridge, as though an enormous hand had pulled it away. It was beckoning to us, inviting us to see what lay beyond.

Nothing could have stopped us from going on. Had we been struck down in that moment, our souls would have broken free and clawed their way up to peer over the edge of that ridge.

We stood as one and approached the edge to the beyond. Our feet found their way. We did not slip or stumble. We were almost there when Connor stopped me with a gentle hand on my good arm. We stood where the mists had lifted, in air that was dry and warm. She held my gaze for a moment before reaching down and slipping her hand into mine.

Together we turned and stepped up to the edge.

The land fell away into a sheer drop, down, down into sand far below. Gray clouds soared high above us, away and bending back down to touch a horizon made entirely of water.

Water that roiled and churned and frothed where it touched the sand.

Water that rolled like dunes.

Water that crashed so loudly it made a sound like wind.

Water that roared.

The scent of salt clung to the air, mixed with another—the smell of water. For the first time in my entire life, I could smell water.

White birds soared and dipped and flapped along the surface. They made a sound like laughing. Something small broke through the surface from below, hung in the air for one shining moment, and then disappeared beneath the water.

Line after line of water rose up, curled, frothed white, and melded into the sand. Clouds cast their shadows, and no land pushed out from a surface of blues and greens and more colors than I had seen in storybooks. It went on and on and on, and there were no words that could describe it.

A force tugged at my hand, pulling it down—Connor. Her legs had folded under her, and she sat on the ground. Her shoulders dipped as though to release a great weight, giving it back to the wind. Her eyes never left the water that somehow had become the land itself, and her mouth drew ragged gasps. She was weeping.

"You should see this," she whispered. "You should see this."

Her fingers still gripped mine. I squeezed her hand, but I knew she was not talking to me.

With the last strength of our bodies, we climbed down to touch the miracle that lay before us.

It was impossible.

And we had found it.

Epilogue

I dreamed of land, of solid ground that stretched as far as the eye could see in every direction. I dreamed of earth that did not move or pitch or roll. I dreamed of a tree that grew out from the middle of that land with bark as smooth as skin and roots that pulled water through its limbs like a heartbeat. Branches of arteries and veins stretched toward a black sky that flickered with balls of fire. A shadow passed over the stars, as though something traveled between them and the earth. A cold wind blew, and the flesh of the tree shivered.

My eyes opened in the dark.

Wood groaned above my head. I shivered and reached down for my blanket, but it was not there. I sat up and reached toward the foot of my bed when I noticed a dark shape standing there.

I yelped and then struck the thin mattress with my fist.

"You cannot keep doing that," I growled.

"I didn't want to wake you," whispered a small voice.

I sighed and fumbled with the lantern on the table next to the bed until it bathed the small berth in warm yellow light.

She looked so small in my old nightshirt. The fabric billowed around her frame like a cloud and fell past her knobby little knees. I had never been so small. She had our mother's frame—delicate and birdlike—as well as her tiny chin and nose. She would never have broad shoulders like me. I looked more like the women on our father's side. She would always be lithe and feminine. I would always be tall and strong, and what our mother had called "too much."

"Can't you sleep?" I asked her.

She shook her head and walked to the side of the bed. Stooping, she picked up the edge of my blanket and handed it to me. I had kicked it off in my sleep.

I moved to make room for her, pressing my side against the wood of the wall. She climbed in and huddled against me for warmth. I pulled the blanket over us and she sighed.

"You are like a mouse," I chuckled.

She wrinkled her nose at me.

I kept the lantern on. Outside, the waves crashed against the hull. Around us, the ship creaked and moaned. We lay in its belly, cocooned in our berth—asea, as we had been for most of our lives.

If only we could stop.

I reached up and traced the spot where we had carved our names into the wall. My forefinger ran over the letters A-N-N-A, then E-M-M-A. Our mother had liked names that ended with A.

I looked up at our night sky, the one we had painted on the ceiling using a book of constellations from our father's collection. Orion ruled over our sky. We had placed him in the middle, painting him larger than all the others, who were clustered at his sides and below his feet. Our father had been disappointed that our sky was not more accurate. We had painted the stars not as they were, but as we wanted them to be.

"Tell me a story," she whispered.

"You should sleep," I answered. "It will be time to get up soon."

She whined and poked me in the side with a sharp finger, as she always did when she wanted to get her way.

I pushed her hand away. "Which one?" I asked.

She snuggled closer to me. "I don't care."

I thought for a moment.

I knew the story I wanted to tell. It had been so long since I had heard it, but I knew it by heart. I knew it as well as I knew our night sky, as well as I knew my sister's face. She had heard it many times before, too, only not from me.

I took a deep breath and began the story our mother had told.

Once upon a time, deep in the desert, there lived a little girl and a lonely wanderer. And though they did not know it at the time, they would discover something no one else had ever seen before. Together, they would open a world within a world. And the rest of us would follow.

THE END